BULLDOG DRUMMOND
ON POISONED GROUND

AIRSHIP 27 PRODUCTIONS

Bulldog Drummond: On Poisoned Ground
© 2019 I.A. Watson

Published by Airship 27 Productions
www.airship27.com
www.airship27hangar.com

Interior illustrations © 2019 Howard Simpson
Cover illustration © 2019 Ted Hammond

Editor: Ron Fortier
Associate Editor: Gordon Dymowski
Marketing and Promotions Manager: Michael Vance
Production and design by Rob Davis

ISBN-13: 978-1-946183-57-6
ISBN-10: 1-946183-57-1

Printed in the United States of America

10 9 8 7 6 5 4 3 2 1

BY I.A. WATSON

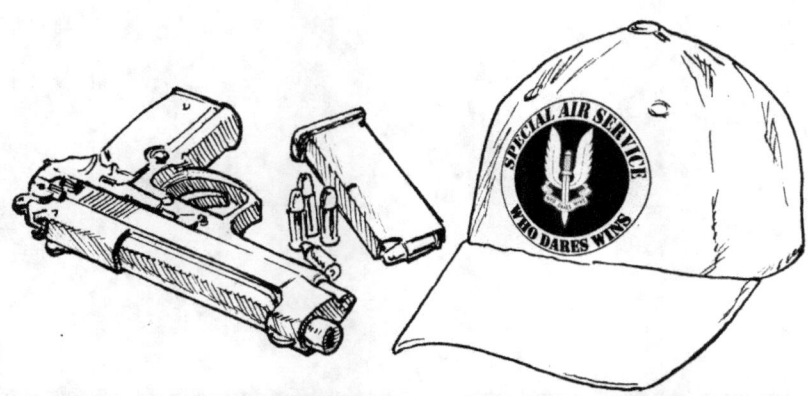

SOME WARS NEVER END

CHAPTER I
IN WHICH HE TAKES BADLY TO HIS LUNCHEON BEING DISTURBED

Captain Hugh Drummond crashed through the exclusive hotel's plate glass window and fell two stories onto the roof of a Citroen C3. The impact would have been bone-shattering, if not fatal, had Drummond not been cushioned by the assassin underneath him.

The man with the machine pistol lost all interest in killing the meddler, so Hugh borrowed his Steyr TMP, rolled off the car, and sprayed a short burst to eliminate the second gunman who was now leaning out of the shattered *fenêtre* of the exclusive Le Meurice hotel.

"I'm going to have to leave a specially good tip," Drummond noted to himself as the third and fourth killers jumped from the window to the first floor balcony and took position to fire again.

He ducked behind a gaudily-repainted metallic orange Porsche Cayenne. The demobilised soldier wasn't a big fan of non-military SUVs and the colour displeased him. If any of the vehicles parked on the Rue de Rivoli was going to get shot up he would prefer it was this one.

Bullets slammed into the vehicle, shattering the windscreen and shredding the bodywork. Street traffic screeched to a halt. Pedestrians scattered for cover.

Hugh thumbed the Steyr *Taktische Maschinenpistole* to single shot and put down another of his pursuers with a neat double-tap just above the line of the bulletproof jacket, just like he'd been taught. The last of the men who'd interrupted his lunch dived off the hotel frontage and landed on the pavement behind a rather nice vintage Bugatti that Drummond had no intention of shooting up.

Although most of the road traffic had ground to a gridlocked halt, four motorcyclists still wove through the jam. That wasn't unusual for the streets of Paris, where suicidal bikers weaving between lanes were a constant menace, but these men all rode identical BMW R 9T Pures and all had the same style of mirror-faced helmet.

And all had calf holsters strapped over their riding boots.

Drummond rolled over the bonnet of the bullet-holed Cayenne five seconds before the place where he'd been crouching became unhealthily polluted with lead projectiles.

"Didn't anyone tell you that this is Paris?" Hugh complained as he rose to take down the nearest rider with a pair of helmet shots. "It is considered very bad manners to try and kill a fellow before he's finished his sorbet. Assassinations should be served along with the coffee and brandy, not before."

The fallen rider tumbled to the road. His bike slid along until it was stopped by a metro bus. The next rider swerved round a taxi and mounted the pavement to flank his prey.

Drummond was ready for the tactic. The remaining man from the hotel attack was still on the ground in cover somewhere nearby. If Hugh concentrated on the bikers he was leaving his back exposed to the last of the sharpshooters. Best to shift the battleground.

Hugh vaulted to abused Cayenne yet again, relieved the dead biker of his additional ammunition clip, and retrieved the R 9T Pure. The retro-styled roadster was built to take a knock and its 110 hp horizontally-opposed twin engine restarted first time. Drummond leaped astride and swerved between traffic before his opponents could reposition themselves.

Rue de Rivali was wide and straight. Directly opposite Le Meurice behind high elegant railings was the Tuileries Garden and the Terrasse de Fuilliants. Drummond swerved left and powered off with the remaining three bikers in close chase. If he kept threading through the standing vehicles he could keep his opponents from getting a bead.

"But someone might end up getting caught in cross-fire," he muttered to himself. It was a lot easier doing this stuff in a war zone without potential civilian casualties to fret about.

Only a hundred yards up the road was a gate into the Tuileries, and beside it a discrete stone stairwell went down into the Metro. Hugh considered taking the bike down the stairs and leading his adversaries on a thrilling chase through the Paris subway, but there were too many bystanders. Instead he hairpinned between the gates into the public gardens. On a warm summer's day there were plenty of Parisiennes and tourists enjoying Catherine de Medici's beautiful park, but they were less clustered than drivers trapped in their gridlocked vehicles.

Drummond swerved back in the direction he had come but on the park side of the railings, away from the Louvre end of the garden, towards the Place de la Concorde and the Arc de Triomphe. He abandoned the straight path of the Allée Centrale and tested his R 9T's impressive acceleration on turf. The other bikers swerved round after him, spreading out to anticipate whatever direction he might run.

From a distance came the irritating discordant wail of French police cars. The historic heart of Paris was well covered with security cameras these days. A major terrorist incident like a gunfight outside one of the capital's oldest and most excusive hotels would provoke a speedy armed response.

Hugh made a note to apologise to the French nation for the desecration of their flowerbeds. He curved off towards the Bassin Octagonale, the great eight-sided fountain at the western end of the park, then slid round to drive directly at one of the three gun-toting riders. The tactic caught the killer off-guard. It was much harder to aim and fire at a mad rider playing chicken at 75 miles per hour.

The bikes crashed into each other beside the fountain. The unfortunate assassin reacted too late and was hurled away with the wreckage of his ride. Drummond timed his leap from the saddle perfectly, splashing down into the Bassin to mitigate his speed.

The other riders approached, but now Drummond was in the water, behind the lip of the octagonal basin, obscured by the fountain's eight twelve-metre water sprays. He took out a third rider with a single head-shot—Hugh was conserving ammunition for his borrowed Steyr. The last biker skidded and came off his vehicle, scrambling for cover behind a group of panicked tourists around a pastry cart.

A shot splashed into the water too near Drummond for comfort. It came from the remaining member of the crew that had broken into a private hotel room to enliven Hugh's luncheon, who had cut on foot to take a sniper's vantage behind a pedastelled statue of some French nymph in classical robes.

Drummond abandoned his water-filled foxhole. He kicked aside a couple of the sun-loungers ringing the fountain and sprinted for cover behind one of the monuments towards the Place de la Concorde. The huge white marble montages would be proof against the 9x19mm rounds the Steyr SMPs sprayed after him.

The original hotel assassin came from cover and hurled a black pineapple-shaped missile. Hugh recognised the Yugoslavian M75 hand grenade at once. The notorious devices had a fuse time of 3 to 4.4 seconds before 38 grams of plastic explosive detonated, spraying 3000 2.5mm steel balls over a kill zone of fifty metres. Vast numbers of them had been sold off to criminal gangs after the fall of Yugoslavia, often for less than the price of a can of lager.

Drummond hurled himself behind the statue's sturdy plinth base. He hoped that the previous gunplay had already warned civilians to take cover. The grenade peppered a pair of nudist gods and a cupid with shrapnel.

He acted in the second after the explosion, while the echo was still booming across Paris. He rolled out from cover, sighted, and took down the grenade-thrower, then dropped to one knee and shot out the petrol tank under the remaining bike-mounted assassin. Another explosion blossomed up from the Tuileries Garden.

Nobody was left at the patisserie cart to take Hugh's money, so he helped himself to a crêpes suzette, left a twenty euro bill, and settled down to finish his lunch while the armed response unit scrambled.

★★★

"If it helps to clarify things," Drummond encouraged M. Brissaud of the French police force, "it was his fault."

The smart-suited diplomat to whom Hugh Drummond pointed managed an embarrassed wince. He showed a security pass to a suspicious officer from the Prefect of Police that got him past orange tape and serious armed men in body armour, and joined Hugh on the rear bumper of a crime scene investigation van.

"Your fault, m'sieu?" M. Brissard asked. The new *Anglais'* credentials proclaimed him to be Mr Toby Sinclair VC, a Third Secretary B3 attached to the British Embassy, a special assistant to the Minister. That made him not only diplomatically immune from prosecution or even rigorous questioning but also politically significant.

"Not at fault," Sinclair replied in perfect French, "but I do bear a certain responsibility for loosing Captain Drummond here on the unsuspecting Gallic populace."

"You know this man who shot up the Tuileries and Le Meurice?"

Drummond, who was not very fluent at any language except English, picked up on the name of the historic $2500-a-night hotel where he had been ambushed. "Le Meurice? Very good beefsteak. I recommend the chef's special sauce."

"Captain Drummond did not carry any firearm. Talk to your crime scene investigators at the hotel. He merely went there for a private dinner with the lady whose room was invaded—although she rather thought he was me, whom she had been deployed to lure there to a quiet little political assassination. Her passport claims she is from Singapore, but she's actually

North Korean. Ask her when she wakes up."

"Wakes up?"

"Captain Drummond did not react well to attempts to inject him with a hypodermic of poison. He rather hit her with the sweet trolley. At that point, as far as we could tell from the wire he was wearing, a number of assailants with Austrian machine pistols emerged from an adjacent suite. The management is quite distressed."

The scene-of-incident officer glanced at the man sat beside the diplomat. Both *Anglais* were around thirty years of age, both fit, both confident. Drummond was the taller and broader of the two, but also by far the cruder-looking, with a Saxon face and a spread out boxer's nose. Sinclair walked with a limp and carried a cane; it was possible that his right leg was prosthetic. The two Englishmen knew each other, were trusting comrades. Even now they sat looking not at each other but in different directions, covering the other's back.

"You claim that Captain Drummond..." Brissaud struggled with the strange foreign name, "was the subject of a murder attempt?"

"Well, *I* was," Toby Sinclair clarified. He rapped his cane on his leg, proving the policeman's supposition that the limb was synthetic. "I'm not quite as quick on my feet as I used to be, so Bulldog here kindly agreed to meet my date for me. I'm not sure how he convinced her he was me; I mean, would you mistake us? *I* don't look like a shaved ape. But he does have a winning smile and twinkly blue eyes that seem to work on ladies' underwear. Anyway, Miss North Korea went for the kill but got smacked with dessert. Everything Captain Drummond did thereafter was survival and self-defence."

"Bulldog?" Brissaud frowned and groped for a translation. "*Bouledogue?*"

"Hey now," Drummond interjected, "Don't you go translating me into French. I won't have it!"

"A nickname," Sinclair explained to the policeman. "When he gets his teeth into something he won't let go—even when it's too big for him to handle and all common sense says to back off."

"We have eight dead men here," M. Brissaud objected.

Hugh caught that. "But the *right* dead men," he insisted. "Le mort hommes de plus good, oui?"

Sinclair patted his shoulder. "Leave the taking to me, eh? Just like old times. By the way, I'm sorry about the idiots with Steyrs. We had no idea that the lady had back-up of that magnitude or stupidity."

"Don't worry, T.S. It livened up my day. A dazzling seductive spy-girl with a hypo of goop is pretty good, and a bike chase through Paris is just jam on top."

"Well, it helped prove we're on to something about the weapons embargo-dodging. It'll be a problem for Interpol now."

"I'd be fine to go hit some more assassins."

"Sorry, Bulldog. I'll be waving my passes and spiriting you off to the Embassy shortly, and then H.M. Government will be giving you a free ticket back to Blighty. Our Continental partners sometimes object when we shoot up their national monuments because you're bored."

"It wasn't because I was bored," Hugh objected. "It was because I didn't get to finish my lunch. North Korea owes me gateau. I shall be sending a note to the Supreme Leader about it."

"Do not invade North Korea," Toby Sinclair instructed him firmly. "Your work here is done, Hugh. Your grateful nation thanks you—again. And sends you home—again. Unless you've changed your mind about joining me at the F.O., the Diplomatic Corps?"

"The Foreign Office has far too many desks and far too many rules, T.S. Can you really imagine me working for any agency with 'Diplomatic' in the title?"

Sinclair failed to suppress a shudder. Drummond continued with his lament. "Everyone wants me to sign up. Dare wants me troubleshooting his international business deals. Algy wants me driving his sports cars. Bangbang wants me running his security consultancy. But I'm just not the settling down type."

"You have a different definition of settling down than most men, Bulldog."

M. Brissaud still had a significant number of questions regarding a major incident in the centre of Paris, starting with, "Who are you, Captain Drummond?"

★★★

"Who is this Captain Drummond?" the man who was currently calling himself Arthur Franklyn enquired as he looked at the front page of *Le Monde*.

"There's a piece about him on page two," the woman who breakfasted beside him answered. Her passport proclaimed her Edith Franklyn, and she was indeed his half-sister, but Franklyn was but a *nom du voyage* suitable for their present travels. "A British ex-soldier. Royal Loamshire

Regiment, rose to the rank of Captain, served almost eleven years before being demobilised."

"And he was able to take out two units of Ryanggang's Special Forces School? Alone?"

"He did. I like the look of him. Ugly men always make the best lovers."

Franklyn folded the paper and set it aside. "I'll commission a dossier on him. There's more to him than meets the eye, more than the press has reported. But for now we must not keep our guests waiting."

Edith nodded to the Maitre D. Apart from serving staff, the Franklyns were the only people in the large breakfast room at the most exclusive remaining tourist hotel in Mosul. Indeed, apart from their guests and retainers they were the establishment's only residents. Nobody else wanted to visit the war-ravaged Iraqi city from which Islamic State troops had been so recently expelled at such bloody cost.

The three men who had gathered there to meet the Franklyns could not have been more different from each other. The first was a smart-looking businessman in a Saville Row three-piece suit unsuitable for the brutal heat, but he gave no sign of discomfort. He was flanked by two attractive female companions in short white dresses, shocking in a nation where women were usually required to be swathed in black from head to toe. It wasn't clear if the ladies were mistresses or bodyguards or both.

"Victor Savvich!" Edith greeted the man, rising to kiss him on both his cheeks, but not the lips he presented to her. "How is the wife?"

"In St Petersburg," the Russian replied with some satisfaction. Viktar Filchenkov was a rising star in Russian hardline politics and he preferred to travel with a different entourage.

"Do give her my love, won't you?"

Edith turned to the second visitor, a dour-faced Chinese man in cool white linens. "Koh Zhenkai," she greeted him, then glanced at the huge hulk of a retainer who stepped two paces behind him. "You brought a date too, then?"

The Taiwanese businessman did not appreciate humour. "This is Gǔ Cāng," he introduced the giant. "He discourages disrespect."

"Gǔ Cāng," Arthur Franklyn interjected. "That means 'Barn'."

The third visitor was a Black man in designer American casualwear, with expensive gold cufflinks and a Cartier watch, all in exquisite taste. He had come alone. He didn't need security other than the pistol and knife under his leather jacket.

"Edie," he hailed Franklyn's sister. "You're still looking fine."

"I know," the young woman preened. "And you're still looking rich. How much more are you worth per minute these days, Mad?"

Nugent Madison II shrugged. "'Bout $700," he judged. "Maybe more. Who counts?"

"You do," Franklyn suggested. "Otherwise you wouldn't be here. Any of you." He gestured to the only table laid out for breakfast. "Come and sit. It's time to tell you what your investments bought."

The visitors took their seats, in the deserted hall of the deserted hotel in the decimated city, and frightened waiters attended them with excellent food. The view over the Tigris to the shelled Old Town was both beautiful and heartbreaking.

Franklyn waited until Filchenkov, Koh, and Madison had been served and the hotel staff had retreated beyond earshot. Victor Savvich's angels and Koh Zhenkai's Barn hovered close but did not have seats at the table. Franklyn sipped his coffee and made his report.

"One year ago, you each ventured half a billion dollars for a good cause. You wanted a new business opportunity and I undertook to find it for you. Now I have."

Filchenkov raised his hands in a 'tell me' gesture.

Franklyn took another sip. "Change brings profit. Disruption means opportunity for those who are ready, those who know it is coming." He gestured to Koh. "You want to establish a stranglehold over the world's financial sector. That's a problem for you; Brexit hasn't destabilised the London stock exchange the way many hoped it would and the British national credit rating remains robust."

He passed to Madison. "Your plans for shifting your extralegal activities into Europe have been relatively unsuccessful. Without a major upheaval, the old firms will continue to control drugs and weapons supply routes, the sex trade, protection and fraud networks and the rest."

The American crimelord nodded. "There's no room while all the pigs are hogging the trough. Some need to be butchered."

"And you, Mr Filchenkov, and your energy cartel, and your political allies, would certainly prefer if internal issues kept NATO and the European Union from getting in the way of your long-term expansion plans."

"We heard this one year ago," the Russian pointed out. "That is why we made funds available to address the situation."

"And now the solution is at hand. I propose the destruction of the United Kingdom."

Edith raised a brow. "But I like Harrods," she objected.

"We must all make sacrifices," Franklyn told his sister. "What I intend, gentlemen, is actually the destruction of London. A strike at the capital, the heart of England, at a time when Parliament is in session, when the royal family is at Buckingham Palace, when the joint military chiefs and senior civil servants are all assembled. Eight million deaths, more than a tenth of the UK's population. What happens then?"

Koh Zhenkai looked interested. "It would be the end of the City," he considered, referring to the world's largest financial market. "It remains in London from the days of empire two centuries ago. It would not return there today. There would be economic war between the New York and Tokyo stock exchanges, and more. And if Britain defaulted on its national debts then the World Trade Bank would be in crisis. There might be global recession. Much opportunity."

"Take out the whole civic infrastructure?" marvelled Madison. "No country could get back up quick after eight million deaths. Hell, I bet Scotland and Ireland and, what's the other one? Well, I bet they'd be quick to break away anyhow. A broken nation, the wealthiest parts gone, collapse of law and order, the rule of the gun? The rule of the guy who thought to bring the guns?" He swore in admiration. "Franklyn, you deliver the goods!"

"It would punch a hole in Western alliances, rupture NATO," Filchenkov predicted. "Especially if there was doubt about what nation was to blame for the damage. A false flag operation? It could set Europe against the US. Or the US versus China? Yes, I can see some possibilities if such a wonderful occurrence were to pass. But can it? There are many safeguards. What method…?"

"That's what I've been planning," the man calling himself Arthur Franklyn promised them. "How best to kill a city of nine million people? How to kill the nation it belongs to? This is how I'll do it."

He spoke for fifteen minutes. He detailed in cold, precise steps how he would accomplish the largest single mass-murder in history.

When his guests were satisfied and departed, he arranged for every servant in the hotel to be slaughtered and the venue burned to the ground.

★★★

CHAPTER II:
IN WHICH THE TIMES INCLUDES AN UNCONVENTIONAL ADVERTISEMENT

Demobilised officer, finding peace incredibly tedious, would welcome diversion. Legitimate, if possible; but crime, if of a comparatively humorous description, no objection. Excitement essential.

Captain Peter 'Dare' Darell set aside the morning paper and rubbed his forehead. "Bulldog? Do you remember that time in Cairo? After the thing with the knife-thrower and the monkey, and that bet with Algy about the belly dancer? And you made me promise that if you *ever* did anything as imbecilic as that again that I should take you into the desert and shoot you to spare humanity your ongoing stupidity?"

"I recall some kind of promise. But then, we had been drinking quite a lot. Egyptian beer has a way of sneaking up on a lad."

"And trickling out of him, in Algy's case. But you were pretty clear that you would like a heads-up when you were heading to Idiotville. Consider this advertisement your visa papers."

"I'm bored, Dare. Bored! You can get excited about exchange rates and business contracts and things. Or you can scheme to get your brothers and sisters and cousins disinherited so you can play boy tycoon with the family billions. But I… I need to be *doing* something!"

"Translation: nobody has shot at you for almost two weeks, not since your attempt to irretrievably damage Anglo-French relations—and Toby's career. I swear, Bulldog, you don't get itchy shoulder blades when a sniper's targeting you. You get restless when nobody is trying to kill you."

Hugh Drummond paused to consider his old friend's assessment. Dare had known him since their schooldays, long before they had made their separate journeys to Her Majesty's Royal Loamshire Regiment and the Special Air Service unit that it covered for.

"I might help people," Hugh argued. "There may be damsels in distress."

"They'll be distressed if they meet you," Dare shot back. "Bulldog, you can't just go putting mysterious adverts in *The Times*…"

"You can though. You just pay them £380 per diem plus the costs of the post office box, and then…"

"I mean, you can't just offer to go off adventuring with an entry to the

Notices column. Especially with this offer to do crime."

"Really? Because plenty of people have sent in offers. I've set Denny and Mrs Denny to sorting them."

Dare felt for Drummond's long-suffering household staff. Denny had been a squaddie back in the Royal Loamshire days; he'd had plenty of experience as Bulldog's batman, but his wife generally had better sense. "Mrs D thinks this is a good idea?"

"No. Mrs D was glaring with every envelope she opened," Hugh admitted. "Why do you think I'm upstairs with you?"

Drummond and Darell were neighbours these days, residents of the same exclusive townhouse flats on Half Moon Street off Piccadilly, London. Drummond had the first floor, with the Dennys in the servants' flat below. Peter had the top floor penthouse. Their rooms were well situated for morning runs in Green Park beside Buckingham Palace and strolls to the Junior Sports Club in St James Square.

"I have no idea why you are upstairs with me, Bulldog. I assume it must be some kind of gypsy curse." Dare had actually helped Drummond outbid all other offers for the four million pound three-bedroom chambers he now occupied. "If the formidable Mrs Claire Denny can't deter you from your slippery slope then I doubt that I can help you."

"As a matter of fact, her system is proving most useful," Hugh insisted. "We have four piles: the scams and sales pitches, the lonely hearts, the tedious, and the unscrupulous."

"And which will you be keeping? The lonely hearts? Those damsels requiring distress?"

"Some did include photographs, though Mrs D has confiscated certain of them. But no, I am hoping for the elusive fifth pile, the exciting adventure offers. It's just that no such entry has yet appeared from the rather large mail-sack delivered by the Royal Mail this morning. It may have done by now."

"Well, do not let me deter you from your life of thrill-seeking and debauchery, old chap. When you have calmed down from your burst of newspaper advertising you can tell me what on earth you did to the Tuileries and whether I shall ever be able to stay at Le Meurice again. For now, I suggest you brave the death stare of your housekeeper and seek your 'diversion'. Good luck with it!"

"You were far more interesting before you became a captain of industry, Captain Darell," Drummond cautioned as he rose and left.

"And you were... no, I've not got anything. Blockhead."

"Ass."

With that comradely farewell, Hugh retired down the plush common stairwell and returned to his own rooms. His former orderly, pug-nosed now-balding James Denny, was still at the dining table classifying replies, but Claire Denny had retreated to the kitchen. The smell of kidneys and bacon were enhancing the atmosphere.

"Anything good yet, James?" the would-be adventurer checked. It was always James, never Jimmy or Jim or Jez; Mrs D wouldn't stand for such abbreviation.

"Young widow in Chelmsford would like her boyfriend's legs breaking," the orderly offered.

"Too commonplace. I am not yet reduced to domestic disputes."

"African émigré requires assistance securing his inheritance."

"Again? That chap is just too careless where he abandons his millions."

"Gent who has firm evidence that the royal family are lizards from the Andromeda Nebula."

"God bless her reptilian majesty and the Space House of Windsor! Come on, James, I can tell from the glint in that roguish glass eye of yours that you have something better, a rose amongst the thorns. Stop tormenting your senior officer and let me see it."

"There is one," Denny owned. He passed over a plain white envelope with a neat handwritten address. Inside was a sheet of bonded writing paper.

Dear Sir or Madam, it began.

"Penned in a fair maidenly script," Hugh observed. "A proper traditional salutation, with an equitable acceptance that my advertisement betrayed no gender. Open-minded and forward thinking. And written with fountain-pen, suggesting…well, I don't know, but she owns a bottle of ink. Or cartridges, if she is of a modern bent. A 19th or 20th century girl, one or other."

I can't tell if your advertisement is a joke. I am just desperate enough to try it and gamble that you are serious. A person who could induce the Times to print so extraordinary a personal notice must have some extraordinary quality, either as a prankster or a genuine dilettante.

"So few people use the word 'dilettante' now, James. We should try and bring it back into fashion. I may put it on my next business cards."

"There's a few words could be put on there, sir," Denny muttered darkly.

In the wild hope that you are genuine, willing to face difficulty and danger for the fun of it, I have a problem for which I have no obvious remedy.

Bluntly, someone is trying to kidnap me, or possibly kill me.

"Interesting, assuming she has not simply neglected her medication," Drummond judged.

I began a new job four months ago, an executive role in a non-profit organisation that does a lot of good in the world. My predecessor vanished abruptly under odd circumstances and cannot be located. I was engaged by the Board of Trustees to get the house in order and troubleshoot certain contracts that had fallen behind deadline. The work is engaging and worthwhile, though requiring long hours and complete dedication.

"So no boyfriend or husband? Write on, dear heart!"

Two weeks ago, I was visited at home by a pair of men claiming to be from British Gas, warning that there might be a leak in the house. When I refused them entry until I had verified their identification passes with their employer, the men vanished while I was phoning. Then, one week ago, I was accosted by two different men in the car park as I returned to my vehicle after work. They tried to grab me, wielding knives, and to drag me into a waiting van. I sprayed one of my attackers with mace and put my heel through the other one's foot, and fled. They might have followed but I also triggered my rape alarm, so they drove off. The police investigated but were unable to trace the van.

"Well now," Hugh admired. "This is the rose, alright. Or an excellent confidence artist who can do a wonderful impression of a rose. Either way I am intrigued."

He read on: *Since then I have thought on three occasions that perhaps my car was being followed, though it may have been my imagination. I noticed an appointment on my calendar to meet a new charitable donor but when I rang to verify the meeting found that he was unaware of any such arrangement. My house was burgled yesterday but I was not at home.*

The police tell me that, contrary to what we see on television, they do not have personnel to place on watch on every potential threat without better evidence than I can offer. There is nothing to link my attackers in the car park with the fake gas men—they were certainly not the same people— or with what looks like an opportunistic break-in to steal my stereo and microwave.

I am becoming somewhat alarmed that I might vanish as did my predecessor. I have no idea why I might be targeted this way. I have no-one to whom I could appeal for help in such an unusual circumstance as this. Hence my writing to an anonymous stranger who placed an unusual advert.

"Quite right," Drummond agreed. "I should have placed my notice months ago, as soon as I was discharged, if I had known it would catch incidents of this quality. I'll plough through a hundred widows in Chelmsford for one lady who stamps stilettos through her kidnappers!"

Mrs Denny arrived with a plate of bacon and kidneys, the sort of heart-calcifying breakfast that was certain doom to any man who didn't use calories the way Captain Bulldog Drummond did. "She sounds like trouble," the housekeeper opined.

"Indeed she does," Hugh approved.

I don't know you, the letter went on. *Before I trust my life to a complete stranger I'd want to get a look at you, make a judgement. I'll be at the Ministry of Sound nightclub on Thursday. Sit at the restaurant bar at 10.30pm and carry a copy of* Lady Chatterley's Lover—*that should help me spot you! If you come and I like the look of you then I'll make myself known. Otherwise, thanks for reading!*

"The Ministry of Sound?" Mrs Denny enquired.

"Very big club at Elephant and Castle, love," her husband supplied. "Started in the 90s—live gigs, three dance floors, three bars, packs in 5,000 punters on a weekend. DJs like Pete Tong and Paul Oakenfold. Not that I'd go to such places nowadays, of course," he added quickly. "Dens of iniquity, oh no!"

Mrs D nudged him. "You just stay away from your old bad ways, my lad! No more trouble, that's what you promised me. No more military police or actual rozzers a-knocking in the night."

Drummond scooped a big mouthful of breakfast meats and reviewed his invitation. "I could potter along there tonight. The restaurant bar?"

"The place recently extended, sir," Denny explained. "New dining venue, a fitness suite, business offices for rent at the back, and a state of the art recording suite. People rate the restaurant. It has Michelin stars and that."

"Well, so long as I am not required to dance. I leave that sort of mission to Peter or Algy. And speaking of the Devil, would you please get me Lieutenant Algernon Everett Longworth on the telephone. I would have speech with him."

"It's before nine in the morning, sir. Lieutenant Algy won't be up for four or five hours yet."

"That's what makes my call so enjoyable. I'm scooping up my kidneys and bacon and retreating to my study. Put the call through to the extension there, please. Excellent breakfast as always, Mrs D. When I'm on death row waiting for my last meal, this is what I'll expect them to serve!"

"There's no more death penalty in h'England now!" Drummond's housekeeper objected. "Not but what they probably wouldn't bring it back special-like for you."

Hugh allowed his domestic support's comments to shimmer off his back and found his seat behind his study desk just as Denny connected the requested call.

"Bulldog?" came a blurry voice. "Unless the British Commonwealth is about to explode and the United Kingdom is about to sink into the sea like the new Atlantis, why the deuce are you calling me at this ungodly hour?"

"I have enquiries in hand, beloved Algy, and the alternative to calling you was to switch on this blasted personal computer and attempt the internet. I decided it was best to leave such unhealthy pursuits to an expert. Kindly undertake some research for me."

Algy Longworth vented a long string of expletives that characterised his former schoolmate and former commanding officer in an unflattering manner.

"Good grief, Algy!" Hugh responded. "Do you kiss your ex-wives with that mouth? How is the lovely Ophelia, by the way?"

"How should I know?" Algy answered sullenly. "The restraining order prevents me from asking her. Meanwhile, her solicitors would quite like half a million a year in alimony from me."

"More than you pay Sonia but a little less than Tanya. You may wish to stop marrying girls before you go completely bankrupt."

"It's too early for you to start prodding my love life, Bulldog. Either go stick your head in a shower or tell my why you're waking me up in the middle of the night."

"To business then. I'm looking for a woman—reserve your wit, Algy, you need to keep what little you have—a woman who might be in a spot of danger. I don't know who she is yet, or whether she's kosher. I'm relying upon your technical wizardry to get me an ID."

"You couldn't just ask her?"

Drummond summarised the letter of application and its writer's alleged circumstances.

"Well, I admit to being mildly interested, Bulldog," conceded the former signals specialist from Drummond's 21 (Mobility) Troop, G Squadron of the 22nd Special Air Service. "Lets see... police reports of two-man assaults on a young woman in a car park, domestic burglaries, senior charity jobs four months ago... Got her!"

"By George, Algy, that might be a new record!" Hugh admired. "And what can you tell me about our mysterious heroine?"

"Phyllis Elizabeth Benton, known to her friends as Filly," Algy summarised. "If you allowed yourself a mobile phone I could send you a photograph. It's well worth looking at. If you like, I could rescue this one and you can take the next."

"Get your own mystery damsel, Algernon. But tell me more about mine."

"She's Chief Executive Officer for Shoreline Conservation Trust. I have their website here, they're a registered charity, been going since the '70s, doing good works for the environment, coastal erosion, protected species and the like. Turnover around six mill a year, run from donations and some government grant, looks like. She replaced a chap named Stuart McCloud last spring, after McCloud upped and vanished."

"There was an investigation?"

"Yes. It's still open, but… let me see, what can I hack that gives me more than press releases…? Ah, it looks like the investigation has concluded suicide and lost at sea, but there's no proof. No further entries on the Approach and Action list. Looks like our boys in blue have made up their minds."

"What about Miss Benton's experiences?"

Tapped keyboard sounds came over the phone. "They're taking the car park event seriously. They've checked CCTV, looked for the van, done a computer match for similar incidents in the police database HOLMES , all the usual stuff. I have copies of Filly's statements here. Shall I e-mail them over?"

"Forward them to Denny. Anything different from what she said?"

"A lot more detail, all recorded in police-ese. Sounds like you have the headlines. No trace of the gasmen, either, but they were ethnically different from the car park maulers. No fingerprints from the break-in either, but then SOCO were only there twenty minutes; what can a Scene Of Crime Officer do with that?"

"So in summary, Miss Filly was telling me the truth as she knows it, someone may well be after her, and she wants me to do something about it? Is it my birthday?"

"It must be. None of us expected your asinine advert to do any good. Now we can expect gunplay and explosions all across London."

"I won't be taking a gun to this nightclub, Algy. Our beloved nation has those pesky gun licence and concealed weapons laws, remember? We don't have a Ministry of Defence hunting license any more."

"You didn't have a gun on Rue de Rivoli either, Bulldog. It didn't limit the number of people you shot."

Hugh was becoming tired with his friends' general assumption that he would leap into danger and cause damage and mayhem. "Is there anything else I need to know before I go on my dream date, Algy? Forward any relevant stuff to Denny and he'll…"

"Explain the long words?"

"Work out what you meant as you slurred through your hangover."

Another voice came over the phone connection. "He's not hung over, Hugh. Just exhausted."

Drummond recognised that voice. "Tanya?" he asked Algy's second ex-wife.

"I have to go, Bulldog," Algy called hastily. "Good luck with the mystery girl."

"And good luck to you with the… Tanya," Hugh replied before the connection broke. Algy had an absolute genius for relationship disasters. But his love-life was never boring.

"I need a relationship disaster too," Drummond decided. "Denny, did Algy send over a picture of the fair Phyllis Benton?"

★★★

CHAPTER III:
IN WHICH FILLY BENTON OFFERS A RANGE OF DIVERSIONS

The lady was sat in a sheltered corner of the restaurant bar, her back to the naked brickwork of the chic converted factory space. She was alone at a two-person table, drinking a Martini, carefully watching everyone else in the crowded eating-place. From her vantage point she had a full view of everyone who went to the seventy-foot long bar that stretched the length of the room.

Drummond settled on a stool and ordered a Stella. The prices were steep here but the beer was good. He made sure Miss Benton could get a good picture of what she was assessing: 5'11½" of muscly, sometimes-battered ex-soldier with a rugged chin and a boxer's nose, broad shouldered and callous-knuckled, ready to stare anyone in the eye and spit in their face if they needed it.

He dragged D.H. Lawrence from his jeans pocket and flicked through to find a spicy bit.

Under cover of studying his book—an activity that made him somewhat conspicuous in the seething press of a Thursday night drink-and-dine crowd on their way to one of the dance-floors—Hugh also studied Filly. He collected blondes, and if she was the real thing then she was an excellent example. She had model good looks but she wasn't trying to accentuate them. She had a nice natural figure that her blue silk midi-dress concealed more than it showed off. Her thick hair was tied back into a braid; not many women could pull off Queen Elsa from *Frozen* but she managed it.

Her behaviour attracted Hugh as much as her appearance. She was checking the room but doing it smart. She wasn't just looking for him but for any enemy. He'd kept the same covert vigil in bars from Turkey to Argentina. She'd spotted him, of course, but she was biding her time.

He let her bide. She was decorative to look at and she had to have time to make up her mind. Choosing a knight in less-than-shining armour was a serious business, especially for a modern young woman who would prefer to slay her own dragons.

Filly noticed the two tanned patrons who entered from each end of the bar and scanned the room even as Drummond saw them. They were almost indistinguishable from the three-score other men who were milling about the place—almost. They didn't quite blend in with the rest of the clientele. They weren't looking to meet friends or to pull. These men had the look of serious professionals. They were here for business.

They wore jackets despite the club's heat, and those jackets had suspicious bulges under the left armpit.

Filly Benton rose, gathered up her purse, and slipped towards the nearest exit, keeping people between her and the searcher who had entered that way. She almost made it before a gaggle of micro-dresses broke towards the bar, leaving her without cover. The stranger saw her and grabbed her in what looked like an affectionate hug.

He had to be pressing a firearm into her side.

Hugh replaced *Lady Chatterley* into his pocket and sauntered towards the tableau. The other searcher threaded through the crowd behind him to reach his comrade.

"Filly!" Hugh called as the lady and her unwelcome companion moved towards the door. "What are the chances of us meeting like this?"

The blonde woman turned back to him with a delighted grin. "Hugh! I didn't think you'd recognise me after so long!"

Drummond suppressed for now his delight that she had researched him as thoroughly as he had her and that she was game for the adventure.

He snatched her from her companion's grip and kissed her soundly.

He snatched her from her companion's grip and kissed her soundly.

Her would-be kidnapper moved to come between them. "You dropped something," Hugh pointed out to him.

"What?" he asked, in an Eastern European accent; Drummond would have guessed Bosnian or Serb.

"Your guard," Hugh replied, slamming home a belly-punch that doubled the man over. "Your ammo." Hugh thumbed the release lever that ejected his opponent's Kahr P45 magazine onto the floor. "Your chin," Drummond added, bringing his knee up to meet the bent-over kidnapper in a jaw-shattering collision.

The altercation did not go unnoticed in the Ministry of Sound bar. People pushed aside. Someone screamed.

The other gunman reached under his jacket.

"Look out! He's got a gun!" Drummond shouted, pointing straight at the remaining kidnapper.

The resultant panic offered excellent cover. Hugh grabbed Filly by the wrist and grinned. "Let me take you away from all this," he offered.

"I could use a drink somewhere quieter," she agreed. "The fire escape is that way."

"Lead on."

A shot ricocheted off the industrial ceiling pipework. Drummond and Filly were left exposed as the crowd dived for cover or hit the floor. Hugh hurled a stool at the shooter. The time it took the gunman to dodge it allowed the fugitives to make it through the fire exit.

They were on an open iron staircase at the rear of the club, with a delivery courtyard below. Filly made to run down the steps but Hugh held her back. There was no time to make it off the stairs and across the open space before their pursuer made the landing and had a clear shot at them.

The fire door burst open again. Drummond shouldered it shut again, hard, catching the kidnapper's right arm in the gap. Bone snapped. The attacker's pistol fired by reflex but then it dropped from nerveless fingers. It clattered on the iron grating and fell into the darkness below. Drummond opened the fire door fully, grabbed the screaming man by his broken limb, and threw him off the staircase after it.

There was a clanging noise below that suggested damage to wheelie bins.

Another shot bit chunks of brick off the wall behind Hugh. Filly swore. "There's at least one more of them down in that yard! This must be the way they intended to haul me out of here."

An alarm was going off now; the door was wired to the security board. The club was evacuating. Similar fire doors on floors below and above opened too as club-goers made their exit. The staircase filled.

Drummond pulled Filly back inside, against the flow of the crowd. They hastened behind the bar and into the staff area beyond. Fire exit signs were lit, indicating another safety route for club personnel.

"Have you made your mind up about me yet, Miss Benton?" Hugh asked his companion.

"You make a good first impression," the lady answered. "I'm tending towards giving you a chance."

"More people may shoot at us."

"You are quite wide and tall. I like that in a meat shield."

This exit opened into a narrow alley onto Newington Court. The pavement further along was filling up with evacuating club-goers. A black Ford Transit van moved slowly along the thoroughfare.

"Would you mind strolling along in that direction, away from the club and the crowds?" Hugh requested Filly. "I want to see if those are bad guys trying to grab you."

"And if they are bad guys trying to drive-by shoot me?"

"Then I shall avenge you most righteously. But if they wanted to kill you straight off they could have shot you in that parking lot, or when you answered your door to the gas board. I'm guessing they need you alive for something. If I'm wrong and they shoot you I will apologise profusely."

"Then how can I decline?" Miss Benton winked at the soldier and headed off the play decoy. Drummond was gratified when the sinister van began to cruise after her.

After all, he and Filly needed a getaway vehicle.

There were sirens in the distance, fire or police. These had a deeper, less annoying tone than the French gendarmerie but they were a bit too American. Drummond still preferred the traditional old-style *nee-naw*.

The van coasted past him as it closed on Filly. Drummond grabbed the side door and hauled it open. A surprised Pole in a badly-made balaclava fell out onto the pavement.

Hugh stamped on him and leaped into the vehicle. A second gunman was there, but he hadn't got his pistol out of its holster. His head made a very satisfying dent in the Transit's panelwork.

Instinct and experience warned Drummond to duck. He dropped down just as taser wires shot over him and embedded themselves in the roof. The man in the front passenger seat made the rookie error of triggering them, discharging electricity through the frame of the van.

The driver was in contact with the metal. He shuddered and lost interest in steering. The transit mounted the kerb, killing parking meters until it stalled.

Drummond retrieved the Kel-Tec P3AT that the downed gunman had never got to use and fired two warning shots into the taser-expert's arms.

It was the work of a moment to haul the screaming wounded kidnapper from the passenger seat to the road. Head-Injury and Taser-Victim-behind-the-wheel were safe enough bundled into the storage space. The fourth man on the road needed another kick to keep him quiet and could then be left in the gutter.

"You seem to be enjoying yourself, Bulldog," Filly Benton noted.

"You looked me up. How?"

"One doesn't usually get away with posting a notice like that in the *Times*. One must therefore have some influence with management or have bribed a staffer. I like to do due diligence. I knew who you were before I wrote to you, but I felt it best not to reveal that or make presumptions."

"You are a rather capable young woman."

"I run an organisation that depends upon charitable bequests. I'm well versed in researching donors and celebrity volunteers." Folly looked at the captured van with its two prisoners and another pair of thugs on the pavement. "This is a little less like a day at the office. What is the protocol now? Does one drive them to the nearest police station or wait for the Flying Squad to appear?"

"One gets in the van before the other van finds us," Drummond advised.

"Other van?"

"We have at least one shooter still unaccounted for, the cheerful fellow who took a pot-shot at me on the fire escape. If, as you so helpfully theorised, they intended to extract you that way, why have a van all the way round here on Newington Court? It makes more sense to park on Gaunt Street, on the other side where that yard comes out. Also, our loud bleedy friend there had a burner mobile phone with just four numbers programmed in. Look, four names—Smith, Jones, Brown, and White. If we assign Smith and Jones to your beaus in the bar, then Brown may be the marksman in the courtyard."

"Which leaves White with another van round the corner," Filly followed Hugh's reasoning. She hastened into the captured Transit, trying to avoid the blood spatters where the previous passenger had ruined the upholstery. "I'm in. What now?"

"Two options," Drummond offered her. "The first is that we drive away, as you suggested, and deposit these unpleasant fellows with the constabulary. When they wake up they can explain to the Sweeney what they intended with you and who set them on. But the rest of the black van blaggards get away. Or…"

"We can try and catch them all?" Folly understood. "Why not, Mr Drummond? The night is young."

Hugh let out a throaty chuckle. It was moments like this that reminded him he was alive.

He backed the battered Transit onto the road, avoided the evacuated crowd that had now abandoned the pavement entirely to totter drunkenly over the thoroughfare, and completed a neat triangle round Southward Bridge Road, past the London Campus of the University of the West of Scotland, and back round onto Gaunt Street.

The burner phone jangled a generic tune, warning of an incoming call.

"Ignore it," Hugh told Filly. "Let them wonder."

"Isn't that the other van?" The blonde asked. She pointed to where an identical vehicle to theirs had edged out of its tight parking spot and was retreating onto the broad dual carriageway of Newington Causeway.

"They are leaving before emergency services arrive. The police here have no sense of humour when it comes to gun crimes, and London has the greatest density of security cameras in the world. Let us follow them. They'll possibly even be expecting it."

The phone tinkled on. "White wants to know what we are up to," Folly presumed. "He's not going to get much joy out of Smith and Jones. Who do you think we are? Could we be Pink?"

"You can be, if you want. I'd prefer to be Green. Or Black."

"Dark Green? Olive? Khaki?"

Hugh swung the captured Transit in behind its twin, heading northeast. Newington Causeway became Borough High Street, clear at this time of night. The vans passed the twin-columned frontage of St George the Martyr and on through Southwark, past the Gherkin and Southward Cathedral and over London Bridge to the north of the river.

"Why would anyone want to kidnap me?" Filly wondered. "I mean, at first I thought a pair of perverts, but I doubt they're this organised with teams in unmarked vans. Am I supposed to disappear like Stuart McCloud did? It makes no sense."

"No. Glorious, isn't it?"

"Not for Stuart McCloud."

Drummond sobered. "I suppose not. Did you know him well?"

"Never met him. When he'd been gone for two months, the Trustees of Shoreline Conservation decided he had to be replaced. They advertised, I interviewed, I was appointed to pick up the mess."

"Mess?"

"McCloud had been Director for donkey's years. The whole charity had grown up around him, depended on him. He had personal rapport with all our key donors, he had the trust of the Environment Agency, he knew the MPs and ministers of state for lobbying. I had a lot of catch-up to do. Still have."

"Was he lobbying for anything special when he vanished?"

"Oh, a dozen things at least. We do work all along mainland Britain and on some of the little islands off Scotland. Anywhere there's a shore, really. We try and shape policy on coastal erosion defences, on preserving areas of special scientific interest—that means places with rare or endangered animals and plants—and we hold contracts for volunteer and specialist work in land reclamation and beach cleaning."

"Sounds worthy but tedious," Hugh admitted. "Sorry. You must be really into that stuff."

"It is worthy, and it can be tedious. But not always. We can't all be shooting up the Tuileries every day."

"Once. I did it once. You, um, saw about that?"

"Put 'Captain Hugh Bulldog Drummond' into any search engine and that comes out first. It turns out you also have a Distinguished Service Order and a Military Cross. They don't give out those medals for nicely-polished boots."

"More for where those boots were planted," Hugh admitted.

"And in whom," Filly surmised. "I couldn't discover the details."

"Official Secrets Act. I did a few classified things in military service. If I told you I'd have to shoot myself."

"Does that line usually work on the girls?"

"About fifty fifty. I can see I'm going to have to work harder with you."

"Bring your A-game, Bulldog. Where are we turning?"

The van they were following had progressed along Lower Thames Street, past the Tower of London, and along Mile End Road through Whitechapel and Stepney. Soon after crossing Regent's Canal, the black van turned right into a tangle of small roads in the urban industrial maze of Tower Hamlets. "Looks like we're heading for home base," Drummond guessed. "By now they'll be wondering what the hell happened back in Elephant and Castle. Did we snatch the cutie? What happened to Smith and Jones?

What happened to our phone? Where did it all go pear-shaped? They'll be worried and suspicious."

"And armed," Filly pointed out.

"A detail. We have right on our side."

The transit they were trailing passed through the gates of a disreputable scrap yard. The high brick walls were topped with rusty barbed wire. Piles of old cars formed borders of a gravel track to a cluster of portacabins. The black van parked up in front of the only lit office.

"We have right on our side and two and a quarter tons of Ford Transit," Drummond clarified. He gunned the engine and aimed his stolen vehicle at the middle side of its twin. "Hold tight!"

The heavy front of his Transit crumpled the midsection of the other like tinfoil. The struck vehicle rocked and toppled onto its side. A brief yell suggested that someone was still inside or had been just exiting when the body had tipped over.

"Stay low below the window line, please," Hugh requested his date. He rolled out of the driver's door, located someone who was still upright and armed, and corrected the situation with a pair of shots to leg and hip.

The only light came from the headlights of the overturned kidnap van and the interior of the portacabin. Drummond was able to get an excellent sight-line from the corner of the overturned vehicle to cover the office door and take down the first tooled-up man to emerge.

"You might want to think about throwing down your arms and surrendering," he advised any others. "So far I haven't actually killed anyone tonight. My patience is running a bit thin. I have you covered and I'm so much better at this than you are. Fair warning and last chance."

The lights in the office went out. Someone still had their wits. Drummond changed position, taking the moment during which his opponents' eyes accustomed to the dark to sprint the distance so he was actually right by the cabin wall to the left of the door.

He heard movement inside before a burly pock-faced thug burst out with an actual submachine gun in his grip. Hugh slammed his borrowed P3AT into the side of the enthusiast's head, dropping him to the ground without a shot fired. Then, on instinct, he fired two waist-level rounds through the cheap cladding of the cabin behind him, at exactly the spot where a second gunman might wait in cover before following the first through the door. He heard a scream.

It went quiet in the junkyard except for the frenzied barking of a dog chained somewhere nearby. Hugh rolled through the open doorway, rising in a Weaver stance to cover the room, but only the badly-bleeding man who had expected a pressed-wood wall to protect him from .380 ACP bullets remained inside. Drummond kicked the kidnapper's weapon into a corner for safety.

He went outside and checked through the splintered windscreen of the toppled transit van. The driver was unconscious. Another occupant had been trying to get out through the side door when the side door became a floor hatch. He was pinned and had passed out from the pain of it.

Drummond completed his circuit and returned to Filly Benton. "I think you might use that burner phone to call the police now," he suggested. "And then I'd better call my neighbour about finding me some legal representation."

★★★

Detective Chief Inspector Mary McIver was not actually on the Major Firearms Incident Squad, or even on the duty roster, but she somehow managed to arrive with the second wave of police who flooded the Tower Hamlets junkyard. "What have you done, Bulldog?" she demanded.

"Thwarted a kidnapping. Captured an armed gang. Saved a lady. You?"

"He did rescue me," Phyllis Benton promised, anxious for her champion not to get in trouble for, well, conducting a small war in a London suburb. "These men came after me, with guns, and…um, I told those other policemen about it."

"That was you at the night club," McIver concluded, frowning at Hugh.

"I was just there for a rendezvous with Miss Benton. Have you been introduced? Mary, this is Filly Benton. She runs a conservation not-for-profit and in her spare time she is stalked by sinister gunsels. Filly, this is DCI Mary McIver, who last time I saw her was seconded to the hard-to-pronounce NaCTSO. What was that an acronym for, Mary?"

"The National Counter Terrorism Security Office," the exasperated police officer responded. "We are the unit that supports the 'protect and prepare' strands of the government's counter terrorism strategy. Which, I am starting to think, mainly consists of convincing you to emigrate to a different country."

"But Hugh didn't break any laws, did he?" Filly protested. "I mean, it was self-defence. A sort of aggravated self-defence and citizen's arrest. Bulldog saved me from those criminals and we had to follow them back to their, their *lair* to find out who they were, so…"

"Save your breath, Ms Benton," McIver advised. "Your boyfriend already called his school buddy, who called somebody in the Ministry of Defence, who called somebody at the Home Office, who called Sir Bryan Johnstone, our Commander at Central London CID, to make it clear that Bulldog is the tabloid papers' blue-eyed boy who must under no circumstances be blamed for the shootout at the O.K. Corral here. It's already stitched up. I don't have to like it. My governor certainly doesn't."

"Why spoil a good story?" Hugh agreed. "Any hope yet of getting a statement out of the sportsmen we bagged tonight? I'd love to know why they wanted to snatch Miss Benson, and I imagine she's a little curious."

"What did they want with me?" Filly also wanted to know.

"I'm afraid that information is part of an ongoing investigation," DCI McIver responded with a mildly malicious satisfaction. "You are the investigated, not the investigator."

"Says you," Drummond objected. "I am working for my lovely companion here. Assuming I passed the entrance exam, Filly? Did I?"

The blonde nodded slowly. "You'll do for now." To the Inspector she asked, "May we go, please? I'll answer more questions tomorrow—or the same ones asked again about ten different ways—but I really don't want to be in this horrible scrap yard any more."

McIver looked like she would prefer both Ms Bennett and Captain Drummond down at New Scotland Yard, in separate interview rooms, preferably without legal counsel in the way; but she knew her Police Handbook and Judge's Rules. "Of course. I'll have patrol cars drive you to your homes," she replied through gritted teeth.

Filly hesitated. "Actually... I'm not really happy about the idea of heading back to my place tonight. We caught these fellows, but they were so organised and well staffed. What if there are more? They know where I live. They've been in my house."

"We can park a car outside," McIver offered. "Or you could come back with us to witness custody..."

"Or," the lady suggested, "I could go home with Bulldog. If he'll have me. Do you have a bed for me tonight?"

"There's a spare room at my flat," Hugh promised.

She hugged his arm. "I didn't ask about a spare room," she purred in his ear.

McIver rolled her eyeballs upwards.

"Don't worry Mary. Your day will come," Drummond assured the Detective Chief Inspector. "You mentioned a ride in a police car?"

***

"It's not a big place, but it's handy for my club, for the park, for the West End and so on," Drummond told Folly as he showed her into his Half Moon Street quarters. "Down there's stairs to Denny's and Mrs Denny's. That's the study, the kitchen, the living room, the spare bedroom, bathroom, my bedroom… Ah, I see you don't seem to require a nightshirt…"

★★★

CHAPTER IV:
IN WHICH COASTAL EROSION IS CONSIDERED AS A MOTIVE FOR CRIME

Arthur Franklyn was Carl Peterson now, an English businessman returned from Saudi Arabia to re-establish commercial enterprises in his homeland. He was sat in William Rupert's office when the CEO of SoarBrite Avionics Ltd. arrived for work.

"How the devil did you get in here?" Rupert demanded. "Where's my secretary?"

"I gave her the day off. And a gift basket." Peterson set aside the newspaper he had been reading. The headline was about a shoot-out at a London nightclub and its conclusion at an East End scrapyard. "You and I have corresponded, Mr Rupert, but we have never met."

The CEO frowned, unsure what to do. If he'd had security he might have called it, but SoarBrite was quite a small firm with few staff. None of them were what might be called muscle, except possibly Mrs Briggs in Accounting.

"I'm Carl Peterson. We exchanged e-mails and letters regarding my acquiring your business."

"And I said no," William Rupert answered firmly. He took his place behind his desk, needing its authority. This Peterson was somehow intimidating just sat quietly in a chair. The man was broad, fit, with a mop of black hair and shot-cropped beard and moustache. His stare was intense and piercing. A faded red line down one cheek looked like an old-fashioned duelling scar.

"I came to make one last appeal in person. I want to convince you. May I make my case? Ten minutes."

"You can talk, but then I want you out of here. I'll call the police if I have to."

Peterson laid two manila folders on Rupert's desk. "SoarBrite Avionics Ltd.," he began. "Your father established the firm in 1962, with a single old crop-duster to hire out to local farms. When you inherited in '86 the assets had grown to seventeen planes and helicopters, mostly fitted out for aerial application of pesticides and fertiliser. Heady days. Of course, fuel and insurance were cheaper back then."

"We're doing fine, thank you very much. You know that, or you wouldn't want to own the business."

"Then came *Directive 2009/128/EC of the European Parliament and of the Council establishing a framework for Community action to achieve the sustainable use of pesticides*—those European Union document titles just trip off the tongue, don't they? Article 9 effectively banned the use of crop-dusting in all member states and overseas territories. 80% of your business vanished overnight."

"We have other contracts, commercial, medical, firefighting…"

"Now you have a sadly diminished fleet of twelve aircraft, only nine of which are airworthy. Two Air Tractors, three Piper PA-36 Pawnee Braves of various vintages, a rather shaky Grumman Ag Cat, a pair of M-18 Dromaders, a Bell 205, a Bell 212, a Boeing Vertol 107 and an honest-to-God decommissioned Boeing CH-47 Chinook that needs a complete overhaul. You are mortgaged to the hilt and about three paydays off being in default."

"We can turn it around. We are turning it around."

"You can't and you wont. So to my business case. In this folder to my right…" Peterson withdrew a certified cheque for twelve million pounds. "This is my best offer for SoarBrite, which I will purchase as-in including its debts and encumbrances. The paperwork is in the same dossier. It's the same as I sent you before except I've upped my purchase price by two million."

Rupert shook his head. "That's a gross undervaluation and you know it. Even if I was inclined to sell, which I'm not, I'd sneer at such a bid."

"In this other folder, to my left, I have some photographs." He laid them out in front of the CEO. "That is the school where your younger daughter is enrolled. That's her, in fact, leaving after class. This is the road she walks down to get home."

"W-what?" William Rupert gasped.

"This is your elder daughter's bedroom. That's her asleep in her bed. Such a pretty thing. That's a knife laid on the pillow next to her."

"How…? You can't do this!"

"This is where your wife does her weekly shop. This is her in that gym she attends. This is her getting changed in the locker room. Her regular routine is on this paper here. These are the addresses of her parents and brother, and of your mother's nursing home." Peterson leaned back. "On one side, I'll spend twelve million to acquire SoarBrite. On the other, I'll spend fifty thousand tops to have your daughters disfigured, your wife raped, your house burned down, and your family destroyed. All you have to decide, Mr Rupert, is which hand do I use?"

Rupert met that terrifying bleak gaze and knew when he was beaten. "I'll sign," he said.

"A pleasure doing business with you," answered Carl Peterson.

★★★

At Half Moon Street, Hugh and Filly were reading the same newspapers at the same time, while enjoying Mrs Denny's special breakfast efforts. The housekeeper evidently felt that any girl who had survived this far with Bulldog Drummond required a hearty start to the day.

"I rather like being the mystery nightclub blonde," Phyllis Benton decided. "I may have to add it to my résumé." The papers had eventually managed to identify the infamous Captain Drummond from CCTV shots outside The Ministry of Sound but his companion remained anonymous for now.

"You can put me down for a reference," Hugh offered.

Filly's comeback was interrupted by a rapping on the apartment door. "Inspector McIver?" she guessed. "There were bound to be follow-up questions."

"Mary would have had to use the intercom on the outer door. I would have given you two to one odds on her turning up before the kidneys were gone, but I'd also have given you the same offer on my upstairs neighbour horning in. And here he is!"

Denny holstered the revolver he had drawn when he went to answer the door and showed Peter Darell into the dining room. "I'm concerned that you might be degrading my neighbourhood property values, Hugh," he told Drummond. "There are reporters outside, being held back by a uniformed constable. You'll be hearing from the resident's association."

"Let them complain to the ground landlord," Hugh responded. He frisbeed a round of buttered toast at his old friend.

Dare caught it adroitly and took a bite. "I *am* the ground landlord. And you haven't even introduced me to your mystery nightclub blonde. Hello, m'dear. I'm Peter, Bulldog's better looking, more eligible friend."

Miss Benton passed him the jam pot. "Nice to meet you, Peter. I'm Bulldog's current case, but I also answer to Filly."

"Algy rather thought it must be you. I'm surprised he hasn't turned up yet."

"This early? Not likely. Algy is another of my inconvenient friends," Drummond explained. "His one redeeming feature is his ability to do technical things, like an idiot savant. Actually, he also makes Peter here look marginally clever by comparison, so he probably has two uses."

"Is this man bothering you?" Dare asked Filly. "If so, just say the word. I have a much nicer breakfast nook."

"But you lack the sublime efforts of Mrs Denny," Hugh countered. "Anyway, Miss Benton is my guest, under my official protection."

"And I already have his sticky fingerprints all over me," the blonde confided. "Sorry, Peter. It might have been beautiful but now it's too late."

Dare tapped the newspapers. "How much of this did they get right, old man? Did you really go and launch a one-man assault against the evil stronghold of evil?"

"It was a one-man one-woman assault," Drummond admitted. "Filly was there all the way, right up to when we rammed the evil league's minivan of doom. But why we had to go to all that effort, why somebody was so blasted keen to carry off a charity director, that's still murky."

The telephone rang. Denny answered it in the hall. "1234? Ah, right-o. Hold on, I'll come down."

"Algy or Mary?" Hugh enquired. Either one would probably have to ring the flat today for access because the intercom panel was secured from the press by the forces of law and order.

It was Algernon Longworth, clubman, playboy wastrel, serial divorcee, and, rather less on the public record, one of the best signals men and field engineers ever to survive the British Army's advanced combat ordinance course. The practical uses to which he had put his specialist training remained protected by a D-notice of press censorship.

But right now it was blithering Algy who stuck his head round the door and banged it on the lintel. "Dash it all, Dare, Bulldog's gone and got the girl again. Next time I'm going to advertise in *The Times* for a mystery blonde. Or possibly a redhead."

"Well, you haven't been divorced by a redhead yet," Dare admitted. "Mind you, the day is young."

Algy introduced himself to Folly, managing to almost drop his mobile phone into Drummond's tea mug. "I didn't just come here to make an ass of myself," he told the lady. "That's just a side-effect. I did a little more digging into Miss Benton's problems and I might have found something interesting."

"Ah. To business then," Hugh decided. "James, clear these dishes off and then come back and sit in on the confab, would you. I think we're going to progress on the mystery blonde's mystery."

The five of them settled round the dining table—Drummond, Dare, Algy, Denny, and Filly herself, watching everything with clever grey eyes. Algy opened up his laptop and offered his information.

"I got to thinking, last night y'see, that maybe the start of this is significant. Not two weeks ago when the fake gas-wallahs started swarming round Miss Benton, but five months before that when the previous Director of Shoreline Conservation Trust did his vanishing trick. So I looked a bit more closely into Stuart McCloud."

"Good thinking," Filly appreciated. "Everyone at work seemed to really like him and miss him. It's an uphill job to win over people who worked with him for so long."

"He built the charity up from a small volunteer organisation to a national operation," Algy reported. "He was sixty-one when he vanished, just five years off retirement and pension."

"I was told he left his office about 5.40 one Friday evening, locked up, and headed off for the Tube. He went straight to Euston station, bought a rail ticket for Greenock, Renfrewshire, changing at Glasgow, and then he presumably travelled there—and vanished."

"Why Greenock, begging your pardon, miss?" Denny wondered.

"We have a project in Greenock and Gourock, restoring the coastline with volunteers, but there was no reason for Stuart to go up there, let alone rush up there. And there was no sign he ever got to Greenock, though the police seem to think he might have jumped into the sea there."

"That's what the incident report says too," Algy confirmed. "He had no luggage with him and he gave no warning that he was heading up north. He never used his credit card again after the Euston booking office. His ticket was used at the platform barrier in London but not at Glasgow Central for the Greenock local line. If he bought a different ticket in Glasgow he used cash, or someone else bought it for him."

"It does sound damned suspicious when you line it up like that," Drummond conceded. "They searched his place?"

"Yes. He lived alone since his wife's death four years before that. Sad sort of fellow, actually. Whole life devoted to saving Mother Nature and suchlike. Bit of a radical in his younger days, marching against nuclear bombs and stuff, .but that was in the 70s and 80s, a long time ago. He was pretty respectable until his sudden disappearing act."

"He still had personal items in his desk," Filly remembered. "A picture of his wife, things like that. I don't think he planned his trip much in advance."

"Something upset him and sent him to Scotland?" Dare reasoned.

"Y'd have to be pretty upset to go to Scotland," muttered Denny.

Algy pulled up some files on his computer. Filly's brows rose and she objected. "Hey, those are confidential documents from the Trust! Those are... are those the application forms for my job?"

"All the recruitment files from your frankly very badly firewalled personnel department, such as it is," Algy confessed. "It wasn't so much that I was hacking as I found the files then realised they were supposed to be protected. But here they are, all the applicants for your job and the shortlisted candidates. There were four of you. Look at 'em."

"Caitlyn Stoker," Filly read. "She was an internal candidate but the board felt she lacked experience. I'm trying to bring her on as my deputy. She could be good with a bit more time. Latif Khan. He interviewed really well and he was actually the Board's first choice, but he turned them down. At this level, interviews go both ways. Some of the Trustees can be a bit fussy and irritating, you know?"

"Oh, I know irritating board members," Peter Darell agreed darkly. The businessman sometimes envied Bulldog's complete disregard for protocol and etiquette.

"I don't know much about this other candidate, except that he was excellent on paper, interviewed well, but something about him put the panel off him. Poor Mr Peterson. But his loss was my gain. I bitch about my job but I do like it."

"Algy, can you chase down this Khan and this Peterson?" Drummond asked his old comrade. "I want to know why Mr Khan didn't accept the post, and what was wrong with this Carl Peterson—assuming that Miss Benton wasn't simply the best person for the job, and no insult intended."

"None taken," Filly promised. "I'm curious myself now."

Hugh went on. "Also, since you have already ransacked Shoreline's database, and perhaps with the retrospective permission of its current Director, can you pull up old McCloud's calendar for, say, the week before he vanished? And his phone log if there is one."

"There'd be an itemised mobile bill," Filly suggested.

"Fine. Take a look for any unusual appointments, any atypical calls or patterns. If we can… ah, now *that* is the intercom buzzer. I believe DCI McIver has arrived at last."

"I say!" Algy perked right up. "The foxy lady from Special Branch? Dresses like a man but has the body of a screen goddess?"

"Out!" Drummond commanded Algy and Dare. "I will not have you slobbering over the forces of the law. Set up in Peter's sty and I'll call you back when we are constabulary-free again, once we have finished interviewing the detective."

"Isn't she meant to be interviewing us?" Filly clarified.

"I see it as a two-way street. Denny, throw these troublemakers out and admit the sublime Mary McIver."

"I see now that I am yesterday's girl," Filly said with an exaggerated sigh. "Whatever happened to the passion in our relationship, Hugh?"

"I'm not convinced I have time to show you passion before Mary gets up a flight of stairs, but if you're game… ah, hello, Detective Chief Inspector. It's a fair cop!"

"If you intend to try and be witty, give me some of that coffee," McIver insisted. She received a steaming mug inscribed with the motto *Who Dares Wins* and took a long swig.

"Did you get any sleep at all?" Drummond asked sympathetically.

"My governor sends you his regards," Mary dodged the question. "Well, his actual words were, 'See if you can't pull that dodgy bugger Drummond up for something, because if there was ever a man that hanging was too good for it's him. And I don't mind if he knows it.'"

"And pass on my best to Sir Bryan. I hope his bunions are improving. And his halitosis. And I don't mind if he knows it."

"You have to admit, ram-raiding a kidnapping ring is bound to set off a few alarm bells in your standard copper," McIver argued.

"But you said that Bulldog was covered," Filly insisted. "A good word from on high."

"That's what has got the Commander's dander up. He's convinced that Captain Drummond is some kind of anarchist mastermind, an arch-plotter fomenting Byzantine plans to disrupt the state and ruin the governor's digestion. Which goes to show he doesn't really know Bulldog at all."

"Because my heart is pure?" Hugh suggested.

"Because you'd get bored ten minutes into your Byzantine plan and punch somebody."

Filly remembered Drummond's comment about interviewing the police. "Any word yet on who tried to snatch me? Or why? Or for whom?"

"Well, we ID'd the perpetrators," McIver admitted. "Eastern European operation, a handy little mob who will be going down for some Post Office raids and a couple of leg-breakings as well as last nights attempt at getting themselves on the UK's most wanted list. Mid-level goons looking to step up to the big time. And strictly for-hire."

"Somebody wanted deniability," Drummond recognised. "None of them know who paid them, right?"

"A third party for a fourth party, naturally."

"What were they paid to do with me?" Filly ventured.

"You were to be held at the junkyard until sent for. Payment was by thirty-k of uncut small diamonds, pretty untraceable, half up front and half on delivery to a venue to be disclosed when they had you."

"That's pretty neat," judged Hugh. "You believe them?"

"Once we got them all separated out, and some of them on pretty good painkillers, it was only a matter of routine and procedure," McIver assured him. "You might not have heard of routine or procedure."

"So we still don't know whodunit. That's irritating."

"One thing that might comfort you, Ms Benton, is knowing that these men were given very strict instructions that no harm must befall you whatsoever, not a scratch, not a grope, on pain of a lot of pain."

Hugh rubbed his chin. "Interesting. And is this the same outfit who were trying to con their way into Chez Benton before? And who tossed the place later?"

"Yes. Their instructions were to look for files, folders, and any kind of computer or PDA."

"My tablet was with me at work," Filly noted. "I don't often take paperwork home. I prefer to stay late at my desk if I have to. Which is most nights, to be honest. I still have a lot of catch-up to do to fill Stuart McCloud's shoes."

"They wanted documents, though," Drummond considered. "Whoever hired them was looking for something, and they didn't find it. That might be why you needed to be kidnapped, so that you could be questioned about it."

"It can't be something on the server at the Trust either," the Director of Shoreline Conservation deduced. "If your friend Algy could just walk in past our electronic defences then we'd also be wide open to less friendly inspection. If what they wanted was there, they'd have got it."

Drummond rubbed his hands together. His mystery blonde just kept on giving.

"If you two have finished your double act extracting information from me, could I get on with taking additional statements now?" asked DCI McIver wryly.

★★★

Police procedural ate the rest of the morning. Hugh and Filly saw the law out of the door with undisguised relief a little after noon—and were immediately occupied again by the return of Algy and Dare.

"We may have got it!" Algy blurted excitedly. "At least we think so."

"And 'it' is?" Hugh enquired.

Dare tried to look modest, but failed. "It wasn't what was there, Bulldog. It's what wasn't. By which I mean, we found the gap where there should have been files. Where files had been deleted and scrubbed."

Filly frowned. "Someone removed documents from our system."

"McCloud removed documents from your system," Algy insisted. "Or else he never put them there at all."

"The accounts for your Trust in 1986," business-savvy Peter Darell said, bringing up the audited spreadsheets on Algy's laptop screen. "Miss Filly, what did Shoreline Conservation do with this flock of sheep that it bought?"

The Director blinked. "We bought sheep?"

"A significant number. It was one of several anomalous expenditures that year. You hired a fleet of sealed-box haulage trucks. And you bought 280 tonnes of methanal—what the rest of us would call formaldehyde."

"That's a pretty large butterfly collection," Hugh considered.

"I've never heard about that," Filly puzzled. "I mean, yes we could use sheep or goats as natural regulation mechanisms to keep down certain parasite plant growth, I suppose. Like some places bring in raptors to keep down pigeon populations. But formaldehyde, that's toxic, volatile, and carcinogenic."

"Is there anyone at the Trust who might remember that time, what McCloud was up to?" asked Dare.

"Thirty years ago? No. But some of our old-timers might know somebody who retired. I'll send some texts."

"So we're saying that a herd of sheep didn't only vanish from the account book but actually, literally vanished as well?" Drummond checked.

Dare hadn't finished. "'85 and '86 were big years for Shoreline. That was the time they stepped up a league, became a national player. Their annual turnover went from tens of thousands to more than two million."

"We began to get government contract work, reclaiming polluted sites and laying coastal erosion defences," Filly explained. "The Department of Environment is still our number one customer."

"There are logistics records for everything else that the Trust moved about that year," Algy reported. "Even bulk transport of sand to restore degraded beaches on the Anglian coast and to shift dredged mud from deepening the Firth of Clyde. There is no record of where that massive formaldehyde purchase went, or what the hire of trucks and crop-dusters was about."

"Do we know who got the transport contracts?" Drummond checked.

"Hold on. There's no names. Only expenditures."

Dare snorted. "There are hundreds if not thousands of truck haulage firms, then and now, but rather less plane or 'copter hire businesses. Even less that are fitted out for aerial spraying. We might be able to track that link."

"Why would a thirty-year-old environmental operation require me to be kidnapped now?" Filly demanded. "What has it to do with Stuart suddenly dropping everything to head to Glasgow? Why should…" She was interrupted by her phone pinging. "Hold on, this is work, with an answer about old-timers." She retreated to take the call.

Denny, who had been hovering in the background as he often did, cleared his throat for attention. "Begging pardon, sirs, but it h'occurs to me that buying that volume of formaldehyde would be like buying a truckload of petroleum or ammonium nitrate or whatever. Someone from the government keeps an eye on it, don't they? Because you can do serious mischief with that kind of stuff."

"And the '80s were smack in the middle of the IRA terror campaign," Drummond recalled. "Oh, yes, H.M. Govt. would definitely keep an eye on 280 tonnes of a dangerous chemical bought by an unlikely purchaser."

"You're going to bother T.S. about this, aren't you?" Dare recognised.

"What's the point of having a chap in the F.O. if you can't call him overseas to have a word with some other chaps in the DoE or the MoD or some other acronym to track down dodgy chemical deals three decades ago. It's not like Toby has anything else to do."

"He's in Paris. There are always things to do in Paris," Algy objected. "And girls."

"Because you can do serious mischief with that kind of stuff."

"Put in a call. See what he can dig up so long after the fact. Chances are that somebody signed off to allow the purchase, and that someone had to know why he was approving it. Civil servants like a paper trail, if only to cover their backs. Follow the paper."

"We might call Hannay," Dare ventured.

"I don't think any of us want to owe the old bastard favours again, do we?" Hugh cautioned. "Let's stick with sending Mr Sinclair ferreting into the corridors of Whitehall. If that doesn't work I'll turn my charms on the fair DCI McIver and see what her suspicious governor can rake up."

"Or I might approach her," Algy offered casually.

"She does her best work when she's not retching in disgust. Anyway, she's Plan B, because she'd probably want to make our little detection party all official, and where's the fun in that?"

Filly, who had been speaking quietly on her mobile, finished her call. "Interesting news," she announced to the room. "We can't place any staff from the early days who would be in the know, but we have one of the founding Trustees still around. Miss Corrie Dalglish was the Chair of Trustees up 'till 1988, when she retired. Dropped out of the world and retired, really, since she abandoned civilisation and took a little crofter cottage in the hills, miles from the nearest settlement of more than twenty houses. And there she dwells in reclusive retreat to this day, though she's still on our mailing list."

"Let's get her on the phone and see what she remembers about sheep and formaldehyde," Drummond approved.

"We can't. She has no phone. She has no mains electricity or mains water. She lives off the grid. But get this: her place is thirty-odd miles northwest of Glasgow."

★★★

CHAPTER V:
IN WHICH HE ENJOYS A VISIT TO HIBERNIA

The Cessna 182 Skylane dropped from its cruise speed of 145 knots and descended over Fyn Lock, a two thousand foot long stretch of water in the lonely Kilpatrick Hills of West Dumbartonshire. The quiet lake was surrounded by rolling plains, green but treeless as far as the misty distant smudges of Bowling and Dumbarton northeast and northwest.

"Good thing you told me there wouldn't be many good landing places, Bulldog," the pilot boomed over the noise of the wind shear. "If I hadn't attached the floats for a water landing I'd be wrecking my undercarriage on that uneven turf."

Jerry Seymour, operator of Falcon Flights, an international air-service for the rich and adventurous, seemed perfectly happy at the idea of a rough landing. He seemed to Filly to be some kind of ginger-haired Hagrid, too big and too Irish to seem believable. There was probably a whole face behind the full hedge-beard and red honker of a nose, but it was in hiding.

'Jez' was another of Drummond's parade of ex-service pals. When Hugh had called on him to get them to Scotland as quickly as possible for a personal call on Miss Dalglish, Filly had wondered just how many retired servicemen her champion might have at his call.

"A fair few," Drummond had judged. "But you've met nearly all the main ones now. There were five of us made up an operations unit—'blades' they called us. Algy was Signals and Tech. Dare did Demolitions. T.S., who I called in Paris, he was Linguistics. You haven't met Ted 'Sir Bangbang' Jerningham yet either, or you'd remember him. And when we needed delivering somewhere, we got Flight Lieutenant Jez 'Never Met a Whiskey Bottle He Didn't Like' Seymour out of bed and made him coax his bus into the air."

"The good old days!" Jez had called them, making an imaginary toast.

"Well, the old days anyhow," Hugh had allowed. "When we were no longer wanted, we all moved on. Dare went into the family business. T.S. got snatched up by the Diplomatic Corps—speaks five languages including his mother's native Danish. Bangbang set up a security consultancy. Algy just went full-time Algy. As you see, Jezzer started Falcon Flights. I did a bit of work pottering around liaising with Mary and co. on target-hardening Britain against some nasty people, until I'd annoyed enough bureaucrats to get my marching papers again."

"But we still come running when he calls," Jez had added. "Al'us have, al'us will. Scotland, was it? Hold on!"

The four-seater Skylane was remarkably fast, skipping 357 miles cross-country from a little private airfield outside London in scarcely more than two hours. Now it alighted on the surface of the loch, shearing twin sprays across the tranquil water as the hirsute pilot managed a textbook feet-wet landing.

By old reflex, Drummond was already prepping an inflatable two-person dinghy to get himself and his companion to shore.

"Thanks for the lift again," he told Jez. "We shouldn't be long. We just have to interview an elderly lady about some stolen sheep. No, really."

"It wasn't me," the roguish pilot insisted. "I've not touched a sheep since that time we smuggled one into the Coldstream's mess hall. Remember that?"

"I deny everything. Never happened. Pop the hatch, old man."

Drummond helped Filly into the inflatable raft and paddled it the fifty feet to shore with brisk, efficient strokes. "You have done this before," the mystery blonde could tell.

"Never with somebody so gorgeous, I promise."

"Oh, I don't know. Your friend Dare is very nice to look at."

They banked the dinghy and dragged it ashore. Drummond checked his GPS wristband. "Your old Trustee's house is about a mile that way, up towards Duncolm, that hill over there. We'd better hurry because I think it's going to rain and yomping over wet turf isn't much fun." He waved Jez farewell and set the pace.

Phyllis Benton struggled bravely to keep up with him. "I'm on compassionate leave, you know," she huffed as they marched uphill. "I was a victim in a major violent incident. I should be home in bed."

"I'll do my best to get you there after this," Hugh promised. "And keep you there as long as I can. But I got the idea you wouldn't want to be left out of the mystery-solving."

"And why should old Miss Dalglish talk to a stranger like you anyway? At least I'm running the charity she used to be Chair of. Hello? Is that a 4x4 driving along that ridge there? Is there a track?"

"It's the way to Corrie Dalgleish's house. Someone else is going to visit her!"

"Right now? Just when we are?"

"Right now. Stay here, low and quiet. I need to move fast and stealthy."

Before Filly could ask more, Drummond had dropped into a crouched lope, a professional hunter's run, paced and efficient. It maximised his speed over distance and kept him aware of his whole surroundings.

Filly was reminded of a big cat hunting the Serengeti, apex predator in a dangerous land. Drummond was dangerous—to his enemies and to her!

The Land Rover stopped outside a dour stone croft, a low single-storey house shadowed from the worst of the wind in the lee of the hill. A dry-stone wall cordoned off a tiny vegetable garden, a battered greenhouse, and a chicken run. Four men hastened out of their vehicle and hurried to the house.

The first of them kicked the door open and shouldered his way inside. Drummond snarled and went after them.

★★★

Luigi Massimo flicked on his ear-and-jaw mike and made his report. "Alpha Actual, this is Alpha One. We are at the location. We have entered and taken possession of the location. Location is secured."

Massimo and his three comrades were all identically dressed in disruptive camouflage combat gear, complete with body armour and helmets. They carried Beretta ARX 160 5.56x45mm NATO assault rifles, Beretta 92FS 9x19mm pistols, a pair of MF2000 grenades, and BM 59 bayonet knives. Their equipment was black market Italian army kit, familiar to them from their training with the 1st Carabinieri Airborne Regiment Tuscania, Italy's anti-terrorism paratroopers; but they had long since left their government's payroll.

"Have you found the old woman?" Alpha Actual asked in Massimo's earpiece.

"We are searching the location now." There wasn't much of the croft to search, just three rooms, a flagstone-paved kitchen with an old stone sink and well-top hand-pump, a tiny bedroom, and a common area that was now occupied by three of the four special forces who had come to take Corrie Dalglish. Massimo was reluctantly forced to add, "Alpha Actual, we do not have eyes on the target."

"Then kindly get eyes on her," Alpha Actual instructed. "Is there any indication that Captain Drummond has actually beaten you there? He set off from Falcon's airfield barely two hours ago."

"No indication of Hostile One," Alpha One reported. "We are establishing a perimeter."

"Well, if you do happen to trip over Hostile One, be very certain not to shoot his companion. If anything happens to Ms Benton there will be significant negative developments in the life of the combat team responsible. Ms Benton is very much required; more than any combat team. Understood?"

"Priority logged," Massimo responded, trying not to sound as intimidated as he was. Arthur Franklyn, Carl Peterson, whatever identity Alpha Actual decided to wear today, he was the most dangerous man alive, and he did not take kindly to failure or insubordination.

"Then get on with your search. Find the old woman and pick up any documentation. Anything."

Massimo noted the pile of *Women's Own* magazines stacked by the huge old fireplace where they could be usefully used under kindling. Other than that and a pile of cut newspaper squares by an old-fashioned commode there was little in the way of paperwork. How could anyone live like this in the twenty-first century?

"Hello in the cottage!" boomed a cheerful voice from outside. "You are trespassing. Come on out with your hands up."

Massimo unslung his ARX and took it off safety. "All units, we have contact with Hostile One! Fan out and locate him, remaining in cover. Alpha Three, you were supposed to be watching."

"I am. I don't see him!"

Alphas Two and Four exited the croft just as the burning rag stuffed into their 4x4's fuel tank burned down enough. The Land Rover detonated like a bomb, flying up from the ground as it split into two blazing halves. The grenade launcher in the rear compartment went up too, magnifying the explosion and sending shrapnel car remnants into the three mercenaries who had just begun their search pattern. Massimo was blown back from the doorway into the common room as the front of the croft was peppered with debris.

"He came in on the far side of the vehicle, our blindspot!" Alpha One reported, though he didn't think any of his team remained in the field. "He'd already set the rag fuse before he called us out."

An oval ball the size of a fist rattled through the entrance and rolled across the floor. Massimo hurled himself down and tried to avoid the grenade—before he realised that it was only a cobblestone.

By then Drummond had entered, was close enough to knock aside the ARX and make the fight physical and personal. He boxed Massimo's ear, crushing the headset, puncturing the eardrum. He slipped Massimo's bayonet out of its sheath and held it at the mercenary's throat. "Game over," he told the Italian.

"No," snarled Luigi Massimo, and pulled the pin from a grenade in his own webbing-belt.

The explosion that blew him to pieces ended the fight.

★★★

"Hugh! Bulldog!"

Drummond blinked away a red haze that blurred his sight and saw Filly Benton leaning over him. He seemed to be covered in rubble and dust—no, in soot. He was laid uncomfortably on a pile of coal, wood, and screwed up wads of paper, and possibly a set of iron fire-dogs. He was in a chimney, in the fireplace at that isolated croft.

He had dived into the hearth as his enemy had detonated himself.

Full consciousness came back to him. The last mercenary had chosen death rather than capture. That made him very fanatical or very scared. Drummond had had less than four seconds to react, and the only cover was the thick stone breast of the rugged old fireplace. If he had hesitated even for a moment he would have been shredded like the rest of the room.

Part of the stonework had collapsed on him, covering him in ash. It fell away as Filly pulled him out of his refuge. Hugh noticed for the first time that a narrow-faced old woman was glaring at him.

"Miss Dalglish," he said, wiping off one hand to extend it. "Sorry about the mess."

"I found her outside, gathering nettles to make tea," Filly explained. "I didn't want to interrupt your playtime, Bulldog, but I don't do the sitting-at-home-waiting thing very well either."

"Yuir young woman tells me that there are sinister doings afoot," the recluse burred. "That's why my front porch is firewood and there's a burning car and three dead laddies decorating the front o' mah house."

"They got here before us," Hugh apologised. "I wasn't sure if they had you trapped in here, so I hadn't time to be gentle."

"Gentle you were not." Cressie Dalglish looked around her wrecked croft. "These spaleens with guns, are they like to be my only visitors bar you, or will there be more?"

"More, I'd say. They had comms systems. They were reporting to somebody in real time. There might be a back up unit, a second wave."

The old woman nodded. "And that plane floating on the loch, yours or theirs?"

"Ours," Filly assured her.

"Right then. Let me feed mah chickens so they'll bide a day or two without me. Then you can take me away 'afore more men with guns come to disturb mah peace. You, Stuart's replacement—what do you know about gathering eggs?"

"I could be taught," Filly offered.

"Right. Hate to let them go to waste. You, muscle man, do what you need to with those fellows you blew up. Be ready to leave in ten minutes."

"Yes, miss," Drummond agreed tolerantly. He might as well gather up some useful equipment if there was anything left intact after the

Land Rover detonation. He doubted pros would be carrying any proper identification.

He was pleased to find that Alpha Four's headset was still functional though.

"Hello," he spoke into the mike. "Anybody home?"

"Alpha Four respond. Report," came the reply.

"Yes, Alpha Four here. I've decided to take a holiday. I fancy Blackpool, or maybe Bournemouth. I don't want to fight Hugh Drummond any more. It hurts too much. Perhaps you should put that in your assessment report, over."

There was a pause at the other end of the comm-link, and then, "Drummond? Is that you?"

"Rumbled. It is I. Or me. One or the other, I get confused. You'd be the villain, then?"

"If you want to class me as such. I prefer to think of myself as an unfettered visionary with pecuniary motives."

"You need new staff."

"Ah, alas poor Luigi. But there are many more where he came from."

"You hired the junkyard boys to go after Filly Benton."

"An associate did. They were also expendable."

Drummond frowned. "I'm going to find you, you know. You won't like it."

"It would likely end badly for at least one of us," Carl Peterson admitted. "You still have the option of walking away. I hear Tahiti is very lovely at this time of year. I'd even purchase your air ticket."

"Because you're my biggest admirer?"

"I do find you entertaining. Perhaps even a little admirable. You really belong in a museum, though. Heroism is rather out of date."

"Whereas villainy is always so 'now'."

"I mean it. I'd prefer not to eliminate you, but if you force my hand I shall act without hesitation or mercy. I will kill you—and Darell, Longworth, Sinclair, Jerningham, Seymour, Denny - and his wife. Consider yourself warned."

The threat was delivered quietly without any boast or bravado; only utter confidence.

"I hear you," Drummond acknowledged. "Now you hear me. Are you listening?"

"Go on."

Hugh pulled the earpiece out, held it to his lips, and blew the shrillest whistle he could right into the microphone. Then he crushed the device in his fist.

Filly and Miss Dalglish appeared from behind the cottage with a travel suitcase and a basket of eggs. "We're ready," the blonde beauty said. "I've explained to Corrie why we came here, about Stuart McCloud and all that, about what we need to know."

"1986?" the old woman asked. "Yes, I can see why y' need to know about that. You need files, too. Those are at my sister's house."

Hugh perked up. "You know what we're talking about? What McCloud was doing?"

"I do. Poor Stuart. I never even knew he was trying to get to me at the end. He knew I still had the records, y' see. Perhaps if he'd been able to telephone me, but… well it's pointless regretting such things now, isn't it? Take me to yuir aeroplane. I'm quite excited at the prospect of mah first flight."

"We can take you to your sister," Filly offered. "And those files."

"Mah sister's been dead these ten years, dearie. I inherited her house and I keep it closed up. Too many neighbours for my taste. But that's where I left the files to bide safe, and that's where they'll be now; at Gairloch in Wester Ross."

"The North-West Highlands," Hugh recognied. "Ross and Cromarty. I reckon Jez has the range." He led the way back down to the loch and the waiting Cessna. "I suppose we'd better radio in as we fly there about the problem at Miss Dalglish's cottage."

"How did they know where to come?" Filly wondered. "And if they knew, why didn't they come before?"

"Well, one possibility is that they have hacked your telephone. You got the address that way. Then we had to wait until Jerry could be spared to pilot us. If they set out as soon as we discovered Miss Dalglish's whereabouts, they might just have made it here in time."

"Oh. Sorry. I didn't think…"

"I'm afraid we'll have to leave your contraption here, Filly. They might also be tracking your location through it. They knew which night club to find you in yesterday."

Filly reluctantly parted from her iPhone and let Drummond shepherd her and Miss Dalglish back to the plane

Jerry Seymour was waiting anxiously. "I heard th' explosions, so I knew you must be having a typical day out, Bulldog. I was just debating whether to come out all guns blazing."

"No need this time," Drummond assured him. He pointed to the northwest. "That way, please."

★★★

The weather worsened towards evening, with westerly squalls off the Atlantic bringing rain and turbulence, but Jez's plucky Skylane kept up a respectable speed, covering a hundred and thirty miles in under an hour; the travel distance by road round the difficult highlands terrain was more than twice that.

The landscape beneath the travellers changed entirely. Bleak endless heath gave way to rugged barren mountains and tree-filled river valleys. To port was the grey strand of the Firth of Lorne and the Little Minch, the coastal waters of western Scotland, and eventually the plane passed the looming peak of Ben Nevis and the long dark streak of Loch Ness. Inverness was a polluted smudge to the east.

Jez dropped lower below the cloud, skimming the complicated crenellated coastline, passing over countless tiny inlets, with the Isle of Skye to the east. As the dashboard clock passed 1800, Seymour scratched his ginger beard and pointed to a bay ahead. "That's Loch Gairloch, which is actually a sea bay. I can land there near the harbour and probably find a mooring. It might be a bit choppy."

Filly glanced with concern at their elderly passenger, but Corrie Dalglish was staring out of the window like a well-mannered schoolgirl on a treat. The old woman stirred. "Have y' enough petrol to drive another ten miles, Mr Seymour?" she wondered.

"Oh, sure. Plenty still in the tank," the pilot agreed. "Why?"

"I want to point something out. It's relevant to yuir enquiry, Captain Drummond. Central, probably."

"Literally five minutes," Jez Seymour promised.

"Where are we going?" ventured Hugh.

"You'll see, young man," Miss Dalglish replied. Now she was the schoolmistress conducting the tour. "Northeast, please. Over Lock Ewe and a bit further till y' come to Gruinard Bay." She allowed her voice to betray excitement again. "I never thought I'd see this place from the sky, y' know. It's a long time since I was there."

"You know this area?" Filly asked.

"I was born here. And as a very young girl I used to picnic there." Miss Dalglish pointed to a prominent island in the bay. "My granny told us the family once lived there in the 1800s, before everyone passed to the mainland. But we used to row out for feast-days, before the War. I remember lots of wildflowers."

"And what has that to do with Stuart McCloud's files?" Drummond wondered.

"Because of what that place is, of course," the old lady insisted. "That, young man, is the island that did not exist on British maps from 1942 to 1975."

***

Cressie Dalglish's sister's house was a tiny two-bedroom terrace on a steep street up from the harbour. It had the musty shuttered-room smell of disused property, though it was still furnished in old lady twee from its former occupant. The surviving Dalglish sister had scarcely visited since it had passed to her, only long enough to engage a local women to "keep an eye on the place" and to settle legal inheritance issues. Now the recluse moved around the kitchenette dusting and cleaning, and once Drummond had found the water stopcock she filled a kettle for a pot of tea.

Jez had retreated to the local pub, but Filly stayed with Hugh to hear what Miss Dalglish finally had to say.

"Stuart and I both come from this area," the former Chairwoman of the Shoreline Conservation Trust explained. "He was born in Kinlochewe, about twenty miles that way. He wasn't old enough to remember Gruinard Island as it used to be, o' course. Not like me. Could y' reach the tea caddy from that shelf up there, Phyllis? That's a dear. Is there anything in it?"

The kettle boiled. Miss Dalglish wrapped a cloth around the metal handle to insulate herself from the heat as she lifted if off the gas ring.

"The island was uninhabited since the 1920s. So when World War II came along and the Ministry of War needed an isolated place, they compulsorily purchased it for £500, with an agreement that when it was no longer needed for the war effort after the conflict the owner could buy it back for the same sum. But that didn't happen. Couldn't happen."

"Why not?" Filly wondered.

Miss Dalglish sniffed the tea caddy and decided its contents were still good. She spooned four scoops into the warmed teapot—one for each guest and one for the pot—before pouring in the boiling water and leaving it to mash.

"The government was concerned that the Nazis were planning germ warfare. That they might bombard our cities with plague or chemical attack. So they decided to develop a similar response, in case. A deterrent, perhaps. They developed a weaponised version of a bacteria called *Bacillum anthrasis*."

Hugh looked up sharply. "Anthrax."

"Quite so. The Vollum Strain, to be precise, named after the Canadian chemist at Oxford University who developed it. Virulent, adaptive, and able to lie dormant for decades, perhaps centuries. Spread by airborne spores and internalised through respiration, ingestion, or broken skin. Symptoms don't appear for at least a day and can be delayed for up to two months post-contact. A first warning is y' get blisters that turn into black-centred ulcers, then fever, chest pain, shortness o' breath, bloody diarrhoea, belly pains, and nausea and vomiting—all kinds of unpleasantness. The worst respiratory infections o' the virulent strains like Vollum kill more than four people in five."

"You seem to know a lot about this," Filly noticed.

"O' course I do. Let me go on. The War Ministry developed Vollum 14578, their very best effort to wipe out Nazis using a weapon o' mass destruction. But it had to be tested in a 'safe, controlled' environment, and somebody picked Gruinard Island. A bomb was detonated there, an anthrax bomb." Miss Dalglish's hand quivered on the teapot lid. "A bomb so deadly that nothing lived on that island. It was quarantined, forbidden for over fifty years. Its very location was omitted from Ordinance Survey maps. Going there incurred a prison sentence—if not a death sentence."

"I've heard of that place," Hugh realised. "As for anthrax, we all had to be inoculated in our unit. Every serviceman is, though nobody knows how effective the vaccination really is. The Iraqis had the Vollum strain in the Gulf War. The old Soviet Union had about 200 tons of the stuff."

"Aye, well, Stuart grew up in the shadow of that history, of the curse of Gruinard Island out there in the bay. When he was a young man he and some others sneaked out there and took samples. The bacteria were still active in the soil, still live. It was one o' the experiences that pushed him to be an ardent conservationist. I think the pot has stewed enough. Pass the strainer."

"So Stuart McCloud knew about the island, had been there when he was young and dumb," Filly summarised. "And then?"

"And then, in 1981, there was a ridiculous movement called the Dark Harvest Commando of the Scottish Citizen Army. No, really. They claimed to, probably did, go to the island and port off about 300 lbs of contaminated soil. A box of it ended up deposited in protest outside the Chemical Defence Establishment at Porton Down in Wiltshire, the government research facility that had run the Gruinard Island test back i' the war. A similar box turned up at the Conservative Party annual conference in Blackpool, but while it was a similar soil type, that one wasn't infected. But it brought anthrax and Gruinard Island back into the national consciousness."

"I'd imagine so," Drummond agreed.

Miss Dalglish poured the tea. "It was decided to eliminate the problem, to sterilise the island. But nobody was quite sure how."

"280 tonnes of formaldehyde might do it!" Filly suggested. "Bulldog, that's what happened! That was the big project that put Shoreline in the major leagues! Isn't it, Cressie? Stuart McCloud pitched for and won the contract to do the clean-up. Aerial spraying of methanal across the whole place, then stripping and replacing every bit of topsoil. That's what all the canister-haulers were for, of course! And it all had to be top, top secret because the whole site was poisonous, politically and literally!"

Hugh received his tea and ventured two lumps of antique sugar. "Nicely deduced, Miss Barton. And for your next trick: what happened to the contaminated soil taken away from the island?"

"Well that… that's where I draw a blank," Filly confessed. "And I bet that's because Stuart and his government contacts scorched the earth behind them—again literally and figuratively. The missing files…" She glanced at Miss Dalglish.

"Yes. Stuart asked me to keep a copy, just in case. He never quite trusted the Ministry of Defence, y' know. It's just a sealed envelope, with the name o' the place where the old topsoil was buried."

"So that's what our baddies are after!" Drummond realised. "A huge supply of the worst weaponised anthrax ever created. Tons of it. They went after McCloud for it, but he slipped away, or he died before telling. Then they went after you, Filly, his successor, expecting that you might get let in on the secret."

"Oh dear," Cressie Dalglish worried. "I'd better find that envelope."

She pottered off into the front parlour. Hugh and Filly sipped their tea. "I don't really like it without milk," the blonde confided.

Drummond's mind was still on weapons of mass destruction. "There's a lot of harm could be done with that amount of anthrax. Even if a few people are effectively vaccinated, you could take out a fair-sized city. Put it in food, in a water supply, in air-con units… there's no proper defence. We stand a chance against nuclear terrorism, smuggled fissionables. We have detection methods, Geiger counters. But this…"

"It's not a problem now, Hugh. Not if we know where the soil was taken, what was done with it. You can tell one of your pals or your glamorous police girlfriend or someone, and suddenly it becomes somebody else's big-budget problem." Filly paused and wondered thoughtfully, "I wonder if we could bid for the contract to move it again? I wonder if…? If…"

"If what?"

"Hugh… Hugh, I'm not feeling so well. I can't see properly."

"What do you mean?" Drummond climbed out of his seat to attend to the wavering girl—or tried to. His legs weren't obeying him.

"Hugh?" Filly called, tumbling to her knees. "B'lldog?"

"Fill…" he replied, before darkness took him too.

★★★

CHAPTER VI:
IN WHICH NOTHING HAPPENS TO HIM

Sir Bryan Johnstone was fifty-one, lean, hawk-faced, and humourless. His professional colleagues at the London Metropolitan Police Criminal Investigations Department believed that if he was ever amused it might be a sign of the Apocalypse. It was clear that the world was not going to end today.

"So in brief," DCI Mary McIver's 'governor' said to her, "in another amateur vigilante display, Captain Drummond blew up a vehicle, causing the loss of life of three unidentified foreign nationals in rural Scotland, and was implicated in the… detonation of a fourth. All of this at and inside the cottage of a retired charity worker who was awarded an MBE for her good works in the field of environmental conservation. He appears to have kidnapped said 87-year old lady *and* possibly the young woman he dragged with him on his last rampage, and taken them to an obscure Highlands township, whereupon he vanished with both of them. His accomplice, a former RAF pilot who now makes a living flying rich big-game hunters and playboys across the globe, claims there has been foul play, though there is no evidence other than his word. Meanwhile, Drummond is conspicuously not available to help us with our enquiries into four more deaths on a murder-board that has now extended to three more whiteboards and a couple of flipcharts. Am I correct?"

Well, I wouldn't say you were brief, was the reply that his senior investigating lead stifled. Instead she said, "We are trying to trace Drummond's movements from Gairloch. There aren't that many road routes he could have taken. We know he didn't use the light aircraft he arrived on. We're looking at local fishing vessels too."

Sir Bryan consulted the documents in front of him. "The airman Seymour," he considered, scanning the witness statement and evincing a traditional Anglo-Saxon distrust of the Celtic nations, "He claims he was at the local pub 'taking a dram' at the time of Drummond's absconding. That's verified?"

"Jerry 'Jezzer' Seymour is quite noticeable. We have a dozen patrons who can place him as the soul of the party. There was a darts wager. He got back to Miss Dalglish's property about 11.25pm and found it empty. He immediately concluded that foul play had occurred and contacted the local constabulary—and the Bulldog Drummond Fan Club."

"So my inbox confirms," Sir Bryan noted dryly. "For an innocent man and military hero, your Drummond is involved in a great deal of random violence, sudden death, and significant property damage."

"He's not my Drummond, sir," Mary McIver clarified.

"But he's your problem. And now mine. We're classifying him as a Person of Interest in the Fyn Loch killings, and we're calling Benton and Dalglish Missing Persons on the locate-and-secure list. Run down the usual checklist, passport control, traffic and security cams, credit card transactions and the like. Find out if Scotland has any numberplate recognition technology like a civilised country, and if so track down any vehicles in the vicinity of Gairloch at the time. The A832 is about the only road that runs through the area. And find out why 'Bulldog' decided to invade a harmless fishing port in the first place."

"We have some new material on the dead men at the croft," McIver offered. "Well, the splattered one. It took a while. The Italian police force is complicated, with jurisdiction divided between the Polizia di Stato and the Carabinieri, and the Guardia di Finanza doing border control and, um, fraud cases. But we have preliminary information that the dead man's DNA may match with a perp on their wanted list for a bullion theft three years back. If so then he's probably ex-Italian military, a mercenary called Luigi Vitale Ezio Massimo. They're forwarding his jacket."

"Do we know when or how these men entered the UK?"

"Not through any regular channel, that's for sure. Best guess would be off a boat at an unregistered disembarkation point. We've reached out to Coast Guard but they're as overworked as usual so it could be a while."

Sir Bryan Johnstone's only hobby was the reading of Sherlock Holmes stories. He admired the Great Detective's ability to piece together arcane clues into a single coherent narrative. It was an ability sorely lacking in real life. "I want Drummond in an interrogation room, McIver. I want answers. A solution. The nightclub, the junkyard, Fyn Loch, whatever went down at Gairlock; they're all tied together. I want to know how. Why? Who? Get it done."

"Sir," Mary McIver replied.

★★★

"See, the thing is," James Denny explained to his unfortunate opponent, "everybody today underestimates brass knuckles. They're all about your knife crime or your gun crime. Nobody gets just 'ow effective a grip of knuckledusters is. I mean, the damage they can do. How much it hurts."

He demonstrated again. The Serbian debt-collector folded over and vomited on the floor.

"Thing is, with brass knuckles, you can just keep going for ages. Strike after strike, all in different places, till your subject's just a pulp of broken flesh without an inch of unbruised body. You can just keep at it, for hours, 'till he tells you what you wants to know."

"Stop," moaned the hard man; at least he'd thought himself hard when he'd been challenged by the balding, unassuming stranger as he left a delicatessen's shop where he'd been collecting protection money. Now he knew better.

"My favourite bit?" Denny went on. "What they can do to teeth. I mean, proper jagged stumps, painful as hell. But before I show you, while you can still talk right and eat without a straw, maybe you'll let me know 'oo hired your mates for the Benton girl snatch?"

"Anonymous…" the debt collector gasped. "Payment in small diamonds."

This time Denny applied an army boot, for variety. "Yeah, I'm not the boys in blue. Somebody 'ad to introduce someone to someone. Recommendations were made. Instructions got passed on. Give me a name or say goodbye to your smile."

The pavement around the Serbian dampened as his bladder control failed. "I heard a whisper, that's all. Somebody asked me, wondered, why the Americans would be looking for a grab team. Nobody even likes the Americans."

"What have Yanks to do with this?"

"I don't know, I swear. But the ones asking about my friends, the ones recruiting? I think it was that Chapter 51 lot, the drugs suppliers out of Los Angeles. That's all I know, I swear it."

"Chapter 51? Never 'eard of 'em." Denny patted his informant's head. "You'd best be telling me straight, old son, or I'll be back looking for you. You wouldn't like that at all."

★★★

Drummond awoke to a different kind of darkness. This wasn't dreamless insensibility but a physical absence of light. The floor beneath him rocked slightly and the creaks around him betrayed that he was on a ship.

He tested his surroundings. His left ankle was cuffed to a welded loop on the metal box in which he was held. The cage was six feet square, solid on all sides, with shuttered hatches on one wall at ground level and two-thirds of the way up. With a little more investigation he discovered a lidded plastic pail—a toilet bucket.

Drummond checked his pockets. They were empty, and his belt and GPS wriststrap were gone.

He tested the ankle-cuff. It was stainless steel police issue, with a zigzag moulded keyhole for a high-end padlock. It wasn't coming off easily. He tried the toughness of the container. The walls were rigid and unbreakable.

"Hey!" he shouted into the darkness. "Hey, you!"

He bellowed for ten minutes before a bulkhead rumbled and creaked open. A minute margin of light intruded through the sides of the cage's shutters. Someone was moving to the crate carrying a torch.

"Where am I?" Hugh demanded. "Where's Filly?"

The upper shutter snapped open, but the bright lamp that shone in made it impossible for Drummond to see out.

"Captain Drummond," came the same voice from the mercenaries' communications gear. "Phoebe Benton and Corinthia Dalglish are also my captives. Their wellbeing depends on your good behaviour. If you are disrespectful, they will be punished. If you try to escape, they will die. My word on it."

"You said you needed Filly."

"No more."

"Because you found where the contaminated soil you want was stored? What will you do with it?"

"I won't play the explain-my-plans game today. Instead I shall take my revenge for your meddling."

"Bring it on. Let me loose and face me like a man."

Carl Peterson snorted disdainfully. The hatch snapped shut, leaving Drummond blinking in the darkness again, his vision blurred with shifting purple retina-spots.

His enemy did the worst thing he could to Bulldog Drummond. He simply left him alone. He left him in the dark with nothing to do, nothing to keep him occupied. The ex-soldier was no longer an important part of the adventure. He could stay in his metal cage, ignored except for two meals delivered daily, and he could rot.

Hugh was no longer relevant. He had been beaten. Let him live with the failure, imprisoned like that for the rest of his days.

★★★

Captain Peter Darell's exclusive Half Moon Street penthouse flat was a lot more fashionable that his downstairs neighbour's. Drummond tended to simplicity and functionalism. Dare's rooms were designed in monochrome with metal tube furniture and rack lighting.

"It's nice," Algy Longworth declared as he stared around. "We should meet here more often. I don't know why we always end up at Bulldog's dump."

"Yes you do," said Jez Seymour.

Dare handed out cooled beer bottles to his two visitors and they waited until the rest of the party got there. Toby 'T.S.' Sinclair arrived by cab straight from the high speed Channel Tunnel EuroLink train from Paris at almost exactly the same moment as Teddy 'Bangbang' Jerningham was dropped off by one of his field staff. They came up the stairs together.

Bangbang's new appearance was a source of ribald comment from his comrades. "Just when we were getting used to that facial growth of Jezzer's," Peter hooted, "you go and become Bob Marley."

Theodore 'Sir Bangbang' Jerningham was always something of a surprise to strangers. Nobody expected the son of a baronet to be Black, of a South African mother. Now, two years after discharge from military service, he had grown his hair out and corded it into Rasta braids. It was a matter of amusement to his former unit-mates and a surprise for clients who hired security from his start-up company, Jerningham Enforcement Solutions.

"I didn't come here for a commentary on my life choices," Bangbang grumped back. "Somebody misplaced Bulldog."

Jez paused mid-gulp with his beer hoisted to his lips. "I was just getting a drink at the sea-front bar," he objected. "Hugh and his dream blonde were taking the old lady to do the exposition bit. You know I always avoid the exposition bit."

"And then they vanished," T.S. noted. "Just like that."

"Well, Miss Dalglish left a basket of eggs."

"Was the house locked? Were the lights off?" Bangbang checked.

"The door was closed but not fastened. The lights were out. Everything was neat and in good order."

"No cups or plates? No books off shelves? Were the beds made?"

"The beds were stripped. The house was disused, see? There weren't many books, only rows of knick-knacks. The kitchen was clean, everything put away."

"No sign of a struggle?" Algy asked.

"I'd have said so if there was. It was just empty. Somewhere between seven and half-eleven, Bulldog, Filly, and the old lady just vanished."

"They were tracked to Fyn Loch," Dare noted.

"Bulldog left Filly's phone at the croft," T.S. reported. "The police have it now."

"Then how did anyone follow Hugh to the Highlands?" Bangbang puzzled. "The timings are tight. You flew direct by plane and landed in the harbour. No one else did. By car it's about 260 miles or more from the Dalglish cottage, five hours minimum on those roads in rainy conditions. If they set out as soon as you were in the air, that offers a window of an hour and a bit to snatch Bulldog."

"Only if they knew where he was going," Algy argued, "which they didn't. It's always possible that vanishing is some wheeze of Bulldog's."

"He'd have left word," Dare suggested. "Some sign. Anyway, at least we know now why he went to Gairloch, what all of this might be about."

"We do?" checked Jez.

"Exposition, I'm afraid, Jezzer. Take another swig and brace yourself. It was that island you overflew, Gruinard Island."

"The Anthrax Island?" T.S recognised. "Shut off after they released the stuff there in the war and killed off a lot of sheep to see how bad it got? Then they found it was so infected they couldn't clean it up for fifty years? The place was only declared safe to visit again a decade or two back, and that was after a pretty expensive and major sterilisation project."

"Yes. You and Bangbang are coming in to this late, so you won't know that Filly's not-for-profit agency bought some sheep—off the books sheep if you can believe it—back about the time the island was being reclaimed. It looks now like Shoreline Conservation were contracted to handle the restoration. The sheep were to drop there and see if they got the plague."

Algy chimed in. "The previous Director of Shoreline, who disappeared six months back, it turns out he had some juvenile cautions for protesting about environmental causes way back in the 1970s. The first were about Gruinard Island. He may even have been part of a silly nationalist group who stole some contaminated soil and sent it to Porton Down. But in any case, he had a bee in his bonnet about Gruinard Island and he was the chap who masterminded the removal of contaminated topsoil and getting the isle fit to be delivered back to its original owners."

Bangbang frowned. "So we're assessing that whoever was after Miss Benton, and her predecessor before her, actually wants an anthrax cache?"

"And nobody wants anthrax for benevolent purposes," T.S. warned.

"Okay, so that's what we know from Bulldog's trip north of the border," Dare pressed on. "Next item of business, James Denny has kicked some information out of the local gangsters about where the money trail on the junkyard outfit goes back to. Algy?"

"Long or short answer?" Algy asked his comrades.

"Short!" Jez insisted, spilling beer-froth into his beard.

"There's an American drug-chain, a sort of super-gang of smugglers and distributors that calls itself Chapter 51—for obscure New World reasons, I suppose. The alleged top chap is… hold on while I get this booted up, ah here we go… is him. Nasty looking cove in the nice suit and designer bling on the left of this shot. That's Nugent Madison II, and he's supposed to control a fair chunk of all the bad things that happen along the California coast. Not that any law enforcement agency has ever proved it."

"He hired the gang that went after Filly?"

"Perhaps," Algy insisted.

Dare was doubtful. "It's not a lot to go on."

T.S. leaned forward. "Show and tell isn't over yet, kiddies. Uncle Toby has a story too. Remember how you wanted to know about how Miss Benton got her job? Well, Algy sent me the job applications and I whispered in the ear of some… well, I whispered. I now know how Phyllis Benton got the post of Director at Shoreline Conservation Trust."

"She was their second choice," Dare recalled. "The first candidate walked away."

"It's always possible that vanishing is some wheeze of Bulldog's."

"Ran away, actually. Latif Khan was warned off. Serious and unpleasant men came to his house. 'Don't take the job, it wouldn't be good for your health' sort of thing."

"So the role went to the number two candidate," Bangbang assumed.

"Well, yes, but not the expected number two candidate," revealed Sinclair. "There was a bit of a row amongst the interviewing panel, evidently. Two applicants were neck-and-neck, and at the last minute a very vocal feminist on the Board made a strident case for giving the female candidate a chance. So Filly Benton squeezed in by the skin of her teeth ahead of her rival."

"Who would have otherwise got the job after Khan was scared away. Interesting."

"Very interesting," Darell agreed. "Algy, can we dig a little bit and find out more about this other applicant? This Carl Peterson?"

★★★

Carl Peterson watched the first bulldozers strip away the turf atop the Skipsea and Atwick Levy, the cliff-buttressing project that helped protect the east coast villages from the North Sea's ever-encroaching erosion. Under two metres of imported topsoil was a concrete raft designed to shore the natural sandstone wall that defined the border between land and sea.

"This area of the East Yorkshire shore, the ancient kingdom of Holdernesse, suffers one of the greatest levels of sea encroachment in the world," Peterson told his sister. "The coast was three miles further out in Roman times. Whole villages have been lost under the waves."

"You like that idea," the woman currently travelling as Irma Peterson recognised. "You like the idea of change, gradual and catastrophic."

"They are playing my tune, yes. But civilisation tends to prefer stagnation. It wants things to remain as they were yesterday, not as they could be tomorrow."

"But tomorrow you might be richer."

"Oh, my dear, tomorrow I shall be richer. Or at least in a few short days." He gestured to the diggers and the waiting dirt trucks. "This is a key step to it. The Gruinard soil will be sifted, harvested for its precious bacteria. Then we shall see what the best illegal bio-laboratory money can buy can do to the finest bioweapon a World War could ever create from the work of a Nobel-winning scientist."

"The timeframe for completion is that quick?"

"Oh yes. There'll never be a better natural biological agent than anthrax, really. Some people like ebola, but that doesn't have the lengthy gestation period that prevents people from knowing they are in a contaminated area. It hasn't the dormancy potential or the capacity to render real estate as unusable as if it were radioactive. If one requires a city-killer, anthrax is the medium."

Irma understood. "It's not enough to kill the people. One has to kill the place."

"Exactly. What will this nation be without half its national monuments, without its technological and communications hub, without its accumulated urban wealth of a millennium?"

"Well, it will certainly change. Catastrophically."

"What our labs can do, what we *have* improved on technically since 1942, is the transmission medium for bacteriological warfare. We can now pair the Vollum 14578 strain to other bacteria that are faster-breeding and more adaptable. The Ames Strain in the USA, sent via letters in 2001, contained two virulent plasmids which encoded into a three-protein toxin and a polyglutamic acid capsule. Less deadly than Vollum but more transmittable. We can marry the two now, for the nastiest of both. We can actually improve upon a classic."

"You always have to go one better."

"Why try otherwise?" Peterson watched the concrete plug being discovered beneath the shifted clean soil. The Gruinard material was locked beneath that. "We should really thank McCloud for this. It was his ambition that made all of this possible."

"Didn't he cut his own throat in a railway station bathroom?"

"Rather than let himself be taken by Christophe and brought to me for interrogation? Yes. Otherwise we'd be a lot further ahead than we are now. We wouldn't have had to make his corpse vanish and we'd not have needed the whole Phyllis Benton gambit. At least now we know what McCloud was intending before he realised himself trapped. He wanted the incriminating documents he had left with Dalglish."

"Incriminating?"

"Oh, quite. You think that the government could not have buried that topsoil themselves? This is a country that encases and buries its nuclear waste, after all, trusting that precautions can keep it from leaking toxic radiation for a couple of million years. In fact they even receive shipments from other countries. What's a little anthrax against that kind of ground-poisoning? But Shoreline Conservation Trust was employed to incinerate the soil, to render it quite sterile in the way that the Russians did with their 200 tons of spores stocked at the Aralsk 7 base on Vozrozhdeniya Island until '02."

Irma knew that her brother could get quite excited about weapons of mass destruction. "The Trust did incinerate many tons of contaminates in the early 90s, didn't it?"

"Yes. But nobody was measuring the volumes. Incineration is expensive. Burial is cheap. And Shoreline had other important projects that were desperately short of funds to accomplish things that were dear to the hearts of McCloud and Dalglish. So costs were cut. Half the extracted soil was sterilised by furnace. The rest was quietly interred under a different Shoreline initiative, and the financial savings ensured the wellbeing of wildlife on endangered Spurn Point."

"Which is why there is still Gruinard anthrax to be had, and nobody is looking for it."

"Except us. And, apparently, Captain Drummond."

"Captain Drummond is persistent."

"And he is neutralised now."

"And his friends?"

"Will be neutralised if they persist."

★★★

"Good afternoon, Captain Darell," Major General Sir Richard Hannay II DSO KCB greeted one of his former command. "You wished to have a word?"

"You know I do. You know why."

"If I do, I always assume it is more polite to wait for people to tell me what they want. Besides, the way those requests are phrased can be interesting in understand the people seeking favours."

"I'm not seeking a favour. We're not playing those games any more. I just need to know what happened to Bulldog."

The septuagenarian military man smiled thinly without any trace of humour. "You don't think that information has value? It is a commodity like any other."

"I'm not here for word-games or clever banter. Do you know what has happened to Bulldog, yes or no?"

"I do not. I can only tell you who has been looking for information about him."

Dare frowned. "He's been on the front pages twice in the last month. Everyone is looking for information on him."

"But only one person has tried to get his classified record. I mean the actual classified record of what you all got up to in the Black Mask Gang, not the decoy classified record. I was quite impressed that someone penetrated that deep."

"You say 'tried to get it'? He didn't succeed."

"We are not all entirely bumblers, Captain. Would you like a name? It will lead to trouble, so you might well find Hugh Drummond there."

"What will this name cost?"

"Your future attention to some matter of significance to Her Majesty's Government and its departments of Military Intelligence," Hannay proposed. "The 'your' in that sentence is plural, by the way. I include Lieutenants Longworth, Sinclair, Jerningham and Seymour in this bargain."

"And if you get us, you get Bulldog," Dare understood. "We didn't like it the last time you called in a favour."

"I did not enjoy asking. But it was necessary. If I ask in future, that will be necessary too."

"Your definition of necessary isn't always the same as ours."

"No. Mine is correct. Do you want the name?"

"Yes, damn it. Tell us. Who's looking at Bulldog?"

"Oh, quite a fascinating character," Major Hannay promised. "In Geneva four years back he was le Compte de Guy. You recall the virtual currency scandal and the fall of the European Audit Minister? Two years since he was Raphael Libstein, and he very nearly set the entire Middle East to war. Last winter he was in Libya making Islamic State look like the soft option, and there he travelled under the name of Arthur Franklyn. We assess he is in the UK now, or has recently been, or soon will be. He will have a new identity here, of course. But he is likely your man."

"Who was he originally?"

"There's the thing. I've commissioned four entirely separate reports on him. Each of them has found absolute evidence of his origins. Each one of them proved entirely wrong. He is not the son of a Norwegian Nazi collaborator. He is not the disinherited heir of Moroccan royalty. He did not grow up as a brutal street-fighter in post-British Hong Kong. He was not a survivor of ethnic cleansing in Angola. He appears on no Interpol list but I rate him the most dangerous man in Britain today."

"What's his interest in Bulldog?"

"Undetermined. It might simply be morbid fascination, like the rest of us."

"Could he have snatched Hugh now?"

"I do hope so," Hannay answered. "That would be a very useful development." He stood up to return to his club. "Good day, Captain, and good luck. You will be hearing from me presently... as it becomes necessary."

★★★

Drummond had no way of tracking time from his irregular meals, but he felt to have a three-day beard growth. He tried talking to his jailors when they delivered food or exchanged his slops bucket but they had orders to ignore him. They knew better than to respond to his taunts or get close when the hatches were open.

The rest of the time he was in darkness. Sometimes he heard movement in the cargo hold where his cage-cube was stored, crates being shifted about, chains rattling, an overhead crane on its runners. There were voices shouting in a language he did not speak—it sounded like Russian. But he was denied information as much as light. Peterson understood how to get to Bulldog Drummond.

Hugh worried about the other hostages and wondered about the parts of the plot he hadn't yet fathomed. He tried to estimate how long it might take his enemies to retrieve the soil deposit they wanted, and what it would take to extract the deadly bacteria for it to be redeployed.

He waited for a chance.

And he waited.

★★★

CHAPTER VII:
IN WHICH THERE ARE NAVIGATIONAL HAZARDS

"Sorry, comrade. If you want me to understand what the hell you're gloating about you'll have to talk in a proper language," Hugh told Viktar Filchenkov, after one of the Russian's lookalike female aides opened the observation shutter on the captive's cage. Drummond had no idea who the stranger was but he knew that his moment had come.

"I said, you are not very impressive," Filchenkov repeated in English, with a sneer. "I came to see the terrible monster who somehow ended Luigi Massimo and his strike team, but all I see is a sweaty ape who had a moment of luck."

"Yeah, I keep having them. Am I supposed to know who you are, sunshine? Is that your backing singers with you?"

Alonya and Viera wore their identical white dresses like models off a catwalk, but they kept their hands free and their eyes alert at all times.

"Franklyn said not to engage with you," the Russian politician scorned Drummond. "I see why now. You are not worth the bother."

"Take me out of this cage and repeat that, Ivan. I bet you won't, though. I can see the murderer in your eyes, but not the killer."

"How stupid do you think I am, Englishman?"

"Stupid enough to feed me straight lines. Franklyn's the brains of your outfit, isn't he? You're what? The clothes rack?"

"He works for *me!*" Filchenkov snapped. "He is a hireling. A superior one, I admit, but *I* am paying *him.*"

Drummond chuckled. "Wow. You really bought that? He is good. So your 'underling' ordered you not to let me out of this box, not to talk to me because you might screw up. And now he's not on the boat so you can swagger a little."

Peterson had indeed left the ex-Soviet cargo ship *Ostap Bender* to attend to matters at the East Yorkshire excavation site, but Filchenkov was hardly about to conform the prisoner's jibe. "This is my boat. My crew. You are my captive."

"And Misses Benton and Dalglish? Where have you got them stowed?"

"Somewhere secure. Miss Benton is quite attractive, is she not? She is in the cabin next to mine."

"You touch her and I stop my good behaviour," Hugh warned. "What's Russian for 'I will feed you your balls'?"

"Perhaps I will tell you as I demonstrate?" Filchenkov offered.

"You won't. You'd bleed all over your expensive Western suit and you'd cry in front of your girlfriends."

The Russian oligarch spat something crude in his mother tongue. "Get him out like he wants," he instructed Alonya and Viera. "He needs a lesson."

"From you?" Drummond scorned. "Bring it on."

He wasn't sure where Alonya produced a handgun from but suddenly it was centred on his chest. Viera opened the cage door and indicated that the prisoner should keep his hands up while she released his ankle-bond.

"Now out," she told Hugh in heavily accented English.

Drummond climbed from the crate, trying to get circulation back into his legs.

"Teach him," Filchenkov ordered.

Viera brought a knee up to Hugh's groin. He was ready to block but even then he was almost too slow. She followed with a nerve punch that numbed his left arm and a crane-swipe that knocked his tingling legs from under him.

Alonya danced in to add a kick to his head that he scarcely rolled away from, and then Viera was back, dropping onto his right leg to pin him so she could deliver a wicked gut-punch.

Drummond caught her, twisted her across him as a shield from Alonya's next kick, and hurled her at her twin to give him some breathing space.

He was barely on his feet when they both came again, flanking him like the world's best-looking tag team, landing blow after blow despite his best counters. They worked together, falling back in turn as he concentrated his efforts then jumping in as he switched to fighting the other. Hugh never connected with a solid blow.

One on one he might have had a chance. Two to one against fighters this well trained he was in trouble.

Alonya managed to plant a foot onto his chest, kicking him back to splinter through a cargo crate of white full-body sterile suits. He used one of the garments up tangle Viera's hands and swivel her away. That bought him enough time to retreat again before the women could corner him.

Filchenkov stood back from the conflict, enjoying the beating his aides were inflicting on the insolent Englishman.

Drummond fell back again, tumbling to crush a pile of discarded cardboard boxes netted to one bulkhead. He snatched up some black plastic packing ribbon and looped it round Alonya's wrist, swinging her to impact with a stanchion-post. That allowed him a breath to beat past Viera's guard and knock her away too.

He reached the object he's been looking for, a commercial staple gun for sealing lids. He swung round to the smug politician and fired a half dozen staples through the air at him. Filchenkov yelped as one drew blood on his wrist.

Viera and Alonya redoubled their efforts, angry now. Viera knocked Hugh to his knees, where he couldn't block a head-kick from Alonya that put him on the ground. Then the women had him pinned and he was helpless to stop their body-blows, again and again until he could scarcely remain conscious.

"*Dostatochno,*" Filchenkov said. *Enough.* He walked over to the floor where his aides had beaten Drummond bloody and looked down at the prisoner.

Hugh tried to spit but he only managed to ooze blood from his busted lip.

"You attacked me," the Russian oligarch snarled, white with fury. "You *hurt* me."

He found the staple gun, bent over the held-down man, and fired three pins into Hugh's cheek. He considered adding one to the eyeball but he knew that Franklyn had said to leave Drummond alone. Finally, he vented his frustration with three more staples below the belt. It wasn't feeding the Englishman his balls yet, but it would do on account.

"Throw him back into the dark," he told Alonya and Viera.

Hugh couldn't resist. He was hurled into his cage, the ankle-cuff clicked home, and the door slammed shut.

He let the vertigo and nausea subside for a while before he started to laugh. He prised the six bloody staples from his body. They were strong steel hoops half an inch long.

They were all he needed to escape.

★★★

By feeding time he was ready. It had taken Drummond much frustrated fumbling to pick his ankle-cuff lock in the dark with makeshift tools. Three staples had broken and a fourth had been lost where he couldn't feel it before he had finally managed to spring the manacle. Now he was only trapped in a barred steel cage.

The routine for delivering his meals was always the same, even if the timings of them were deliberately random to increase his disorientation. Two armed guards came, one to cover him with a firearm while the other received his full latrine can, replaced it, and handed in food that tasted as dull as the thin cardboard container it came in.

The system relied on the prisoner being shackled to the rear of the box. Drummond could not reach out and grab at an arm without going full stretch and offering plenty of warning to the guard aiming the pistol. Except that now Hugh wasn't restrained like that.

This time when the sailors arrived, Drummond was prepared. As the guard pushed the clean slops pail through the lower hatch, Hugh shifted to the side, grabbed the man's wrist, and hauled with all his strength and speed. The guard's head impacted the metal door; he grunted and then he slumped.

Hugh dipped below the line of fire of the top hatch, in the lee he wouldn't have been able to reach if he had still been cuffed. The lower hatch was too small for him to escape, but it was fine for reaching through and commandeering the downed sailor's sidearm.

Then it was a matter of sharpshooting. Drummond popped up at the top hatch and placed one careful round in the other sailor's right forearm. The guard screeched and lost his grip on his gun.

"Don't try anything," Drummond warned. He hoped his tone would get the command across if the Russian seaman didn't understand his language. "Come here. Open this door."

If the guard did anything else, Hugh could drop him. The man spread out his good arm in the universal gesture of surrender. He approached the cage and shot back the latch-clasps that held it shut.

Drummond pressed his shoulder to the gate and pushed it open despite the unconscious men that lay across it like a doormat.

"Get in the box," Hugh ordered Gunshot Wound. "Take him with you. Give me your spare ammunition. Now tourniquet that arm if you don't want to pass out."

He sealed the guards in his former cage and thoughtfully left them his meal in case they got peckish.

Now it was time to case the ship. He knew it was some kind of commercial cargo vessel, quite large and not new. The boxes it carried were a mixture of industrial and scientific equipment, including a lot of those white sterile suits. "Almost as if they expected to be heading into a biological contamination zone," Hugh muttered.

He defined his objectives: first secure the ship; signal for aid; when it was safe, liberate Filly and Miss Dalglish.

The *Ostap Bender* was a Panamax bulk-break cargo ship—that is, it met the Panama Canal Authority's size specifications for fitting through the two older sets of locks, the upper limit for most commercial freighters of its vintage, and it carried boxes and containers. Over 900 feet long, with a 100ft beam and a 25ft draft, the vessel weighed in at 50,000 dead weight tons. The shallow cargo hold in which Drummond had been kept was the only traditional storage space. Everything above that was steel cargo containers on a low deck, with a capacity for 3000 twenty-foot equivalent boxes. The *Ostap Bender* was fully laden.

For its size, the ship was relatively low on crew. Drummond was able to get almost to the bridge before he encountered anyone else.

A regular seaman backed out of a mess room, chattering to comrades, and almost bumped into Hugh before he noticed him. Drummond pressed his borrowed Lebedev PL-15 pistol into the sailor's temple and indicated he should step quietly back into the mess.

He took the six off-duty crew by surprise, and such was his authority—or perhaps the expression on his well-bruised and swollen face - that none of them objected when he shepherded them into the adjacent galley and shut them in the meat locker.

None of them admitted to speaking English, so he couldn't get any sense when he asked about a captive blonde or an old woman.

Bridge, boiler, and funnel were all amidships. There was a keycode on the hatch onto the command deck, so Drummond politely knocked. When someone answered he slammed his boot into the door and caught the unfortunate sailor behind it.

The bridge was long and narrow, spanning the entire width of the superstructure. There were two armed guards there, with holstered sidearms identical to the pistol Hugh held. The difference was that his weapon was primed and aimed. He took the men down without hesitation, then turned his gun on the four-man bridge crew."

"Somebody had better speak English or all of you are taking bullets," he warned them.

"I am speak of English!" the watch commander answered hastily.

"Then tell your people to back away and get against the rear wall. Now!"

The crew complied. Nobody wanted to be a hero when that savage face was staring at them.

It was dark outside the wide ship's windows, with only running lights to show the distant perimeters of the vessel. Bridge lighting was muted red for night running, though the navigation computer was doing the actual steering right now.

"Where are we?"

The deck officer pointed to charts. "*Islandiya*… Iceland."

"We're heading to Iceland? Or we're there?"

"In one hour, perhaps?"

"Docking where?" There were naval charts on the map table, with the cards for the southern Iceland coastline from Reykjavik to Djúpivogur, but a red cross indicated an unnamed destination in one of the minor inlets between Hvalnee and Seley.

The deck officer clamped his mouth shut, pale and frightened.

"What's your cargo?" Hugh asked. "Is this where you're delivering it?"

The watch commander nodded. "Tools. Medical supplies. Vehicles. Cutting equipment. Many things."

"Things that might exploit a city crippled by a bio-attack," Drummond speculated. "Again, what's here?"

"We do not know. We follow Gospodin Filchenkov's orders."

"Filchenkov? Is that the streak in the suit with the two lethal bimbos?" The Russian seemed puzzled by Hugh's colloquial slurs. "Is he an older guy dressed well, with two female companions?"

All the crew nodded. If they didn't follow the language they understood the figure of eight shape he made with his hands when describing Alonya and Viera.

"He's a big man back home?"

"Rich. Powerful. Many friends."

"I'm really not one of 'em. Where is he?"

"Master cabin."

"With his ladies? I guess he gets horny when he has someone beaten up. He seems the type. What about any other passengers? A pretty blonde and an old lady?"

The crew agreed there was an attractive girl in the stateroom next to Filchenkov's, but they knew nothing of Miss Dalglish.

Drummond snarled. "Right. So this crate is heading for a secret location that doesn't appear on the regular charts, carrying a bunch of kit that could be used to equip a small army, and nobody knows about it but us." He looked at the radio, an expensive state of the art digital model, newer than the bridge it was fitted in. "Get me through to the coast guard," he ordered.

The crew exchanged unhappy looks. "We cannot," their commander explained. "Silence of radio."

"You will. Push buttons or I pull triggers."

"Cannot!" the sailor insisted, frightened. He mimed typing on a numberpad. "Key code. Only captain and Gospodin Filchenkov."

"Looks like I need a word with your boss, then." Hugh smiled unpleasantly. "Fellahs, down the hatch. You're going into the meat locker. I'm going to the master cabin."

★★★

The *Ostap Bender's* guest cabin doors were wood-panelled over watertight steel, and they required key-cards. There was no way to break in without heavy cutting gear. Instead, Hugh hefted the fire extinguisher off the companionway wall, leaned it against Filchenkov's door, tapped deferentially, and retreated to the stairwell.

Alonya answered the rap, cautiously opening the door a fraction so she could see who was interrupting her employer's sleep. Drummond fired a single shot into the extinguisher bottle, detonating it in a spray of CO_2 that caught Filchenkov's aide right in the face.

She staggered back, still managing to squeeze off a couple of shots from a designer pistol that Hugh didn't recognise, but the powder cloud effectively blinded her. Drummond closed the distance, kicked the door wide, shouldered past her and dropped into a defensive roll. Viera sprayed bullets where he had been a second before, pockmarking the teak-clad walls with shot-holes.

Drummond fired back, catching her in the hip. She dropped behind the bed, knowing its steel frame would give her cover, and pulled Filchenkov down beside her.

Alonya grabbed Hugh from behind, trying to lock his arm, but he was braced on one knee. He caught her and heaved her over his head, sending her crashing into a coffee table, shattering antique Romanoff china. As she reached for a concealed knife, Hugh made a hard call and fired a single round through her forehead.

Viera leaped from cover, heedless of her own safety, orienting her pistol on Alonya's killer. Drummond shot out the cabin light, plunging the room into gloom and shifting position to avoid the woman's shots. He jumped her, relying on his bulk to slam her back into the bedhead.

She raked for his eyes, struggling to bring her gun to bear. He headbutted her nose, and as she fell back he loosed an identical round into her forehead too.

A tilt of the ship swung the cabin door wide again, playing a rectangle of light across the bullet-riddled wall. Filchenkov looked over the devastation, at his dead aides, at the man he had tormented free and armed before him. He tried to reach for Viera's discarded gun.

"No." Drummond caught the oligarch's wrist and snapped it. "You're with me, Ivan. This way."

Viktar Savvich Filchenkov screamed but could not resist, because the Englishman was dragging him by his broken hand. He stumbled over Alonya's corpse but Drummond had no mercy and gave him no quarter.

There was already shouting on the crew deck one level below, and the sound of men moving.

"This way, comrade." Hugh pushed Filchenkov ahead of him up the stairs back to the command deck. He had propped the bridge door open so he could regain entry, and now he hastened his prisoner inside as the first guards came into view below. A rattle of bullets ricocheted off the bulkhead beside the intruder.

Hugh tossed the politician down beside the dead bridge guards and kicked the door shut. There was an internal bolt that closed off this control cabin's reinforced door against piracy. Right now Drummond was on the most secure place in the ship—but there was no way out.

He checked the auto-navigation instruments and saw that they were closing on the programmed co-ordinates. The first glimmer of dawn showed the dull edges of a fjord bank. The ship was manoeuvring down one of the innumerable inlets on the Icelandic coast. The display screen named it but Drummond could never have pronounced it. There were too many þ's and ð's.

"What's our destination?" he asked Filchenkov.

"I'll see you die slowly in a concentration camp for this," the Russian promised.

Drummond hit him and slammed his head back into the wall. "Where are we going?"

"A staging area, that's all," Filchenkov answered reluctantly. "A place to gather men and supplies while we wait for a long-planned opportunity."

"The anthrax attack? I'll stop it."

"You won't. It's not aboard. It's been recovered, claimed, but even I don't know where it's been taken." There were thumping sounds as people beat on the bridge door. "There's nowhere for you to run, Drummond!"

"I'm not running." Hugh hit him again. "I'm sailing."

He checked the controls. There were a lot of dials and switches he didn't understand, but the big speed lever was pretty obvious. He grabbed it and pushed it back to полной - *Full*.

The auto-nav began bleeping and flashing red warnings. Drummond hit the *Ignore* options. When it asked if he required manual control, he selected *No*. He just wanted to get to the final destination faster.

A bullet hit the observation window in front of him, starring the reinforced safety glass.

"I can make you rich," Filchenkov offered. "You could leave here with Miss Benton and be a rich man."

"Stop boring me. When I get bored I punch things. And Folly better be okay too. I warned you about her."

The boat rocked as its hull scraped a mudbank. Automatic navigation was having trouble with these narrow waters at ever-increasing speeds.

"You'll wreck us," Filchenkov warned.

"That's what I do," Drummond agreed. He found some more safety overrides and flipped them off. Like most vessels that sometimes traversed dangerous international waters, the *Ostap Bender* had safeguards against hijacking, but they all assumed that the bridge was the crew's final sanctuary. From here one man could override engineering, fire suppression control, everything.

"Decode the radio," Hugh told his prisoner. "I need to make a call."

The Russian stumbled to the starboard control desk. He seemed to lean on it for support, but actually he was slipping out the concealed weapon under the console.

Hugh saw Filchenkov orient the PP2000 SMG and knew he couldn't avoid seven hundred 9x19mm parabellum cartridges per minute; nobody could. And Filchenkov had the drop on him.

He decided he'd take his murderer out with him. His hand jerked by muscle memory and tapped two rounds through the Russian, centre-chest.

Hugh didn't die. It took him a heart-pounding moment to realise that Filchenkov hadn't thought about thumbing the PP2000's safety slide off. The Russian oligarch had people to do things like that for him.

The clamour outside the bridge compartment was matched internally by an ever-growing number of collision alarms. The boat swayed alarmingly as it course-corrected and juddered, scraping across the shallow fjord bottom. It was surging forward at twenty knots and still accelerating.

Hugh spared a worry for Filly, locked in one of the staterooms below. At least she was amidships in the best-protected part of the vessel. He was glad that no one had thought to grab her as a hostage to force his capitulation. He was deliberately keeping the crew busy.

More stars and cracks appeared on the windscreens. A deckhand tried to climb up the outside of the superstructure but was knocked off as the *Ostap Bender* rocked over another shallow submerged bank.

One last manoeuvre brought the ship's prow almost due north. The fjord ended in a shallow rise with rock ridges. Cradled between two promontories were a collection of new concrete buildings and a larger array of the kind of metal portacabins and container crates that were stacked atop the *Ostap Bender*. A whole secret training camp had been set off entirely off the grid.

A long sturdy pontoon dock had been floated out to moor the boat. By the time the autopilot gave up and returned control to a nonexistent human operator there was no way to stop the vessel from beaching at speed. Hugh held the steering wheel and made sure the 80,000 tons of ship and cargo were aimed square at the secret base. To be fair to the enemy he sounded the collision horn as the *Ostap Bender* speeded in.

The massive ship actually seemed to skip as it left the water and crashed through the first of the buildings. The collision appeared to happen in slow motion because the scale was so massive. Drummond saw the front end of the *Ostap Bender* simply crumple like foil, its for'ard twenty-foot containers flying into the air like scattered Lego bricks. The front third of the ship bent and disintegrated, flattening Filchenkov's hidden headquarters and whoever happened to be in there.

The base gas tank went up, sending a plume high into the grey dawn, much more effective than any flare. A bloom of that size against the frozen Icelandic landscape would show up on satellite.

The *Ostap Bender* began to slew sideways, swiping more of the structures, spilling the rest of its top cargo. The deck pitched thirty degrees to port. The remaining seamen who had been trying to attack the bridge lost all interest in gaining entry, scrambling for their lives. Drummond still held the wheel though helm control was gone; it felt like the thing to do.

The gas explosion sent burning debris across the ruin of the base and over the ship that had detonated it. Some of the scattered containers exploded. They had evidently included weaponry. A large chunk of machine debris shattered one of the reinforced bridge windows. Icelandic morning chill filled the cabin.

The boat tilted further, but then it ground to a final halt, its front end gone, a row of flames spreading along its starboard rail.

Drummond recovered the PP2000 that Filchenkov had withdrawn from under the radio console. He deliberately disengaged the safety catch before he pulled back the bridge door bolts and headed back into the ruined boat.

There were shouts ahead. Men with weapons either charged Drummond or just wanted to get past him. He couldn't tell which so he shot them down.

He returned to the passenger deck. Filchenkov's door remained open and Alyona's corpse had been tossed into the entrance. Drummond had to step over her to search the room for the politician's master key card.

The emergency lights began to fail. Hugh swiped the lock on the adjacent cabin and kicked open the buckled door. "Filly?" he called out. "Are you okay?"

He saw the crumpled blonde laid on the floor where the crash had tossed her. She was unconscious but breathing.

And she wasn't the right mystery girl. He was young and pretty, with wavy yellow hair, but she wasn't Filly. Hugh had no idea at all who this was.

"Well, I'll ask you when you wake up," he told her. "I can't leave you here."

She had a nasty cut on her forehead where she'd tumbled into a reinforcing strut. Drummond cleaned the wound as best he could and slung her over his shoulder in a fireman's lift. He kept his gun-arm clear.

He made his way back to the bridge, locked himself in again, and waited for the authorities to arrive. He chided himself for not stopping off in the mess and grabbing a sandwich.

***

About half an hour later, twenty minutes before the coastguard arrived, forty minutes before everybody arrived, the young woman woke up. She groped at her forehead and her hand came away bloody.

"I bumped my head," she acknowledged, speaking English like a native. "Ouch."

"Sorry about the reckless driving," Hugh told her. "I got a bit carried away."

"What happened? I've not seen you before. Why is this boat on a tilt?"

"Good questions. I'm Captain Hugh Drummond. I was kidnapped aboard. I escaped and decided to scuttle the ship. I expect rescue will arrive soon, so just sit tight and nurse that headache."

"Thank you, Captain Drummond. I was also kidnapped and held here. It never occurred to me to crash the ship. I wish it had."

"Speaking of kidnapped ladies, you don't happen to know anything about a couple of other missing persons, do you? There's an elderly bird called Connie Dalglish and a fetching young lass by the name of Phyllis Benton. Ring any bells?"

"I can't help you with Connie Dalglish, I'm afraid. Never heard of her. But as for Phyllis, yes. Hello. I'm Phyllis Benton."

***

CHAPTER VIII:
IN WHICH INSPECTOR McIVER DOES NOT GET A BISCUIT

DCI McIver finished her shift only two hours late, her best time that week. At 20.55 she clocked out of New Scotland Yard on Victoria Embankment—the third version of New Scotland Yard, right next door to the original New Scotland Yard –and found a cab. Her mind was still on her long half-day struggle with HOLMES, the Home Office Large Major Enquiry System computer that was the major research tool of the modern British police force; like the character it was named after, it was comprehensive but quirky. There was some traffic on Westminster Bridge but the trip to McIver's Lambeth maisonette took less than twenty minutes.

She let herself in and was surprised to hear voices. Her medical student brother Danny was supposed to be on call at Chelsea & Westminster Hospital tonight. "Mum?"

"In here, love," Janice McIver called from the tiny living room. A police widow's pension didn't buy a lot of space in central London. "I'm just entertaining your caller."

"My caller?" The DCI was instantly suspicious. She had no social life. She didn't do callers.

A Person of Interest was stood beside her mother, admiring Mrs McIver's cabinet of photographs and memorabilia. "Evening, Mary," Hugh Drummond greeted her. "I never knew you won ribbons for pole vaulting."

"You!" Detective Chief Inspectors of the London Met. didn't carry guns when they were off-duty. She hadn't even brought a taser home.

"It wasn't affirmative action," the intruder told her. He pointed to a framed certificate and photograph. "Youngest DCI on the force? Completely earned. You should know that."

"I tell her that," Mrs McIver insisted. "If you knew the crap she has to put up with."

"Oh, he knows," her daughter growled.

"Your dad would be proud," Drummond told her, sincerely. Pride of place amongst the displayed photographs was a uniformed shot of Police Sergeant Gabriel McIver, draped with the silver, blue, and red-striped ribbon and three inch silver disc of the Queen's Police Medal—awarded posthumously for gallantry.

"I'm just entertaining your caller."

"What are you doing here?" Mary demanded. "I have to caution you…"

"I'm having a cup of tea with your mum," Hugh said. "Also a biscuit. Home made, very good."

"Well thank you, Captain," Audrey McIver responded, smiling. "The secret is how you mix in the chocolate chips." She gestured to her elder child. "Well, there she is. I'll leave you to chat."

Mary's mother departed with a this-looks-promising-it-could-be-a-winter-wedding glance. DCI McIver gritted her teeth. "Do you know that there's an All Points Alert out on you?" she demanded as soon as the living room door closed. "It's like you want to be arrested!" Then, as she saw the purpled bruises and cuts on Drummond's face, she added, "What the hell happened to you?"

"I got beaten up by some mean girls. Can we talk?"

"I want you to talk. You do not have to say anything. But it may harm your defence if you do not mention when questioned something which you later rely on…"

"This isn't an interview under caution, Mary. It's me telling you what's going on and looking for your help. Do you want to know what's going on?"

"Yes. But I'm also a police officer, and I have a duty."

"Well, I've nothing against a copper chasing a villain. Do you really thank that's me?" Hugh helped himself to another cookie and dipped it in his teacup.

McIver made a frustrated noise. "*Why* are you here? How are you even here? You vanish without trace in the wilds of Scotland, you're missing for four days, there's some bizarre rumour about a classified incident in flaming Iceland…!"

"I was kidnapped. Well, first I was drugged, then I was locked up on a cargo freighter, then I was beaten up by girls, then I escaped, then I rammed the boat into the criminal mastermind's secret base—sadly, no volcano, even though it was Iceland as you say, so I have to mark them down for that. Then, given that it's pretty clear the archvillain of the piece has flaming good intel on damn near every part of my life, I declined to wait around for the authorities after all and arranged a trip home by unofficial channels."

"Unofficial channels?"

"Pretty unofficial, yes."

"Your little circle of army buddies?"

"Nope. They're being watched too, I reckon. They won't know I'm back until you tell them. You'll need to re-interview them all, but work in the code-phrase 'nothing but the plain truth'. That way they'll know to slip their leashes and head to our secret rendezvous point."

"Of course you have a secret rendezvous point. Who doesn't?" McIver glared at Hugh. "Why shouldn't I just haul you in right now for obstructing justice and anything else I can think of? You left four more bodies at a croft in Dumbartonshire, and you may have abducted a seventy-three year old Member of the British Empire."

"I didn't, but I know who did. Look, Mary, it's really simple… Do you trust me? And if so, are you going to help me?"

The DCI stared at the trophy cabinet, at the photograph of Gabriel McIver QPM, at the picture of her police graduation and the certificate promoting her to the rank of Chief Inspector. She looked at Drummond's hopeful, battered face. "What are those six holes in your cheek?" he asked, apropos of nothing.

"Staples," he told her cheerfully. "You can kiss them better later if you like, and I have six more below the waistline if you're feeling enthusiastic. But first, can I count on you?"

"I hate you," Mary McIver agreed.

★★★

Eighty-five miles up the winding Thames from London, the old river cuts through the rural Goring gap, forming the boundary between Berkshire and Oxfordshire. Ten miles past Reading is the village of Goring itself, spread along the north bank of the wide peasant waterway. As the sun lowered on the day after Drummond's unexpected visit to McIver's home, the DCI drove her police-issue Ford Focus through the gates of a riverfront cottage property there.

"You own this?" She asked Hugh, who lounged casually in the front passenger seat. "How much does a place like this even cost? How didn't we flag it when we checked your assets this week?"

"It would be about five million on the market," Drummond estimated. "It's hard to get property with private Thames moorings anymore. The reason you didn't find it is because it wasn't bought in my name. Legally, this is yours."

McIver stamped hard on the brake, jerking the car to an abrupt halt. "It's what?"

"Well, we couldn't use any of my 'known associates', so we went with someone who wouldn't be looking for her own name on the title deeds. Congratulations. You're a homeowner."

"Bulldog, do you have any idea the kind of trouble that Internal Affairs would have with this? How compromised...?"

"I've never compromised you, Mary. And it's not for want of offering. Anyway, trust Dare to buy an off-the-books cottage without raising any red flags. Hell, I bet half the neighbours round here are tax-dodging offshore shell corporations. Would you like to look around?"

"What's that motor boat in the slip? Is that yours too? Or mine?"

"It's Algy's. That'll be how the lads got here. After you tipped them off, they'll each have gone their separate ways, made their arrangements, shed their tails—or better yet, established firm alibis—and then met up to motor through Teddington Lock and so up to Chez McIver."

"So the gang's all here."

"I'm not keen on repeat recaps, so I thought it might be best if I got you all in the same room before I spill the beans."

"Will that include where you've been since you ate us out of biscuits last night?"

"All will be revealed, as the actress promised the bishop. Come and admire your kitchen."

McIver had brought a taser this time. The fact comforted her. She gritted her teeth and followed Drummond into the riverside cottage.

"Hugh!" Jez Seymour yelled in greeting. "So it turns out that you're not dead!"

"Bulldog!" T.S. echoed the greeting. "You owe us explanations."

"And beers," Bangbang insisted. "Several beers."

"But you can start by explaining why you have a revised mystery blonde shacked up here," Dare insisted.

"Absolutely," agreed Algy. "Why are you stacking up spare blondes? Is there going to be a shortage? Nobody warned me. Anyway, I prefer tall, athletic brunettes. Hello, DCI McIver!"

"I have a taser," the police officer responded.

"What happened to Filly, then?" Jez demanded. "I'm not saying I don't admire the replacement, but..."

Dare gestured to the slim, attractive young woman who was enjoying the sun patio. "She won't tell us who she is. Your orders, evidently."

"Operational security. Is James Denny here? Ah, James, good to see you. Could you find a glass of something decent for Mary? She's off-duty and I rather think she's a dry red sort of girl, am I right?"

McIver shook her head. "I'm fine staying sober and finding out what the hell you are up to, Captain Drummond."

The alternative blonde, realising that her rescuer had arrived at last, set aside her paperback and joined the others in the lounge/dining room. "Is this everyone?" she asked.

"All except for Mrs Denny, and she is holding the fort back in London for now," Hugh confided. "How did Mrs D take the police search warrant, James?"

"It was not a pleasant experience for any of us," Denny answered, wincing. "Claire can be a little bit caustic when people disarrange 'er kitchen. Fortunately, I believe the modern police force retains counsellors and the like to 'elp officers overcome psychological trauma."

"I told the governor a premises search was a waste of time," McIver insisted. "But if we hadn't covered it, any review would have picked it up as a defect in methodology."

"Then perhaps we could get on?" the new mystery blonde suggested, in tones that the absent Mrs Denny might have approved.

"Just so," Drummond agreed. "We need to all get on the same page. Everybody sitting comfortably? Then I'll begin. Mary, gentlemen, may I introduce you to Miss Phyllis Benton."

"That's not Filly!" Algy objected. "Filly is…"

"An impostor," Mary realised at once. "Of course! You said your regular associates were known! She knew them."

"Hold on…" Dare objected. "How can this be Filly?"

"Phyllis," the young woman corrected him. "And Ms. What kind of woman allows herself to be called Filly? Sometimes I answer to Fi."

"*Ms Fi* was scrobbled four months back, just after she got shortlisted for new Director of Shoreline Conservation Trust. Faux-Filly turned up for the interview and scooped up the job."

"With an impressively deep online cover," Algy admired. "Someone altered Facebook photos, Snapchat, all that kind of thing. It can be done, but it's a professional job. Very sexy."

"They wanted to get an agent inside the Trust to look at records pertaining to the Gruinard Island contract," T.S. reasoned. "Except there weren't any, not any more."

"The old lady had them, all right," Jez confirmed. "But when Bulldog went to collect them from her…"

"Faux-Filly dosed my tea. I even watched her take the caddy down from a top shelf for Miss Dalglish. Then I got taken to a Russian cargo hulk and, well, I'm worried about where Cressie Dalglish ended up."

"I was held at some kind of farm," actual-Phyllis explained. "I didn't see outside but I could smell animals. Sheep, I think, and some cows. Then a week ago I was transferred to the *Ostap Bender* and locked in a cabin."

Bangbang raised a hand. "We are sure she's the real thing, then?" he checked with Drummond. "I mean, we're convinced that she's not the impostor, trying to make us think Filly was the fake?"

"I dug up her school yearbooks and some family friends," Hugh reported. "That's part of where I was today, Mary. Fi is Phyllis, Filly is fraud."

"And she knows all about us now," Dare recognised. "Damn, she's good."

"So *she* hired those junkyard gangsters to go after her, so as to have a really great meet-cute with Bulldog," realised T.S. "Then he had a reason to take her back to Half Moon Street and 'keep her safe' all night long."

"And keep her close while we all found the hidden site that she was looking for," Algy added. "She played us all really well."

"Like a cheap fiddle, if you don't mind me sayin' so, sirs," Denny judged, "or even if you do."

Drummond slammed his empty beer bottle down on a side-table. "No, you're right, James. She led me by the... the nose and she got what she wanted. No wonder the bad guys had orders not to let any harm come to her for any reason."

Fi wasn't happy. "So this 'Filly' stole my name, stole my job, stole my life, and now she's stolen something that the Trust tried to bury?"

It was time for the full story of Shoreline Conservation's Gruinard Reclamation Project to come out, including the new information that not all the contaminated soil had been incinerated. Then there were Major Hannay's revelations to pair with the developing investigations of Captain Drummond's associates.

"Once we knew to look, I took another go at that Carl Peterson who nearly got Ms Benton's job," Algy explained. "Now *that* was another excellent cover, but I finally cracked it. There were layers and layers of backstory for him, references, work history, tax returns, academic record, even newspaper and magazine subscriptions, but... I don't think he actually exists. He's not real."

"Compte de Guy—Arthur Franklyn—Raphael Libstein—now maybe Carl Peterson," Hugh listed off. "We need to find this guy."

"His home address is an empty property," reported Bangbang. "No sign it was ever occupied since it was bought about a year ago. But the hunt is on."

"He's had six days now to get to wherever McCloud and Dalglish hid the soil they were meant to have sterilised," McIver worried. "Bulldog, I have to report all this in. This is Major Incident stuff."

Drummond shrugged. "Fine. But then what? We both know that the NaCTSO protocols playbook is woefully thin on the bio-terror options. We can up security levels at airports and subways and major public events. We can deploy more anthrax particle detectors, through not that fast. There's a finite stockpile of vaccines and treatments that have never been mass-tested and have controversial claimed side-effects. And that's before whatever Peterson does to gin-up his haul of death."

"What do you suggest then? I can't just sit on this while you… what? What can you do that the state can't?"

"The state didn't ram a boat into the terrorists' base," Fi Benton pointed out.

"Yes, Nice one, Bulldog," Dare approved. "Um, this might be the time to mention where we got Franklyn's history from, to link him to the Peterson identity. I went to Hannay. I didn't know what else to do."

"The Major?" Drummond shrugged. "We'll survive it. Probably."

"Not necessarily," Toby Sinclair VC noted. He tapped his prosthetic leg. "Not entirely."

"I mention Hannay because if we tell anyone in government, he's the one," Dare argued. "Hell, doesn't he sit on the Cabinet Office Briefing Rooms meetings anyhow?"

Sinclair agreed. "It's true he's a COBR regular, whatever the national crisis. If you want to warn the right people and not tip off the wrong ones, he's your man."

Fi wasn't familiar with the jargon. "Cobra?"

Drummond explained. "C-O-B-R., though the press like to report it as Cobra. It's the name for the top-level emergency committee that gets pulled together when there's a major threat or incident to Great Britain and Northern Ireland. It's the group that tells the PM and the Cabinet what their options are, then makes things happen. Composition varies by crisis, but there are a few old hands who are regulars, so to speak. Threat of widescale anthrax attack? That's a COBR problem. Alright, T.S., pass the word. Make sure Mary gets a credit, though. I want her back covered."

"Will do," the Foreign Office representative agreed.

"There's one other bit, sir," Denny chimed in to Drummond. He relayed his discussions with Eastern European muscle-for-hire and the connection with Chapter 51.

"The Americans?" McIver recognised. "Bad people."

"You know about them?" asked Algy, edging closer and risking the taser.

"About eighteen months back they made a determined bid to grab a slice of the UK drugs market, here on the ground, not just as a supply chain link. They've pretty much saturated their west coast US territories and are looking to expand. But they got ejected from London, Liverpool, and Edinburgh pretty hard."

"Maybe they're looking for round two?" Bangbang suggested. "Think about it. Mass chaos after a major terror event? Police well distracted, disruption in criminal hierarchies? Good time for a prepared crew to carve out some new turf."

"Nugent Madison II is the name what keeps coming up," reported Denny. "'E's supposed to be their big boss-man, but nothin's ever been pinned on 'im and stuck."

Algy resorted to his laptop. "Yes, this chap is slick," he decided. "Shady enough to be the ringleader, clever enough to have deniability in court."

"Could he be Peterson?" Darell wondered.

"Not without major Michael Jackson levels of pigmentation changing. This is a photo of him walking free from a failed prosecution for human trafficking. Hannay's intel had Franklyn and co. being White, didn't he?"

"But he may be close to Peterson, like Filchenkov was," Drummond speculated. "Another sponsor, maybe? And he might be our next way in."

"Does this involve a lot of flying?" Jez asked.

"Not right now," Hugh admitted.

"Well then..." The hairy ginger pilot reached for another beer.

"The reason I called you all out here to Mary's cottage secretly..." Drummond began to explain.

"It's *not* my cottage," the DCI insisted.

"The reason for secrecy is that Peterson directly threatened all of you, by name. And Mrs D, actually. Filly has either met you or heard about you. She knows what you do, and Peterson is evidently well able to trawl through at least some classified data on us. If he works out that I'm back and that I'm using the old firm, then he'll go after you, and maybe the people around you."

"Actually, Tanya kind if dumped me. Again," Algy admitted.

"No, Bulldog is right to take this seriously," Bangbang told his comrades. "We're all out in the open now, public. We're easy targets. We need to be very careful. *Very* careful. And I run a security firm!"

"Is this why you had us avoid the Icelandic authorities and hide out here?" Fi asked Hugh.

"Yes. I trust all the people you see here, but not too many others. I'd like you to stay in cover here. We'll send Mrs Denny down to keep an eye on you. Try her fried bacon; never has cholesterol poisoning been so sublime. Meanwhile, the rest of you head back to your daily lives and do the secret identity thing. Except for Algy. Nobody will lift an eyebrow if he disappears off on a binge. Him and James are with me."

"Oh, jolly g.!" Algy approved.

"The rest of you will need to do some covert mission prep. and assemble a few assets. Mary, you're going to be busy too."

"Being interviewed by the Independent Office for Police Conduct?" the DCI gloomily predicted.

"Fighting evil," Drummond promised. "Alright, boys and girls, this is what we are going to do..."

★★★

CHAPTER IX:
IN WHICH BAD THINGS HAPPEN TO BAD PEOPLE

"Nugent Madison II," Assistant Special Agent In Charge J.K. Green repeated over the secure transatlantic line from Washington. "Bad guy's bad guy. We want him quite a bit, but we've never had a case worth taking to the Attorney General. Three agencies have tried, and done nothing but waste public money and land the government with punitive lawsuits."

"I've got his stats and files here, but I wanted a personal picture from someone I trust," DCI McIver confessed. She and Green had liaised together for over a year when they'd been assigned to joint counterterrorism co-ordination. "We think this guy might be on our soil now, under a different name. You keep tabs on him?"

"When we can. But we've had two agents put into the hospital, and there's a missing vice cop somewhere too. Madison doesn't play softball. But nor do his attorneys. You can't harass an unconvicted man."

"It says in the file that he's from money."

"Sure. He's Nugent Madison the Second. His poppa was first generation Black wealth, crawled out of poverty to become a millionaire in shipping and retail, big ties with the teamsters and such. Junior inherited the lot when senior apparently misjudged an easy road-bend on a dry bright day and splattered his car across an underpass. Shipping and retail offers a great infrastructure for drug and people-running."

"Chapter 51?"

"Was one small clan of neighbourhood thugs till Nugent adopted them. Give punks like that some proper training, serious weaponry, real organisation, and you have a damn army right there on the streets. An outfit like that can expand rapidly into other territories, and before you know it they have half of California playing them tribute. We estimate the Chapter 51 turnover on west coast alone in excess of four billion a year. Four *billion*—that's more'n half the Agency's entire budget for the whole US."

"What's Nugent's control over them like? Is he really in charge?"

"He's the main man, I'd say. It's all hearsay, but he's famous for not bothering with bodyguards. That's not just bravado. He's world-class at unarmed combat and he's proficient in pretty much all kinds of firearms. He might be Olympic-standard if he ever tried to qualify. Word is that he's taken down a few challengers mano-a-mano, sometimes with his bare hands. And he's not pretty about what he does to them. But, as his lawyers say, there's no proof to take before a jury."

Mary McIver winced. "If he's over here, you're welcome to have him back, J.K."

"Keep him," the Special Agent offered. "What's your interest right now anyhow?"

"Oh, I'm not asking for me. I'm asking for a friend. An unusual, should-be-retired mutual friend, with impossibly strong jaws and no sense of proportion."

"Oh." Green caught on at once. "Well damn! Does he know what he's getting in to?"

"Does he ever? Does that stop him?"

"No. I'm glad I'm on this side of the Atlantic, though. Nugent and him? Damn!"

"It is worrying."

"Sure. But also the best news I've had all month. Our strong-jawed acquaintance tends not to worry about attorneys or, well, odds. I'd say it was suicide but, well, I've seen him go."

"He put an ad in the paper, asking for interesting problems he could tackle."

"If I'd seen it, I might have pointed him at Madison. Except I couldn't, because it would be illegal. You're helping him?"

"The Metropolitan Police can do nothing to assist a private citizen in a vigilante vendetta against a foreign national who has never been found guilty of any crimes," McIver stated for the record.

"Right. Say hi to him for me. Keep me in the loop."

"Oh, I imagine you'll be able to keep up to date. You get the Reuters news feeds, right?"

★★★

Pietro Kaaleste was one of the new breed of European crimelords who had prospered in the days of relaxed border control between EU states. He came from the Estonian underworld that had blossomed since the collapse of the Soviet Union and had elbowed his way to a slice of the gaming and prostitution businesses in Wandsworth, Lambert, and Southwark, south of the Thames. These days his sidelines of credit fraud and hardcore video porn brought in almost as much as his traditional rackets.

He enjoyed fast cars and owned fifteen of them. His pride and joy was a €2.4 million Lykan Hypersport from the Arabic W Motors. The twin-turbocharged flat-six engine offered 750-horsepower, for 0 to 100km/h in 2.8 seconds and a top speed of 245 mph. It had diamond-encrusted LED lights, gold-stitched leather, and a Virtual Holographic Display instrument panel. It was one of only seven in the world.

At some point around 12.45am, intruders disabled the sophisticated security around Kaaleste's garage and set timed explosive charges on each of his car collection except the Hypersport. That vehicle's anti-theft system was hacked and the car was removed. By 1.10am, a 30° ramp had been quietly constructed in Kaaleste's driveway, while seven state of the art security cameras looked on blindly. Loose guard dogs had eaten drugged meat.

At exactly 1.11am, Kaaleste was awoken in his master bedroom by the sound of the Hypersport's horn. Neighbours in the exclusive houses adjacent also heard the racket, and the vehicle's throaty revving. Only a few seconds later, the pride of the Qatar motorshow had been driven at the ramp at an estimated speed of 147 miles per hour. The driver had presumably exited as the car hit the incline and had landed in a cushioned fall on a children's bouncy castle that had been positioned for the purpose.

The Lykan Hypersport had leapt from the ramp in a well-calculated parabola that had smashed it through one of the first floor windows of the master bedroom, demolishing both exterior wall and the internal partition to the en-suite bathroom. It brought down part of the ceiling before the floor also collapsed, dropping the remains of the car into the kitchen below.

Thirty seconds later, the garage exploded.

Pietro Kaaleste survived because his emperor-sized four-poster bed was on the other side of the room to the intruding vehicle's incursion. He suffered minor injuries from shrapnel glass and respiratory problems from the debris dust cloud but was otherwise unharmed—at least physically. His dignity and his temper were casualties of the attack.

"I want to find whoever did this and slice them slowly," he told his lieutenants. "They sent a message? We send a better one! Find them! Find out who!" The trouble was there were so many possibilities; but if Kaaleste was to keep face and retain his status there had to be consequences.

The police were an unwelcome presence in his ruined home, but they were inevitable. Kaaleste and his solicitor stonewalled quite effectively. The crimelord had no intention whatsoever of leaving this matter to the investigating authorities.

One question gave him a vital clue, though. A woman DCI who had nothing else to do with the investigation arrived, showed her badge to the scene-of-crime lead, and asked Kaaleste just one question. He declined to answer, but that enquiry gave him the target he needed.

"Do you have any association with, or have you had any negative business dealing with, a Mr Nugent Madison II?" asked DCI McIver.

"That Yank dude with the attitude that we kicked out a year ago?" Kaaleste didn't answer, but could have. "No. But I'm sure going to."

★★★

While fire engines were still responding to an unusual call at the Kaaleste residence, it was business as usual at the former petrol station on Fulham High Street. The forecourt pumps were gone now, the garage priced out of business by cheap supermarket offers, and the site was operated by DCZ Taxis, operating twenty-three cabs out of the single-storey former pay-point and convenience store.

The name on the ownership deeds of site and company was DCZ (Holdings) Ltd., registered in Jersey where the tax laws were quite different, but if anyone had been diligent enough to chase through the shell companies and offshore holdings, the site would turn out to belong to Himmat Rao Kandi, an Indian investor with a diverse portfolio of holdings across Hammersmith, Fulham, Ealing, and Hounslow.

Mr Kandi's main return on the business was not from the hire of his vehicles, however, but on their use as anonymous delivery systems and even retail points for a variety of illegal products from the Golden Triangle. DCZ Taxis shifted almost a million pounds of heroin and its derivatives every month; a cash-based business like a cab company was a great way of laundering the proceeds.

Kandi had received an offer for his entire operation from Nugent Madison II when Chapter 51 had been looking for a toehold in London the previous year. Madison could replace the Asian supply chain with his own South American contacts and invest more in home-made lab products to supplement DCZ's menu; but it would have cut Kandi out from a lucrative ongoing trade and it would have angered his partners in Laos, Myanmar, and Thailand. When Madison had tried to push, the Mekong River boys had been quite ready to push back. Nobody went too far because nobody wanted a war.

Until 2.05am, that is, when the tired dispatcher at the Fulham High Street site heard an ominous rumble, and then the ground began to tremble. He looked out from his sealed booth and was horrified to see a huge metal object rolling onto the forecourt.

An old VCR-linked security camera later proved the intruder to be an FV510 Warrior Infantry Section Vehicle painted in desert camouflage colouring, the same kind of tank that the British Army deployed in the Gulf, Iraq, and Afghanistan. GAE Sankey/Defence and its purchaser BAE Systems had built 789 of the FV510s for the British Army and 254 for the Kuwaitis; it was not clear where the tank on Fulham High Street had come from, to whom it belonged, or who had borrowed it.

At two in the morning most of the taxi fleet was back home, lined in front of the cabin on the hard-stand where the petrol pumps had been, sheltered by the awning that still bore the logo of the former station franchise. The tank began at one end of the first row and rolled right over the line of cabs, crushing them under its caterpillar tracks. The FV510 weighs 25.4 tonnes, the police incident report noted. Late night cabbies lounging and smoking in the waiting room rushed out to protest, but the tank executed a near 180 degrees pivot and came back along the other line of taxis.

Some idiot amongst the drivers had a handgun. His bullet bounced off the Warrior's thick armour plating and nearly killed one of his co-workers. When the tank's secondary armoury L94A1 coaxial 7.62mm chain gun swivelled towards him he dropped his Saturday night special and fled for his life.

The tank turned again. This time it was evident that the target was the cabin. The FV510 crashed through one of the supporting beams holding the forecourt gantry in place; the awning crashed down atop the ruined vehicles but the tank ignored it. Inside the caller's booth, the panicked operator realised that there was no time to open the safe and extract the quarter million pounds of packaged product hidden there. He scrambled away and got out just as the Warrior demolished the building.

The floor-standing safe was certified to Eurograde 5 and EN1143-1 standard. That meant it could withstand 400 minutes of attempts by thieves using heavy cutting tools to breach it and 100kN of force to move it, but the industry standards had not anticipated the secure container being driven over by an army tank. The safe withstood the weight for long desperate seconds then burst like a beetle under a shoe.

Clouds of white powder billowed out and coated the demolition site.

The tank backed out of the wreckage, regained the road, and returned the way it came, past traffic and security cameras that were experiencing an unexplained and temporary blackout.

Somehow a 44-foot long tank vanished into the London suburbs without any trace of where it had come from—or who had borrowed it.

The next morning, during the police responders' triumphant discovery of a major if somewhat compromised horde of Class A drugs and the subsequent arrest of Mr Himmat Rao Kandi, a female DCI asked the same question of the livid suspect that she had of the car-less Mr Kaaleste. Had Mr Kandi had any dealings with an American called Madison?

Mr Kandi had some specific and unpleasant instructions for his solicitor to pass on.

★★★

Local entrepreneur Harry 'the Hedgehog' Soames was 'old school', one of the East End boys in the tradition of the Kray Twins, a hard man who gave hard knocks to anyone who crossed him. He ran the ponies and the ladies in the Docklands, Tower Hamlets, and Spitalfields, along with a number of modelling agencies that promised special futures to good-looking girls from the provinces, with exotic international travel guaranteed.

Local rumour said that the Hedgehog, named because he was "a prickly bastard", had been known to personally take a chainsaw to people who had crossed him, or to their near relatives. No body parts had been found to prove the story. Harry Soames was a major investor in the new building developments on Canary Wharf.

Harry had come up the hard way, the bloody way, from being a foot-soldier in the 90s working protection and enforcement for the old generation of "dodgy geysers", stepping into middle management in his thirties when the Jamaicans and the Bangladeshis had tried to walk in and take control of the rackets, and then helping the old guard retire whether they wanted to or not, taking proper authority ten years ago. He wore sharp-edged finger-rings because he liked to punch subordinates who asked stupid questions.

The heart of Harry's empire was the Duchess, an early Victorian hotel-turned-knocking shop, right round the corner from Brick Lane Market, Shoreditch. The Duchess of Hoxton had been a grand venue once, catering to the rich farmers who came in for Spitalfield Market and to travellers via Liverpool Street Station, but somewhere between the world wars the old place and the surrounding area had fallen into disrepute. The hotel became a whorehouse and the Duchess became a whore.

Some people said that the Hedgehog was birthed right there in one of those seedy by-the-hour rooms, by a mother who was included with the rent fee. They didn't say it in front of Harry, though; not when he had his finger-rings and his chainsaw.

The Duchess was the first big place that Harry bought as he rose in the world. It was still an entertainment site, a 'massage parlour' and 'conference centre'; but the top floor was his, his palace, his stronghold, and from it he looked out over a neighbourhood that was his.

Until 4.47am. That was when a Liebherr LTM 1200-5.1 Mobile Crane stolen from a waterfront demolition site rumbled up to the old hotel and raised an old-fashioned, almost obsolete wrecking ball on its 72 metre telescopic boom. "In the Duchess," a voice came over its powerful speaker array. "You got five minutes to evacuate by the rear. Not the front. That way you get shot. Git out the back!"

Witnesses later described the voice as being American-accented, "like from those Westerns." Algy Longworth would have been flattered.

Harry the Hedgehog was not a man to go down without a fight. He sent his boys out first while he prepared a sawn-off double-barrelled shotgun to follow them. The first foot-soldier through the door was punched back inside with a bullet through his right shoulder. The second fell with a shot through his lower thigh. The attackers had a sharpshooter.

"Get out there!" Harry roared, using his shotgun as incentive. Another two of his boys took flesh wounds but by then six of them had scrambled through the front door, ranging out to take shots at the driver's cabin and the crane control booth.

The crane's smoked glass windscreen shattered, revealing that the cab was empty. The LTM 1200 had already been perfectly parked. The metal cage around the crane operator protected him, 25 feet off the ground. His booth windows had been additionally armoured by welded-on steel mesh that made them effectively bulletproof to small-arms fire.

"You was warned!" the crane's speakers boomed. The boom's long armature swept back, taking with it that ominous 6,000lb eleven-foot oval of steel. Wrecking balls were hardly ever used these days, replaced by controlled detonation and other demolition techniques, but there were still a few around. They had unmistakable authority.

"No!" the Hedgehog shouted, loosing both barrels at the crane controller. The heavier rounds dented the steel mesh but didn't breach it.

The sniper, somewhere beyond the crane in the darkness, put down two more of Harry's men with uncanny non-lethal shots. The rest saw the swing of the crane's ball, calculated its trajectory, and began to run.

Harry the Hedgehog nearly stayed in place, played chicken. He was livid, his face bright red. He seemed ready to head butt the incoming wrecking ball. Only at the last moment did he drop to the ground, allowing the three tons of steel to pass over him and crash into the frontage of the Duchess of Hoxton.

The ball bit deep, shattering the decorated facade, demolishing ground and first floor halls almost to the rear courtyard, then causing more damage as it ripped back on its chain in a devastating arc. Retaining walls of old piled stone could not resist it. Part of the roof gave in and clattered its slates to the pavement. The upper floors, no longer properly supported, tumbled down onto the levels below.

Harry screamed in fury. He rose to charge the crane but realised that the elevated cabin on the folding jib was out of his reach. He fired again but his shots could not get through the booth's plating.

The ball fell again, another sweeping arc that ripped out more of the hotel's guts. Harry almost choked in the demolition dust. Somewhere in the distance was the blare of emergency services.

One last swing caused the whole structure to collapse. Harry the Hedgehog scarcely managed to scramble out of the way of the falling debris. He was left beside the ruin of his headquarters, plastered in dust, clutching an illegal weapon that had proved entirely useless and shown him to be impotent.

Pre-set smoke grenades went off, filling the whole street with thick choking smog. Only someone with infrared night-sight goggles could have penetrated that cloud to quit the stolen crane and join the hidden sniper for a well-planned exfiltration.

"What is your relationship to Newton Madison II?" a too-cute looking plain-clothes copper asked Harry Soames before he was taken off by ambulance.

"Madison, eh?" the Hedgehog replied mildly. "Why'd you ask?"

"Just routine," DCI McIver replied in the same causal tone. "You didn't hear about the problems with Pietro Kaaleste and Himmat Rao Kandi yet? I guess you will. Do you know them? Do you know if they have any association with Mr Madison?"

"Why?"

"Well, they both suffered significant property damage tonight also. Mr Kandi is under arrest."

"And what's this Madison to do with it?"

"You tell me, Harry."

"I'll tell you nothing but this, fuzz. My relationship to Newton Madison, darlin'? I'm gonna bloody kill 'im!"

★★★

"The bosses are hiring," the anonymous middleman told the rough hardcases who had assembled in a freight warehouse by the docks. "Good pay for serious trouble. The bosses are going to war."

"'Oo with?" someone asked.

"The Yanks. Them West Coast Gangsta N---s!"

James Denny signed on with the rest of them.

★★★

Special Agent Jerome J. Green read the Reuters feeds from BBC, ITV, and Sky News with a special kind of schadenfreude. Then he poured two whiskeys and drank them both: one for himself and one for a friend across the water.

★★★

CHAPTER X:
IN WHICH HE ANNOYS CHAPTER 51

Newton Madison II swept a row of vases and ornaments off the mantelpiece of his expensive hotel suite. "Why the hell are they blaming me?"

Carl Peterson folded the tabloid newspaper that was filled with pictures of the last night's incidents: GANGLAND WAR ERUPTS IN DEMOLITION ORGY. "Because Bulldog Drummond is not as stupid as he pretends," he suggested. "And not as dead as we might have hoped."

"That shipwreck in Iceland?" scorned Irma Peterson, formerly Filly Benton and Edith Franklyn amongst many others. "That wouldn't stop Bulldog. He caused it. He probably extracted little Phoebe as well, before he ruined Victor Savvich's day."

"It's pretty clear now that he's back in England," Peterson agreed. "And he knows enough to stay clear from obvious contact with his regular stooges; although his man Denny is unaccounted for and so is the idiot savant Longworth. I have an enquiry in with a police force technical contact that should track him presently."

Madison would have broken more things, but there were none left. "You're saying this Bulldyke..."

"Bulldog," Irma corrected him. "He's definitely male."

"This f----d used a car, a crane, and a f----g tank to take out some Brit operators and framed me for it?"

"He is creative," Peterson admired. "That's why we involved him to help us find the anthrax cache. Although I did not instruct my sister to sleep with him for it."

"You don't instruct me who to sleep with, period," Irma assured her brother. "Getting close to Hugh Drummond was just a perk of the mission. I'm sorry that it's over."

"But Drummond is still out there, with his face in my business!" Madison persisted.

"He is." Carl Peterson raked a toe over the remains of an antique Dresden Shepherdess amongst the broken china on the carpet. "He was sealed away, well out of it. Filchenkov must have disobeyed my instructions."

"I don't care who's to blame. I care how we're gonna clear up his mess! Right now I've got a whole bunch of pissed-off players gunning for me and mine. Not just the natives, either. I'm getting heat from the Triangle and from the Indians. What few holdings I did have over here are burning, and

"But Drummond is still out there, with his face in my business!"

art copyright 2019 H. Simpson

now I'm taking casualties back in LA and San Fran. I mean my factories getting shot up, some legit holdings taking hits. Now Chapter 51's got to push back or we look like pussies."

"Isn't that rather what Bulldog wants?" Irma enquired. "You and your rivals all locked into a little private war, blowing the hell out of each other?"

"It's a neat job," Peterson judged. "You have to walk away, Newton. You have to be the bigger man."

The US gang boss disagreed. "If I back down I'm not the bigger man. I'm dead. No respect means no authority, means no control, means no money, means no life expectancy!"

"Life expectancy? What do you think the life expectancy of Kaalesti, Kandi, and Soames is, given what we're planning? Why waste time and resources when you're already going to take them out in just a few days with eight million of their neighbours?"

"Wasn't killing them with almost everybody else kind of the point?" Irma supported her brother's case. "How many of the local 'operators' that are opposing you will still be around soon? And then the long-distance players who rely on them for their UK network will have to come to you if they want to continue."

Madison Nugent II was slightly mollified. "I'll have to push back, but I'll keep it low key. Keep it rattling rather than exploding. If I can. How far off are we from the big day?"

"Koh Zhenkai says that Dr Lakington estimates ninety-six hours until go," Peterson revealed. "Evidently Lakington is so happy with the new mutation of Vollum-21136 that he's got a disturbing permanent erection."

"I didn't think Lakington could get any more disturbing," Madison admitted.

"Does he know that we lost Phyllis yet?" Irma wondered. "Wasn't getting her for his 'experiments' part of his deal with us?"

"We might yet retrieve her for him," Peterson considered. "If not, there are many other women he can play with. He can have his pick of the survivors."

Madison returned to his point. "What about Drummond, though? I want him. I want to hurt him. Hell, I have a whole damn show planned out!"

"Have at it, Nugent. I shall watch with interest."

"You won't help?"

"I may set a few things in motion, but Bulldog Drummond is beyond the terms of our present contractual parameters. Unless you would like to pay me another, say, twenty-five million?"

"For one broken-down ex-soldier?"

"Oh, he's a very fine broken-down ex-soldier," Irma assured the boss-man of Chapter 51. "I reckon that Carl's offering you a bargain."

"I'll take care of 'Bulldog' myself then," Madison glowered. "And you can take your contractual parameters…"

Whatever he was about to snarl choked in his throat as Peterson looked sharply at him.

"Good hunting, Nugent," said Irma.

***

"Have you known Captain Drummond long, Mrs Denny?" wondered Fi Benton. The rescued charity administrator felt the need for human interaction after four months of captivity.

Mrs D. paused in her kneading of cake-mix. "For coming up to a decade now, I suppose," she considered. "'E was C.O. of my James' unit, see, and then James was detailed to be his orderly."

"You knew James before that, then?"

"Lord, yes! James was the boy next-door-but-two from me back in Ealing. The scrapes that lad got into! We played in the same street, went to the same school, fell out, made up, hit puberty, and well… Eventually I found I was Mrs James Denny! What a thing! People allus said 'e'd get me into trouble."

Fi reviewed the story. She wondered how many gaps it covered up. "So you were married when James joined the army then?"

"No. I wasn't speaking to James just then on account of 'is no-good thieving criminal habits. 'E got out of a prison stretch by agreeing to enlist, you know. I wasn't best pleased. But I must say, it directed 'is unscrupulous ways to different ends. And 'e did keep coming back, which is more than you can say for most men."

"He's been with Captain Drummond for a long time too, then."

"Doing things as can't be said under the h'Official Secrets Act. Why, when we settles down to write of an evening, we spends 'alf the time working out what we can say without getting locked up for it."

"Writing?"

Mrs D chuckled, the first time Fi had heard her laugh. "You wun't think it to look at us? Thick common nobodies from the bad part of London? But all them times James was off with the Loamshires or, well, wherever with 'ooever, 'e'd write me these little stories and send 'em to me. And after a time I got to writing 'em too, and sending 'em back. And if I say so myself, they weren't 'alf bad. And when James got 'imself discharged a couple of years back and I said to 'im, 'Lad, it's time you made an honest woman of me,' and we settled in with the Captain at 'Alf Moon Street, we'll, we just kept up the writing, natural like."

"But you have to beware the Official Secrets Act?"

"Write what you know, they says. Well, what James knows is mostly classified mission stuff. So we turns it into fiction, changes names and dates and things. We're planning a book about the Captain, you know, but we'll 'ave to call 'im something else. Greyhound Gibson or something. And I'll be Mrs P."

"And I'll be the silly girl who got kidnapped and didn't do anything useful in the story," Fi Benton considered. "Honestly, I felt so helpless all those months at that horrid farm. And now I'm locked away again, in hiding, and I have nothing useful to contribute at all!"

Mrs Denny laid her pastry as she wanted it, trimmed the edges, and slid her pie into the oven. "You can't help as what 'appened to you. And you have to be sensible now and stay concealed or it'll 'appen again—or worse. But perhaps there's stuff you can do as will give you some agency— that's what we calls it in a book when a character has some choices what change the plot. Agency. Do you want to be an agent, Ms Benton?"

"Definitely. But how?"

"Well, as you've 'eard, the Captain and the rest are tryin' to crack this Carl Peterson fellah. Whatever was 'appening in Iceland's gone for a burton, but that was just one string to 'is bow. There's this American gangster, but I gather my James 'as that in 'and. But nowhere has anybody come across a farm except you. Knowing about that place would be useful. Maybe a new line of attack to cut another bowstring, so to speak."

"You think I might know something useful? I already told you, I was locked in one room all the time. The window was covered on the outside with wooden planks and sacking so I couldn't see out. Nearly all the people who came in with food and things were masked. When I was first brought there and when I was dragged off to that ship I was hooded."

"Still, there's things to think on," Mrs D insisted. She washed off her hands and arms and hung up her apron. "Do you want to think them through? Can you?"

Fi swallowed hard. "I can try," she agreed.

Mrs D sat her on the sofa, facing the French windows with their view of the terrace and the lawn down to the Thames. "Start with the thing what scared you the most," she prompted.

★★★

"Hello? Is that Mister Nugent Eye-Eye?" asked the British voice on the telephone. "You're looking for Bulldog Drummond?"

"Nugent Madison *the Second*!" Madison snarled into his Savelli Champagne Diamond smartphone. "Who the hell put this bozo through to my private line?"

"He's got a lead on Drummond," explained Iceman Lattif, who was co-ordinating the payback for the Brits' attacks on Chapter 51 properties. "Sounds like it could be for real. But he won't talk 'cept to you."

"There's a reward," the caller insisted. "Everyone knows it. One million dollars for information about where Bulldog is. Right? Well I know and I want the money."

"And who the crap are you?" Madison demanded.

"I'm anonymous. Well, I know who I am, obviously. But I don't want Bulldog finding out I told you. He has a lot of friends."

"What made you think this bozo knows more than any of the million other time-wasters we've heard from?" the gang-boss interrogated Iceman.

"He knew about that Russkie ship crashing and about them Scottish places. And he claims he knows where Drummond is right now."

"I know where Bulldog is, and where he's heading to," the voice on the line promised. "But I want my million dollars. Or bucks. You call them bucks, right? I want my million dollar-bucks."

"Is he for real?"

"Or is it buck-dollars? Buck-dollar greenbacks? Anyway, I want mine in Bitcoin."

"Oh, you do, do you? And how can you prove that what you're saying isn't bull to scam my money? You trying to scam my money, boy?"

"No. I'm trying to get the reward you promised. Word is out, 'on the street' as you chaps like to say, 'on the mean streets', that you're looking to find Bulldog. So I know and you want to know. That's the basis for a contract. Isn't it?"

"What do you know? How do you know?" Madison demanded.

"I might have made a few travel arrangements for him, bought tickets, hired rooms, that sort of thing. You pay me, I'll tell you where Bulldog is and where he'll be at 9pm tonight. That's 9pm British Summer Time, not

California Time. And you'll transfer my money. Wiring it, it's called, isn't it? That's what you'll do. I'll send you details of how to log in and shift the... the *moolah* to my Bitcoin wallet. When I get it, you get Bulldog."

"There won't be any transfer until I know your info's good."

"There won't be any info until... well, you know how this goes. But look, here's the thing. There's a provision in the electronic transfer software for this kind of issue. You transfer the funds to an irretrievable account—that means you can't get it back. But it's a locked account—that means I can't take the money until you send off a second permission code. You deposit the e-greenbacks so I know you won't back out. I give you the info. When you've got Bulldog, you release my reward. It's the modern equivalent of tearing a banknote in half and leaving a bit with each fellow. Deal?"

Madison thought that his annoying informant could go whistle for the release code when this was done. "Deal. But if this isn't the real thing I will find you and cut you."

"That's very fair. Um, do you have an e-mail address I can send you the coin wallet details to?" asked Algy Longworth.

★★★

"The scariest thing was the one man who came to see me that didn't wear a mask," Fi told Claire Denny. "He was about fifty, maybe, and he wore a lab-coat and those old-fashioned horn-rimmed glasses. He didn't speak at all. He just stared at me for perhaps five minutes. Then he turned and left. He came three times and did that. He terrified me."

Mrs D asked some clarifying questions that pegged the visitor as Caucasian, wearing black laced shoes, with a watch on his right wrist.

"The rest all wore black masks that covered their whole heads. Like those ninja hoods you see in movies," Fi went on. "Nobody ever spoke. If they wanted me to move they pointed. And they had knives. Always knives, straight and about seven inches from hilt to tip."

Mrs D established that Fi's jailors were both men and women, but none of them was over 5'10" tall. That as much as the 'ninja hoods' suggested they might have been Oriental.

"My room wasn't very big. It had one sloping wall like an attic, where the blocked dormer window was. The sash was screwed down so I couldn't open it, even when the room got hot. The door was always locked and there was a bolt on the outside. I could hear it scraping when they opened it. Food was simple, mostly rice and fish or meat stew, sometimes with a piece of fruit. Drink was always water. Cutlery and plates were plastic. Twice a week they brought me clean clothes, always the same cheap stuff you get in supermarkets. There was a pile of second-hand paperbacks in the room, all trashy romance stuff I wouldn't normally read. I loathe that kind of pap."

Under Mrs D's questioning, Fi worked out that the farm was an old one, with plastered walls and creaking floorboards. Her room had faced east. The farmyard smells were strongest at sunrise, and she could sometimes hear vehicles coming and going, often trucks, sometimes five or six a day. She occasionally heard planes overhead, often with buzzing engines like light aircraft.

Mrs D enquired about Fi's original kidnap.

"I was shopping. I was at a mall. I felt a sharp prick in my neck and… that's all. I never saw anyone. When I woke up I was cuffed to a chair with a hood on my head. A woman asked me a lot of questions that I answered for her. All things about my life. I suppose now she was this fake 'Filly' person waiting to take my place. I owe that bitch."

Mrs D noted that 'Filly' had known exactly what to ask to usurp Phyllis Benton's life. 'Filly' had skills and training. "I wish I 'adn't given her such a nice breakfast now," she confided in the real Phyllis.

"I wish she'd choked on it. I really think that's all I have for you, Claire. Creepy staring man, old farm-house, masked kidnappers, scheming bitch."

"Everything helps. I'll pass it on. Mr Darell 'as some of 'is staff chasing up farms for sale or hire in the past year or so. If your place was near a private airfield then that might narrow things down a bit. Every little helps."

And then the blinding revelation came to Fi. "Those romances! Those trashy books! *Her Master's Voice* and *The Squire's Command* and *Passion of a Virgin* and all the rest. They had price stickers on them. Second hand price stickers, 20p, 25p, that sort of thing. They were from an Oxfam shop!"

Mrs D nodded in satisfaction. "That's interesting. Were they all Oxfam labels?"

"I think… some of them were stamped with Salvation Army?"

Claire Denny clapped her hands together. "Now you're talking. My old dad, 'e's a right Salvationist, and I still drop a fiver in the red collecting kettle when I sees one. Thing is, there's about six hundred and fifty Oxfam shops in Britain, but less than forty Sally Ann shops now. 'Ow many places 'ave both, near an airstrip?"

"Not many?"

"Let's 'ope so."

★★★

"It's gone in," Algy Longworth reported to Hugh Drummond as they sprawled comfortably in the common lounge of a cheap bed and breakfast in Chelsea. Hugh had hired the entire house for the duration and had sent the proprietors on holiday to Spain.

Algy had hooked his laptop up to the big TV so they could both see the contents of the screen, though Hugh had a limited understanding of what his technical friend was doing. Algy also had a Bluetooth headset at one ear, which was doubling as a telephone. "Hello, Mister Nugent? Have you got it?"

One of the windows on Algy's computer changed, filling with a screed of fast-scrolling code-lines. "He's got it," Algy grinned. Into his headset he said, "Is it working? Can you find my coin wallet?"

Bulldog watched his old comrade work with an appreciation for excellence. Algy was a well-known blithering idiot when it came to relationships, personal finances, self-expression, or anything involving tact, but his computer skills were superb. He had been signals-man in Drummond's 'Black Mask Gang' SAS unit, a role that included hacking and deciphering any number of enemy systems; Algy had seldom failed.

"He opened the program and it has installed my malware," the well-known blithering idiot reported. "I'm in his computer now. Any minute now I should be able to... yes, there we are. That window, bottom right. That's his desktop. That lady should find a bit more clothing."

"She seems to be finding ways of staying warm," Hugh observed. "Don't computers have anti-virus things to stop people from doing what you're doing right now?"

"That stuff only stops about sixty percent of attacks, the common stuff. You can't always defend against new methods and malware, until it's been discovered. I only wrote this program last week. Nobody has ever heard of it. I'd explain what exploit I'm using but you wouldn't listen anyhow." Down the phone he said, "Right, I want your dollar-bucks now. Then I'll give you Bulldog." And back to Hugh he added, "He's haggling. He wants to only transfer half now, half later. Do I agree?"

"Reluctantly," Drummond advised. "It's not like we'll get our hands on the cash anyway, however much we settle on."

Algy bartered, his voice querulous and outraged. In an aside to Hugh, he added, "Actually, now I'm in his system, if I can just get him to do one account transfer I can probably ID his bank account, maybe more than one, and perhaps spoof his authentification. It'll be two-factor, but with the other stuff we know... You're bored again, aren't you?"

"I'm just enjoying the magic show. No need to reveal how the tricks are done."

Something else on screen changed. A red zero changed to an amber $500,000.

"Yes, I see it," Algy told Newton Madison II. "Jolly good. So I'll tell you what I know and you'll put the rest in when you've got him? You promise?"

Drummond rolled his eyes. He was almost certain that Algy was only playing the fool right now. Almost.

Another pair of windows on Algy's display were scrolling numbers and code as the Trojan software interrogated Madison's computer and the Chapter 51 network. A third box contained a bar with a white line moving steadily to the right as the contents of the gang-boss' hard drive were downloaded.

"No, I don't want to get off the pot," Algy said down the line to Madison. "Why would I want to do that? I'll tell you what I know, right now. Do you need to get a pen and paper?"

Hugh suppressed a snort of laughter. Mr Longworth was enjoying this far too much.

"Well, 'I know so much' as you put it because I'm the chap who buys the train tickets for Bulldog Drummond, as it happens. That's how I know that he's on the high speed train from Leeds to London right now, arriving at King's Cross in twenty-four minutes. Yes, that's tight, but I had a devil of a time convincing your Icepick—sorry, your Iceman—that I was the genuine article. Anyway, you're not likely to catch Bulldog in a crowded rail terminal, are you? And he's in disguise. You can't tackle every nun and lady in a burka. It's not done. People object."

"I'm in a burka now?" Drummond checked his jeans and t-shirt combo.

"You might be. For a given value of burka. Who can tell?" Algy toggled his mike back on and continued. "It doesn't matter whether you get him there or not. I also know where he's going. I made another payment, you see, to the owner of a shipping warehouse in the old undeveloped part of the Docklands, to use the place as a discreet venue for a meeting that Bulldog is arranging. At 9pm tonight he's gathering a lot of muscle to, well, I don't know what exactly. To go against you, perhaps, or else to go against somebody else and get you blamed. Sorry, I don't know what some of those words mean, Mr Newton Two."

"I bet you do," Hugh scoffed.

"Yes, I can give you the address. You just paid for it, remember? Well, paid half. Or put half in escrow—that's what it's called, yes? Can you hold while I Google 'escrow'?"

"Keep it this side of farce, Algy."

Algernon Longworth stuck his tongue out at his former commander. He gave the address to Madison. It was the same venue where Denny had been recruited the night before and was due to assemble with the others who had been hired to push back against Chapter 51. It was a nice, isolated location where British and American ne'er-do-wells could punch, stab, and shoot each other to their heart's content without endangering civilians.

"And I'll get my e-cash as soon as you've got him?" Algy asked down the line earnestly. "Hello? Hello? Well, the rotter's hung up on me!"

"You still appear to be in his computer system, though," Hugh noted.

"Well, yes. I suppose I should have a little bit of a rummage about and see what I can find there. Chapter 51 accounts, incriminating e-mails, that kind of thing. And then I'm going to take a crack at that bank account and see if we can't syphon off an offshore account or two to cover operating expenses. I think Ophelia's bloodsucking solicitors will be coming at me for a seven-figure sum this month, so any contribution that Mr Madison can make would be very welcome."

Algy turned his attention back to his keyboard, making little encouraging noises to himself as he did unpleasant and illegal things to Chapter 51. Hugh knew it was best to leave him to it.

Drummond still had one preparation to make, though. He fished out one of a dozen burner phones from a supermarket bag next to him and dialled up the private number for Harry the Hedgehog.

"Just thought you'd like to know," he warned without identifying himself, "that Chapter 51 knows about your meeting tonight at the warehouse. They're planning to hit it. Prepare accordingly. Toodles!"

He cut the call and stamped the phone into oblivion.

"Now just find me any references in Madison's files to Carl Peterson or Viktar Filchenkov. And then find me where Madison is heading for next."

★★★

CHAPTER XI:
IN WHICH ONLY
THE SALVATION ARMY IS PEACEFUL

"I am a suspicious man, by calling and nature," Sir Bryan Johnstone told his subordinate Detective Chief Inspector. "Some people think I like a good mystery. They are in error. I like a good mystery *solved*."

"Yes, governor," Mary McIver agreed.

"I don't like anomalies. I don't like not understanding why people do things. I especially dislike not knowing why my officers pay seemingly-random visits to incident sites and ask the same leading question each time."

"Ah. Yes, sir."

"It makes me wonder whether Captain Drummond is not behind the current wave of underworld violence and anarchy that is cluttering my in-tray and disrupting my digestion. It makes me consider whether one of my trusted colleagues is working with him to bypass the processes of the law."

"Sir."

"There have been thirteen reported incidents so far that are assessed as related to last night's excitements. Those are the reported incidents, note. Who knows how many back-alley scraps and private feuds have not come to official attention? Moreover, every face with a record of violent conviction seems flush for cash today. Wicked men have been recruiting lesser wicked men, McIver, to do wicked deeds to each other."

"Sir."

"And I am left to speculate that this… cascade has been provoked by Captain Drummond, who is not lost in the Icelandic fjords, as he would be had he any manners, but has resurfaced to hasten my inevitable cardiac event. And I wonder whether my CID staffer has decided that she is no longer on the side of law and of order but has joined with the ranks of tank-using, hotel-wrecking, garage-bombing outlaws."

"No sir."

Sir Bryan eyed her. "That's good to know. An arrest of Hugh Drummond would certainly restore my faith, McIver. Have you some useful line of enquiry you might pursue to that end?"

"Only got one tip, governor, but it's a bit iffy."

"Do tell."

"I heard there might be a bit of a barney between some of the rogues gallery tonight. Down at the Docklands. There's a warehouse there, hired for... well, wickedness, I suppose. I have reason to believe that Captain Drummond is involved."

"Have you reason to believe that he asked you to inform me of this, so that I can have armed police officers secure the perimeter and arrest the whole damn lot of them?"

"Sir," McIver answered neutrally.

"Well, multiple arrests for assault with a deadly weapon, carrying an unlicensed firearm, public affray, and doubtless a large number of parole violations will have to do for now," the Commander accepted. "Mary, go withdraw a combat vest and firearm. You're getting some overtime."

★★★

At seven-thirty that evening, the watchers that the man calling himself Carl Peterson had deployed on Bulldog Drummond's associates reported in that three of them were on the move. Darell, Sinclair, and Jerningham all left their residences and travelled by separate routes to a rendezvous at the Junior Sports Club in St James' Square, where they had a drink in the bar.

From there they progressed on to the Royal Opera Arcade off Haymarket, the world's oldest enclosed shopping arcade, where they enjoyed craft beers at the London Beer House. By nine they were downing pints in the Tom Cribb, which was named after the famous 19th century bare-knuckle boxing world champion, and after that they moved to The Imperial and to The Moon Under Water.

Their tails were still trying to work out what their quarries' plans were. The three men staggered into a Brewmaster above Lincoln Street Tube Station, and then patronised The Porcupine long enough to down long glasses of Tim Taylor's Landlord. As midnight approached, they decided to return to sample more of the excellent beverages available at the Beer House.

The watchers had to endure a follow-up session of competitive wall-pissing before the three revellers wobbled back to the Junior Sports for a nightcap and some strong coffee.

Dare, T.J., and Bangbang sipped their caffeine in the happy assurance that they had diverted at least some of their enemies' attention away from what their active comrades in the field were doing. Sometimes a man has to sacrifice his kidney function for his brothers-in-arms.

But by that time several other things had happened…

★★★

While their pub-crawling allies were still at the Tom Cribb, Hugh Drummond and James Denny shared oxtail soup from a thermos in an old Land Rover Jeep, while Algy Longworth played on his laptop in the back.

"See, this is why I don't carry a mobile phone," Hugh told his orderly. "Geolocation? Might as well carry a flag around with the words 'Here I am, Shoot me now!' painted on it in bold red letters.

"Madison had it switched off," Algy argued. "I had to hack his computer to hack his phone account to reset his password to activate phone tracking. He might not even know he's got it installed, but it comes as standard with all those expensive smartphones."

"And we know where he is?"

"Yes. Right now he's on North Woolwich Road, near enough to keep an eye on what's happening, far enough to be deniable and do a runner if he needs to. Want to see him?"

"You can do that?" Drummond shivered.

Algy activated Madison's phone's camera. It showed a blurred image of the side of a Black man's nose. There was audio as well. "*Is everybody in position, Iceman? What do you see?*"

"*I guess everybody who's coming to the shindig is here now, boss. There's two guys on the door but the rest are inside getting their instructions. If you want to give the word we can… shit!*"

The gunshot was audible across the phone connection, then the line dropped.

"I reckon 'Iceman' just worked out that 'is ambush 'as been ambushed, sir," Denny chuckled.

"I reckon you are right, James," Hugh replied. "Algy, put Madison's nose away and let's be after the man himself. James, drive. Take us along North Woolwich Road and let's have words with the villain of the piece."

More gunshots were audible now without telephonic help. Algy politely pulled to the side of the road to let four police cars with flashing red and blue lights zoom past in the direction of the noise.

"See, the thing about that warehouse," Drummond explained in a pleased voice, "is that it's very strategically located. There's not that many isolated warehouses left in the Docklands now it's all been developed for yuppie homes. Not many docks, for that matter. But with all the new development in Woolwich and Silvertown, most of the old rat-run back streets are gone or blocked off. It's made it so that those warehouse compounds can only be reached by a few easily-blockable roads. Set up cop-cars at those choke-points, cover the Thames with police launches, and there's not a lot of places for bad lads to run."

"Shame that," Denny said insincerely.

"It's time to call the bad guy," Hugh decided, reaching for another burner phone. "Hey, Newton? Drummond here. How's your day going? Spotted my trap yet? I'm coming to get you."

"Drummond?" came back the angry American snarl. "How did you get this...? What are you pulling?"

"You mean apart from getting your goons and your enemies' goons all shooting each other up in a nice tidy corner where the police can bag the lot of them? I'm taking you down, old lad. You're a nasty piece of work who deserves a good thumping, so I'm going to deliver it. After that you can tell me all about Carl Peterson and his anthrax plot."

Madison delivered a stream of obscene invective down the phone and hung up.

"Swearing shows a lack of imagination and limited self-expression," Drummond declared, repeating a lesson drubbed in to him by his schoolmasters long ago.

"He's moving," Algy reported. "Madison's in a black Lexus LS V6 sedan. He's disabled his phone now but I'm monitoring the car's satnav data. He's heading off up North Woolwich Road, towards London City Airport. He has two chase cars with him, a pair of 4-wheel SUVs."

"He won't go to the airstrip," Drummond predicted. "Too many delays before a private plane could launch. Get us behind them, James. Algy, what range do you need to do your technical wizardry?"

"I can take out those SUVs from fifty yards. Here's a trick I prepared earlier, because I found their purchase documents and got the VIN numbers. Those models have a unique transponder chip code for their electronic anti-theft systems, and they're usually very secure. But if you contact the dealership and prove that you're the owner and say you've lost your key fob, they'll issue you with replacements, custom-programmed with the coded anti-theft system activation signal to disable the engines. Then you plug that fob into a transmitter with a better range than five feet and... yep, I just triggered them."

Ahead in the road, two 4x4s stalled as electronics, fuel pumps, and distributors shut down. The SUVs skidded to a halt. A black sedan swerved around them and carried on.

"Madison's car has been upgraded," Algy warned. "His security system is custom. I can't remote-trigger that one."

"'S cheating anyway," Denny complained. "Ruins a proper car chase, does messing with computers."

"Yes, where's the romance in that?" Hugh agreed. "But that's the modern world for you. Get us up behind him, James. Now his escort has been taken out he's got to know that something is wrong. Algy, keep tracking him."

"Right you are, Bulldog. He's ignoring the turn to the airport like you thought, racing along Albert Road. That'll take him past Royal Victoria Gardens and across the marina bridges to Becton. Once he gets to the roundabout there he could head off in any direction."

"Albert Road is the place for us, boys," Hugh confirmed. "High wall between road and houses to the left, low railings to the park on the right, and nobody much about at this time of the evening. James, invite him to a tour of the gardens."

"Tour it is," Denny agreed. He revved the Jeep up to sixty miles per hour and smashed straight into the rear offside corner of Madison's Lexus. The black car was spun off the road, crashing through the park railing and narrowly avoiding a tree. The Jeep bounced the other way, mounting the opposite kerb, but Denny brought the vehicle under control.

"That car's armoured," he warned.

The Lexus wasn't stopped. It sped up, running along the garden lawn on the far side of the trees that lined the road. A rear window dropped three inches and a gun-muzzle pointed out.

Denny swerved the Jeep, took out more railing, and closed for another collision with Madison's car. Bullets starred the Land Rover's nearside panels and windows but did not penetrate the chassis.

Bulldog replied with a Glock 17M, a generation five updated model of the regular British field pistol that the FBI had adopted as standard in 2017. He placed double-taps of 9x19mm Parabellum bullets into the Lexus' offside wheels but was disappointed to discover they were fitted with solid-filled projectile-resistant tyres.

The two vehicles slammed into each other, sparking as their sides ground together, churning out sprays of turf as they each tried to shift the other aside. Drummond's Jeep was perilously near the line of trees.

"This is getting a bit hairy," Algy noted. "Bulldog?"

"Paint grenade," Drummond called, holding his hand out like a surgeon. Longworth slapped the homemade device into his hand. Hugh slipped open the Jeep's roof-panel and lobbed the bomb to hit the other car's windscreen.

The device shattered, spewing white paint to obscure the driver's view. The Lexus veered right. Denny kept on it, clashing again as it speeded up to try and break away.

A different muzzle appeared from the rear passenger window. This was unmistakably a Remington model 870 pump-action shotgun, and 28-gauge shotshells were a much more serious threat to the lightly-armoured Land Rover.

"Duck!" Drummond called as the weapon discharged, shattering driver's side window and the windscreen with one shot. A second shell penetrated the engine compartment but didn't impair the vehicle's running.

The Lexus was still driving almost blind, though. The wheelman hadn't seen where Denny was pushing him. At the western end of Royal Victoria Gardens is a picnic area with benches, a children's play area with swings, and a large paddling pool. The black car bounced through the tables, losing speed, and mounted the lip of the pool to splash into eighteen inches of water. Its momentum brought it all the way to a juddering impact at the far side of the pond but it hadn't the clearance to climb out.

The Lexus came to an abrupt hard stop. Its occupants were hampered by air bags.

Denny swerved the Jeep to a halt inches from the water. Drummond and Algy rolled out, splitting up to run in at the black car from different angles, keeping up a steady fire as they splashed through the wading pool to pin the occupants of the enemy vehicle. Approaching from behind they could avoid easy shots from the topped car's side windows, and the reinforced rear window did not open.

One of the rear doors cracked open so that the Remington could be used. The other side door had evidently been deformed by the crash and was stuck. The front passenger door opened too, but the bodyguard there tumbled out and fell into the water, his head bloody from where the air bag had driven his own gun into his face.

Drummond covered the distance to the back door in seconds, emptying his Glock to keep the marksman too busy to aim. Another 28-gauge shell whizzed past the fast-closing soldier; but then Hugh was kicking the door shut, trapping the weapon's barrel until half a dozen slams had deformed its muzzle.

The driver broke out, holding his own pistol two-handed. Algy pitched into him with a rugby tackle and the two of them went down into the shallow pool.

Newton Madison II pushed aside his car door and discarded the useless shotgun. "Bulldog Drummond," he recognised his opponent from the newspaper headlines. "I have surely been wanting to meet you. Is it guns, knives, or fists? Or won't you face me man to man?"

"Oh, I'd be delighted," Hugh promised him. He doubled his hands into hard balls. "Let's go bare-knuckle. James, put your gun down. Newton's going to be a sport."

Madison proved him wrong by palming a knife he'd had up his jacket sleeve and trying to carve it through Drummond's belly. Bulldog stuck to fists and landed a solid box on the gang-lord's ear that knocked him to one knee in the water.

Madison swore, rose, and came again, moving smart. He switched the knife at the last moment, a move he'd killed men with before. Drummond wasn't fooled though. He deflected the blow with an outward arm-sweep then hooked a foot round Madison's left leg while the knife-wielder was overbalanced.

The gang-lord fell backwards into the paddling pool. Drummond stamped on the knife—he'd aimed for the wrist—but it still cost Madison his weapon. The lithe American rose more cautiously, his lips drawn back in a mad snarl, his own fists closed and ready.

"Going to try a fair fight?" Hugh mocked him. "That'll be a new experience for you, I bet."

Algy Longworth finished off the driver and dragged his unconscious form to the patio. Denny had already secured the head-injured bodyguard with plastic ties.

Madison had training. Some serious martial artists had tutored him, that much was clear. Drummond spotted a blend of Wing Chun, Muay Thai, and Taekwondo, and estimated that his opponent was black-belted or equivalent in all of them. He was pushed back by a series of hard attacks that were more difficult to deflect in eighteen inches of water.

But all those disciplines were offensive techniques, relying on strikes. Madison was used to dealing out punishment. Drummond let him exhaust his first adrenaline surge, then tested how the gang-lord coped with grappling attacks. Jujutsu and Aikido were more effective when the opponent's motion was slowed by being knee-deep in liquid.

Madison wasn't ready for being joint-locked. Drummond caught another devastating *chum kiu* uppercut before it made contact, dragged the American's arm further along his attack line, and forced him into a submission hold. Madison found himself being pressed down, his head only a couple of inches above the water.

"You can stop now or I can break your arm," Hugh told him.

Madison slipped a razor blade from his other cuff and went for Drummond's femoral artery. Drummond snapped Madison's ulna to stop him. Hugh dropped hard onto the screaming gang-lord's back, pinning him under the water.

"He doesn't seem to understand how to fight as a gentleman," Hugh told his comrades. "I had to be harsh."

"He don't seem able to breathe underwater, neither, sir," Denny pointed out practically.

"Good point," Hugh accepted. He hauled the battered Madison up by the scruff of his neck. The American was half-drowned and barely conscious. "Let's abstract this fellow before the constables arrive, shall we? There are a few questions I'd like to put to him regarding Carl Peterson and some hundred tons of missing earth. James, help me patch up his arm with a splint. Algy, check the Lexus and see if there's anything useful there."

Longworth wasn't going to bother taking Madison's switched-off phone—after all, he had already thoroughly hacked it—but it woke up and rang just as he was about to discard it. Drummond was busy levering his wounded prisoner into the car and Denny was breaking out the first aid kit. Algy answered the call.

"Algy?" came a woman's voice that the playboy recognised.

"Tanya?" There were many possible reasons for good or ill that Algy's second wife might call him; there were no good reasons for her to call him on Newton Madison's phone. "What are you...?"

"Algy, I..."

The woman's voice was silenced. A man spoke instead.

"Mr Longworth, as you will surmise, I have invited your former spouse to come and visit with me."

"Who the blazes is that?"

"Who do you think, Mr Longworth? Who would know you had hacked Madison's phone because he had previously done so himself? Who would be monitoring your exciting car chase that way? Who would determine exactly when to call you as you bundle your captive into your bullet-spattered Jeep?"

Algy looked around. "You're watching us?"

"Indeed. I could have you taken down with sniper-shots right now, all of you. But it might put my ally at risk, and I have a contract with him. So I'll make an exchange. Bring Madison—unquestioned—to Drummond's Westminster flat at midnight tonight and the former Mrs Longworth won't become the late Mrs Longworth."

Drummond has spotted that something was wrong with Algy. He came back to find out what the problem was.

"Give my regards to Captain Drummond, would you?" the speaker on the phone said. "Tell him that Carl Peterson has not forgotten his promises."

Then the line went dead.

★★★

CHAPTER XII:
IN WHICH THE PETERSONS TAKE AN INTEREST

Do you think he'll go?" asked Irma Peterson.

"I believe that Hugh Drummond is loyal to a fault when it comes to his friends. He has been Longworth's best man three times, supported him through three divorces, and saved his life on several occasions. He won't let him down now. You disagree?"

Irma Peterson selected a purple grape from the fruit platter before her, popped it into her mouth, and only answered when she had swallowed it. "He'll go. He might have some sort of trick up his sleeve. He's hardly as dim as he looks."

"Well, I haven't slept with him, but I agree with you. That's why I've worked to narrow his choices. He has little time and a lot of pressure. Fortunately, the Metropolitan Constabulary will be somewhat busy tonight tidying up the Docklands fiasco. He won't need to worry about a police watch on his flat. Still, I look forward to seeing what he comes up with."

"You like him too," Irma accused before picking another grape.

"I admire him," Carl Peterson admitted. "The way one might admire a volcano or a hurricane, for its ferocity, it's implacability, it's unpredictability. And because Bulldog Drummond has many admirable traits. Unfortunately, those traits make him a hero in an age that doesn't really have a place for such men."

"Hugh's postbag seems to disagree with you."

"Give my regards to Captain Drummond, would you?" the speaker on the phone said.

Carl watched his sister carefully. "You realise that your Hugh has now become too great a liability? After this war with Madison I can't just sideline Drummond. He has to go."

"I'd prefer if you didn't kill him. He amuses me."

"Find other amusement. I can't afford Bulldog any more. I've sent Rosca."

"Christophe? Then you really mean it!"

"He volunteered. I think he is offended with Drummond for sullying your honour."

"Christophe desperately wants to get me in bed," Irma recognised. "Killing Bulldog won't get him any closer."

"I suspect Rosca doesn't see it like that. Anyway, I've deployed him. It's done. Besides, even if our finest assassin didn't end your hero's life, he'd die with eight million Londoners two days from now."

Irma pushed the fruit dish away from her. She'd lost her appetite.

★★★

"What is the score?" Sir James asked DCI McIver.

"One hundred and forty-one arrests, ninety-five illegal firearms, a hundred and two concealed bladed weapons, twenty-seven suspects shifted to hospital, five corpses discovered in and around the site, and an estimated three thousand hours of police overtime," she answered. "At least the newspapers won't be saying we're doing nothing to tackle gun crime and street violence in the wake of this week's incidents. But your in-tray isn't getting any lighter."

"Oh, I imagine the bulk of the work will fall on the senior officer at the scene, the one who unearthed the information. The one who acted on information received. Isn't that so, Detective Chief Inspector?"

McIver recognised that she would have to pay her penance. "It'll be my pleasure, guv," she surrendered. "On the upside, amongst those we've pulled is Harry the Hedgehog himself, with a nice little flesh wound, and a tasty American chap with the street-name Icepick who managed to get himself shot in the pelvis. J.K. Green says the FBI will happily take him off our hands as soon as there's an extradition order."

"No sign of Captain Drummond?"

"Nothing I'd take to court."

"You are referring to the car crash and firefight off Albert Road?" Sir James supposed. "The two gentlemen secured at the scene are quite lawyered up and prefer to remain silent. Their missing colleague is most likely an illegal immigrant called Newton Madison II. I believe you were asking after him."

"He's a Person of Interest in several enquiries, sir."

"I should certainly like to talk to him. See if you can rustle him up, would you. Perhaps you might have another tip-off."

"Yes sir. Give me about, oh, four to eight hours to finish up with the Docklands take-down and I'll get right on it."

★★★

"What do we do, Bulldog?" Algy asked again, trying to control the panic in his voice. "It's Tanya, Hugh! We have to do something. But what?"

"We'll make the trade," Drummond assured his friend. "I've talked to this Peterson over the radio and when I was in that ship-cage. He seems to take his word very seriously. I wouldn't trust Madison to stick to a hostage exchange bargain, but I think Peterson might."

"She'll be terrified. She's not cut out for all this. She hated it when I was a soldier. And I couldn't tell her what I was doing or when I'd be back. No wonder she got rid of me. And I still got her into this!"

"Stay strong, Lieutenant. Can't have you going to pieces on me now. Tanya's relying on you. Shape up!"

Denny turned into Park Lane, at the wheel of an anonymous BMW X3 that had been waiting in the same lock-up garage where a bullet-riddled Jeep was now hidden. "Not far now, sirs. Is there a plan, yet?"

"Take us in round the back," Hugh decided. "Curzon Street, Trebeck Street, Shepherd Street, White Horse Street. Drop me off by the stand of trees near The King's Arms. From there I can get into the flat and see if there's anything nasty waiting for us. You two will circle the block, keeping moving, with Nugent still trussed in the boot, until you see my bathroom light on and the shade half down. Then you make for the garage and have our guest up to 17a as fast as you can."

"And if it's not alright, sir?" Denny asked.

"If the blind is all the way down, then it's a trap and they've got me. Veer off, warn the others, make best speed for Goring, and get Mrs D and Ms Benton out of there. Then use your initiative to head somewhere I wouldn't anticipate so they can't drug it out of me."

"And Tanya?" Algy asked.

"I'll do what I can for her."

"And if this Peterson bloke turns up for an exchange?" enquired Denny.

"We make it. We won't have Madison to interrogate but we've already got his files. And there's a lead Mrs D turned up with Fi regarding charity shops of all things. We have to accept that Peterson outflanked us on this one. It's the battle, not the war."

"No tricks," Algy insisted. "Not 'till Tanya's safe."

"Agreed. But if they try something then all bets are off. And there is one insurance policy I'll be taking in with me."

"The Glock?" Denny asked, "or something from the lockbox in the mews garage?"

"The latter. Don't worry, Algy. Peterson would be disappointed if I didn't take some precaution. He'd lose all respect for me."

The BMW rounded the corner into the narrow passage of White Horse Street. Double yellow lines forbade any parking on the one-way route; two cars could only pass if one was half onto the kerb, entirely blocking pedestrian traffic. At eleven at night the cafes, cobblers, and barbers were all shut. A lone wine bar was operating, with a few patrons clustered outside, but otherwise the road was quiet.

Denny scarcely stopped the car. Hugh jumped out and crossed into the shadow of the alley that led to the old mews behind the row of Half Moon Street townhouses. Once such courtyards had been common in London, but the Blitz and property developers between them had made them a rare feature now. Drummond found shelter in a doorway and waited for five minutes to spot anyone else lurking nearby.

Either there was no one or the lurker was very good. Hugh slipped into the small tree-filled space that his flat's rear windows overlooked. He ignored the service door to his property, instead letting himself into the two-car garage where he kept his favourite vehicles, a classic Rolls Royce Phantom Coupe for style and a Chevrolet C4 Grand Sport for speed and power.

There, under the workbench, was a box of old tools. Hugh pulled it out, revealing rotten old coconut matting beneath it. Under that was a fingerprint-lock floor safe, and in there were the items he needed.

There were six of them; deep bronze-coloured steel spheres 2.6" in diameter, topped with black matte safety clips and ring-pull triggers. Embossed on the side was GREN HAND HE L109A1, SM (for Swiss Munitions) and a unique serial number. The L190A1 was the British Army variant of the Swiss military's *Hand Granate* M1985. Each grenade contained 155 grams of TNT and would detonate into 1,800 fragments that were lethal to everyone within ten yards.

With them was a webbing belt from which they could be hung. Hugh spent fifteen minutes working by torchlight to bypass the clever safety catches and ensure that he could explode the entire belt with one sharp tug on a piece of string. He thought of it as the Luigi Massimo Memorial Tactic.

If Carl Peterson wasn't a man of his word and Drummond was to die, then the soldier intended to take out Madison too, and whomever Peterson sent to collect him.

He departed the old mews stable and let himself into his house. The dwelling was in darkness. Darell was out with the boys, the Dennys were both absent, and the occupants of the second floor were enjoying the good weather on the piste in Seibelseckle. Hugh listened again, but he heard only the sonorous beat of the grandfather clock in the entrance hall.

He did not take the tiny modern lift up to his first floor rooms, preferring to quietly ascend the main stair where he had clear firing lines at any intruder. He reached the landing to his flat and checked behind a rather pleasant watercolour of Rome; the concealed security panel claimed that there had been no breach of the property.

Hugh still entered his rooms cautiously. He had left other tell-tales as warning of intrusion, including some good old-fashioned hairs stuck across doorways and drawers. There was no sign of visitors.

Satisfied at last, and with twenty minutes left until midnight, Drummond half-drew the bathroom shade, made sure he was out of sight-line of the window, and flipped on the light.

Unsatisfied, he went back downstairs to let Arty and Drummond in with their injured gang-lord and to make one last bit of preparation in the lobby.

★★★

Dr Henry Lakington, Fi Benton's creepy observer, was currently watching other things of interest. He stood with Carl Peterson and Koh Zhenkai one the safe side of a thick glass screen. Sheep occupied four cubicles on the other side. The other four cubes contained nine people in each.

"The tests are quite encouraging," the chemist told his employers. "Cubicle one contains a dozen Scottish Blackface sheep, the same breed that was used on Gruinard to test Vollum 14578 in 1942. These animals have been infected with retrieved samples of the same. The contamination rate and development of symptoms is broadly in line with observations made then. The recovered anthrax spores remain as potent as they were when they were first released."

"You were right, then, Mr Franklyn," the Taiwanese financier told Peterson.

"The second ovine batch, in cubicle two, were treated with the vaccine developed since the 1970s, widely touted as a "cure" for anthrax contamination. Vaccination for anthrax is not new, of course; Louis Pasteur was doing it in the 1870s. The modern MDPH-PA, 'Anthrax vaccine adsorbed', has proved mostly effective, although it is weak against inhaled spores. The US Strategic National Stockpile keeps six million units of it at all times, enough to treat a million people. Our own laboratory sample sets are necessarily small, but I would assess it brings an 80% kill-rate down to 25%."

"That's still a significant amount of damage," Peterson observed, "but not sufficient for our purposes. Several tons of anthrax vaccine are also stored across Britain in case of an outbreak."

"Yes. Armed forces being deployed to potential combat zones are routinely inoculated these days," reported Lakington, "despite the controversial issue of potential side effects and efficacy. But here, in cubicles three and four, we see this practically tested. The nine men in this cube are unvaccinated, and Vollum 14578 has infected all of them. Two are dead already, and we expect a death toll similar to that of our woollier specimens." The scientist paused to snicker at his small joke. "These other nine are ex-servicemen who received vaccination. There the infection rate is just 44% and we expect only two of those men to die of their symptoms."

"Disappointing," pronounced Koh Zhenkai, staring indifferently at the suffering sick men who could not see him through the one-way observation screen.

"Ah, but then we come to our improved product," Lakington promised. "The sheep in cube five and the men in cube seven have been exposed to my new Vollum 21136—although really it should be called Lakington 388. This strain is significantly more robust, a proper upgrade for the 21st century. Untreated sheep and men alike have a one hundred percent infection rate and I confidently expect a 93% mortality index."

"You haven't finished your tests?" Peterson asked.

"Oh, this is the fourth batch, purely for confirmation," the chemist promised. "Of course, since we retained the delayed onset feature, some subjects will not get overt symptoms for several days yet. They will be infectious all that time."

"Nobody will know who is a carrier," Koh appreciated. "Society will shut down. Britain will be quarantined, walled-off from the rest of the world by frightened governments and their militaries."

Peterson nodded. "And who will send aid when they fear that their nation may be the next target? Stocks of ineffective vaccine will be hoarded, international travel banned. There will be food riots and fuel shortages. People suspected of carrying the bacterium will be burned alive by frightened mobs. And once a country has descended to such depths, has learned its true face, it can never go back to what it was before."

Lakington continued his presentation, indifferent to the consequences of his work. "Finally, look to cubes six and eight. The cube six subjects have been exposed to Vollum 21136 with no prophylactic. Those in eight have been given the best modern vaccinations available, the intramuscular injections approved by the US FDA in 2008 after the postal anthrax attacks over there."

"And the result?" Koh breathed.

"I am pleased to announce that all the subjects in cube six will die, and at least eight of the nine in cube eight who were inoculated. Our tentative kill-rates are 97% and 88% respectively. This represents a reasonable success within the margins you specified."

"Thank you, doctor," Peterson told the scientist. "I know it's been a rush job, but your work had been exemplary."

"I look forward to seeing it tested through widespread practical application," Lakington assured him. "You have solved the distribution problem?"

"That was always the easiest part. I have acquired a collection of crop-dusting and fire-fighting aircraft, light planes and helicopters. They are already fitted for aerial droplet spraying over wide areas. The day after tomorrow they can enter London airspace and begin to release their cargo over the city centre. I expect some of them will actually be shot down; major cities have taken precautions since 9/11, and Drummond will have appraised somebody in power of my ambitions. Even half of the craft will be sufficient to spray 84,000 gallons, 2,645 tons of newly-cultured anthrax across twenty-five square miles."

"From Buckingham Palace to the Tower of London," anticipated Koh Zhenkai. "From Hampstead Heath to the South Bank of the Thames. And it will persist. It will cling to buildings, to pavements. It will drift. It will pollute the river, seeping into the water table all the way to the coast."

"The British had a similar plan in World War Two," Peterson noted. "Ironic, since the bacterium was first identified by a German in 1875, the Nobel-winning Robert Koch. Operation Vegetarian prepared five million livestock pellets and cattle-cakes to drop over Germany, as well as the aerial anthrax bomb tested on Gruinard Island. But then the Manhattan Project rather one-upped it, and weapons of mass destruction went another way."

"I have significantly improved on Operation Vegetarian," Lakington promised. "And on Little Boy and Fat Man."

"The 2001 post office attacks were very limited," Koh declared, "but decontamination of the Brentwood postal facility took 26 months and cost $130 million US. Cleaning government buildings in Washington DC cost $41.7 million. The total clean-up bill from that quite contained series of events was over one billion. Imagine the resources required to restore a whole city? There is not enough money in the world!"

"It's the end of London," Peterson agreed, watching the infected prisoners behind the glass with their black open sores. "That's the point of the exercise, isn't it? The whole area and miles around the drop-zone will become uninhabitable for a century, maybe much longer. The entire south of England will be blighted. Billions lost in property, millions of casualties, loss of central authority, devastation of the economy, collapse of law and order, international political upheaval. As promised."

"The necessary volume of product will be cultivated for shipping by the day after tomorrow," Dr Lakington declared, "but I would prefer a 48-hour safety margin. Given that extra time I could double the amount of cultured anthrax available for you to deploy."

Peterson shook his head. "That won't do, doctor. You have been busy in your lab so perhaps you have overlooked the date; or perhaps you are not a follower of current events. The day after tomorrow is our absolute deadline. You understand why, Mr Koh?"

The financier worked it out immediately. "It is the official State Opening of the UK Parliament," he realised.

"Correct. The reigning monarch of Great Britain and Northern Ireland marks the beginning of a new session of Parliament, making a speech from the throne to both the House of Commons and the House of Lords. Since the ruler of the Commonwealth processes to the Palace of Westminster in a state carriage, the route is lined with a hundred thousand tourists and well-wishers. The press televise the whole thing. Many important dignitaries will gather for the event. Every MP is expected to be present, with the senior judiciary, military, and foreign diplomats. Security forces will be on high alert, which means there will also be a great number of police, military, and anti-terror specialists gathered in our kill-zone."

"The chance to test Vollum 21136 is unprecedented," Lakington enthused.

Koh Zhenkai was also keen. "This chance to change the world is unprecedented."

Peterson's phone rang. He checked the Dark Matter KATIM device, a cutting edge 256-bit encrypted instrument with a hardened Android O/S that would have caused Algernon Longworth many hours of useless toil to attack, and accepted the call from Christophe Rosca. "He's there? And Madison?"

"Drummond went in alone first, as predicted. Then Denny and Longworth brought the American inside. Madison looks to have a splint on his arm. His mouth is taped shut."

"Improvements," Peterson considered. "Did they find the micro-camera in the entrance hall?"

"No. It would take a serious security sweep to detect that. You didn't give them time."

"Then they are confirmed *in situ*?"

"Confirmed. I have them."

"Then hold for my signal. Thank you, Mr Rosca."

Peterson shut down the call, checked the time, and saw that it was nearly midnight. "Excuse me," he told Koh and Lakington. "I have another appointment."

***

"I say, Bulldog," Algy called as Madison's captured phone pinged, "It's a text alert. For you. From your girlfriend!"

He held out the touchscreen so that Drummond could read the all-caps message: HUGH, IT'S A TRAP. GET OUT OF THERE NOW! FILLY.

"Proper warning?" Denny wondered. "Or is that supposed to flush us from a prepared position into the open?"

"Oh, we're in a trap," Drummond judged. "Don't know if Filly's a part of it though, or if she genuinely does retain a vestige of affection for the outfit who supplied her with bacon and kidneys. Hope so."

The flat's landline rang, an old-fashioned bell tone. Hugh took the call. "The Old Firm!" he announced himself.

"Captain Drummond," Carl Peterson recognised. "Exactly as amusing as ever. You have Newton Madison II? Put him on the line."

"He's a bit damaged and a lot handcuffed," Hugh warned. "Hold on while we rip off some carpet tape."

The wrathful Madison made a noise of pain and anger as his gag was torn off, and added to his collection of obscenities.

"Your chum wants a word with you, Newton," Drummond told him. "I'm putting this on speaker. Algy, how do I… ah, thanks."

Peterson spoke to the captive. "Newton, kindly confirm that you are more or less intact and that you have not been interrogated in any way."

"I'm here. I've got a busted wing that these guys are going to pay for. They've asked me jack and I've told them less."

"Excellent. Then Captain Drummond and Mr Longworth have kept their side of the bargain. I'm sending a text now to have the delightful Tanya released in Trafalgar Square in the next minute or so, along with sufficient cash for her to take a cab back to her Knightsbridge home."

"Wait!" the gang-lord objected. "I'm not free yet!"

"That wasn't actually the bargain I made, Newton. I agreed to release the lady if Drummond brought you to his flat by midnight. I was quite specific. I never expected to get you released. Why would I? Your idiocy has already inconvenienced my plans and your usefulness is significantly impaired by the loss of your UK network and of Chapter 51's offshore funds."

"My… what?"

"Your captors have thoroughly gutted your organisation and shown you to be a prize chump, Nugent. You've become a liability. Our partnership is terminated. Drummond?"

"Peterson," Hugh replied, his hackles rising as he sensed what was coming.

"This isn't personal. Terminal, but not personal. Well played."

In the flat across the road from number 17, Rosca shouldered an RPG-7 portable, shoulder-launched, rocket-propelled grenade launcher. He fixed the PGO7 2.7x telescopic sight on Drummond's lounge window, where his target's main cord-fixed landline telephone point was, and loosed the 40mm OG-7V anti-personnel fragmentation warhead at his target's apartment.

The gunpowder booster charge thrust the ordinance forward at 115 metres per second, leaving a faint blue trail between the buildings. The rocket motor launched and propelled the missile towards its top speed of 295 meters per second. It punched the 4lb grenade-lance through Hugh's reinforced plate glass as if it had been tissue paper and detonated on the far wall, sending out lethal shards that punched through brickwork into adjacent rooms.

Rosca wasn't done. He selected a TBG-7V thermobaric warhead and snapped that into place on his shoulder. This shot went through the adjacent study window, exploding in a balloon of flame that filled the entire floor and blossomed out of front and rear windows. The floor of Drummond's apartment collapsed down into the Dennys' ground floor service flat. Fire and security alarms halfway along the road began to sound and flash.

Rosca lifted another TBG-7V and put that through the front door of 17 Half Moon Street just to be certain. It took out the staircase and turned the entire bottom half of the building into an inferno.

"Did he get out of the back?" the assassin checked with the marksmen he had positioned on the roof of the mews.

"Negative. The trip-charges on the rear door only went off when the fireball hit them."

"The signal from Madison's phone?" he checked with his operations support.

"Silent."

Only then was Christophe Rosca satisfied to text back to Peterson that the targets were dead.

★★★

CHAPTER XIII:
IN WHICH THERMODYNAMICS AND GRAVITY HAVE THEIR SAY

A hundred and twelve miles north and west of Half Moon Street and fifteen thousand feet off sea level, Flight Lieutenant Jerry Seymour piloted a 1947 Supermarine Spitfire Mk 11 over the rolling plains of Norfolk. This was the same model as the plane in which Squadron Leader Martindale had set a world speed dive record of 606mph, Mach 0.92, in April 1944, and was one of only fifty-four Spitfires that remained airworthy of the 20, 351 such aircraft once built.

It was Jez's pride and joy, a pilot's craft, a work of engineering genius, as responsive and rewarding to drive today as it had been when it had been the mainstay of the RAF in and after World War II.

Jez liked to keep the Spitfire in its original condition, in its traditional olive livery with the red dot and blue circle on the wings, but today he had bowed to the 21st century enough to temporarily attach powerful infrared ground surveillance equipment and a top line digital recording unit. Reconnaissance surveillance had been one of the Spitfire's primary design functions and Jez felt that the old bird wouldn't object to playing the part one more time, with some helpful upgrades for night flight and electronic observation. And who would expect an eccentric hobbyist flying an antique to be conducting espionage?

He checked the modern electronic display. His course was eastsoutheasterly, passing over the quiet parishes of Tharston, Forncett St Mary, Forncett St Peter, and Aslacton. He was just under ten miles from Norwich, one of the flagged locations that included both Oxfam and Salvation Army charity shops and was within most aircraft's flight reach of London. In the war that the Spitfires had helped to win, the flat country had virtually become one giant airfield in defence of Britain and many private landing strips and former Ministry of Defence airfields still remained today.

The terrain below was a spider's web of lights, of houses and street-lamps strung out across the farmed landscape, surrounded by tracts of impenetrable darkness where woodland or crop fields sprawled; or those areas would have been impenetrable except for the Vexel UltraCam Eagle IR lens on the Spitfire's undercarriage. That was working fine to interpret low-light data and thermal imaging to offer a real-time view of what was happening in the shadows.

There were three licensed airstrips in regular use in the locality that could have generated the traffic that Fi Benton had heard during her captivity. That she had only heard noise in daytime suggested a smaller field for shorter-range craft, excluding the commercial landing pad for an import/export freight business near Long Stratton. A private hobby field in Wreningham was only used at weekends. That left a hire firm called SoarBrite that scraped along doing aerial surveys and some ground-spraying and firefighting. On Mrs Denny's list of potential sites it had ranked third-highest.

Jez was checking them all. He noticed that SoarBrite's hangar sheds were still active this late at night, with multiple people moving about. The thermal bloom of multiple light plane and helicopter engines and systems was unmistakable. Fully a dozen aircraft were down there and some were being serviced and tested.

That pinged an alert in Jez's mind no less telling than the warble from his surveillance program. He banked the Spitfire round and dropped to 5000 feet to get a much better look at the airfield. His camera recorded the details of recently-renewed equipment, expanded fuel silo, and half a dozen pantechnicons lined by the security fence.

The software chirped again, drawing the pilot's attention to another set of readings a half mile further west between Forncett End and Hargate. That was farmland, complete with the usual cluster of agricultural buildings well off the main road. There was a sprawling main farmhouse, a couple of milking sheds, a stable, long hay barns, and all the other structures and storage that a working agricultural base might need. But what working farm today had nearly two hundred people on it, and some of them patrolling the perimeter fence in pairs? What cattle shed's thermal and electromagnetic signatures were not caused by a herd of penned bovines but by high-tech machinery and enhanced power cables?

"Well now, hello there," Jez greeted the estate he overflew. His sensors recorded it all: the perimeter wire and electric chainlink, the recently-upgraded entrance road that might better take heavily-laden lorries, the bright thermal bloom of a working incinerator, the electronic hum of significant equipment in the converted barn that was drawing a lot of current. "Hello, villain's lair!" the pilot called out. "You're busted!"

***

In the farmhouse below Jez's Spitfire, Coninthia Dalglish glowered up at her midnight visitor.

"How are you doing?" Irma Peterson enquired of the elderly lady.

"Still a prisoner of murderers," Miss Dalglish replied. "Yourself?"

"Still a *femme fatale* luring men to their dooms."

Miss Dalglish made a very Scottish noise that conveyed in one throaty expression an appreciation for dark humour, disapproval of the humorist, and acceptance of a bleak and uncaring fate. "Yuir brother hasn't killed Captain Drummond yet, then?"

"What makes you say that?"

"Because y'd be a lot more upset, lassie. Yui've had every chance to murder yuir young man since this began. Y' could have killed him in his sleep. Y' had him drugged to oblivion. Y' had him locked helpless in a cage."

"We had reasons for keeping him around then. Those reasons have expired, and so must he."

"An assassin has been dispatched tonight, hasn'ae he? Hugh Drummond is his target. You are waiting restlessly for word of success or failure and y' don't quite know which would be which."

"You have been talking to my brother."

"Actually, I've been talking to the Barn."

"The...? Wait, you don't mean Gŭ Cāng, Koh Zhenkai's massive doorstop? I didn't even know he spoke, let alone spoke English."

"Oh, he's a lethal killer, I'm sure, but he's been brought up tae respect old age. He's been supplying me with gossip about Captain Drummond's progress—and a rather pleasant green tea. I think he's hoping tae meet your hero—to kill him, naturally."

"He's not my hero," Irma insisted. "I rather gave him away. Literally."

"And yet tonight when yuir brother has sent his best killer to terminate the Bulldog, you are wandering the building disturbing old women you have kidnapped."

"But not innocent old women. If you and McCloud hadn't played your con-trick to finance your charity, if you'd incinerated all the contaminated topsoil as you were contracted, we wouldn't be here."

"We did what seemed proper tae us at the time. I regret it now, have regretted it for a long while. I'm sure Stuart did too, far before it was the death o' him. It was the death of him, wasn't it?"

"The same person who has gone to eliminate Hugh was following McCloud when he decided to end it all. Unfortunately we had no idea of whom he was running to. Hence the charade with Bulldog."

"A charade you enjoyed, Miss Bent... Miss Peterson. Yuir're probably not really Irma Peterson either, are y'?"

"My brother and I left our original selves behind long ago, and we don't miss them. Now he's Carl and I'm Irma; at least for a bit. But yes, it was nice pretending to be Hugh's heroine for a time."

"Y' are afraid for him. And of him."

"I'll leave you to get what sleep you can, Miss Dalglish. Forty-eight hours from now we will both be accessories in the greatest mass-murder in history."

***

The ground floor of 17 Half Moon Street was an inferno. The first floor, Drummond's flat, was shredded by shrapnel and the rear wall had partially collapsed. The floor above, belonging to the absent skiers, was sagging down to fall into the flames. Only the penthouse, Peter Darell's apartment, remained partly intact until the fire breached it.

That was where Drummond, Algy, Denny, and Madison were. It had been simple enough for Algy to carry out Hugh's request to rewire the property's British Telecom landline mastersocket to divert all calls from 17a to 17c.

"I didn't expect the rocket launcher," Drummond admitted. "Nice touch."

"That bastard Franklyn jus' tried to kill me!" Newton Madison II gasped, his eyes wide and desperate. "Let me loose! I'm not gonna burn here!"

"More likely the building will collapse first," Drummond considered.

One wall of the penthouse living room where they had set up camp was gone, bringing some of the rafters down with it. "We can't get past it to the landing," Algy shouted over the roar of the flames below.

"I can get us through," Hugh promised. "I have a beltful of hand grenades. Everyone into the kitchen. I'm taking out this wall between us and the bedroom."

"Because we don't need all the supporting walls we still 'ave," muttered Denny.

Hugh uncoiled his improvised suicide belt and laid it along the base of the partition wall. He jerked the go-string and dived for the kitchen for cover beside Denny.

Another blast rattled the crippled building. More of the ceiling came in, showering the apartment in ceiling plaster and lath-boards. A kitchen smoke alarm valiantly meeped its unnecessary warning.

Drummond peered out from cover. The way was clear to bypass the fire-choked hall by stepping straight through the wall and the remains of Dare's wardrobe.

Algy checked the way out from the master bedroom. "The entire stairwell has gone. There's no way down!" Algy warned.

"There's the external fire escape here at the rear," Denny reminded them.

Hugh shook his head. "The bad guys will have rigged it. I know I would. We're going up, over the rooves."

"You're insane!" Madison cried.

"Cut him loose, James. He'll find it hard enough to climb with that busted wing anyhow."

Denny sliced through the plastic binding cuffs. "Watch yourself," he warned the American.

"Over the roofs?" Algy checked unhappily. "You've planned this?"

"Dare and I had all the exfiltration routes figured ten minutes after he moved in. This one is about the only way left to us, across the shingles, using the apex ridge and chimneystacks for cover. Denny, you keep an eye on Chuckles the One-Armed Wonder. Algy, you check my six. Let's go."

He opened the sash window in Dare's bedroom and peered over the sill. Peter liked to doze in at weekends so his sleeping area faced away from the main thoroughfare, overlooking the small tree-filled triangle and the mews garages at the back of the property. From this vantage it was possible to identify the pattern-camouflaged hitmen atop the two-story former stable block, placed to kill anyone fleeing the burning building.

"That's unfriendly," Drummond muttered. He aimed his Glock and squeezed off three double-taps in rapid succession. Three men grunted, twitched, and slid off the tiles. Their hunting rifles clattered to the gutters and stuck there. The assassins rolled all the way to the ground.

"Clear," Hugh called back, and led the way through the window to the lowest angle of the roof. Some of the slates had fallen, rattled from the earlier abuse the brownstone had taken, making traversing the slope in the dark more dangerous.

Denny peered down at the blaze that shone out across the courtyard. "Mrs D. isn't going to like this," Denny predicted.

"Not a big fan myself," Hugh told him. "I'm feeling the need to express my opinions to Carl Peterson and that blighter with the grenade launcher."

Madison slipped and almost fell, landing hard on his broken wrist and yelping like a dog hit by a car. Algy grabbed the crime-lord and hauled him back from the roof's edge. "Steady, old bean. Don't die until you spill all the beans about your nasty plans."

Newton Madison might have come back with a rude or tough retort, but it was a long way down behind him, and getting hotter.

Drummond made a hand gesture. Algy and Denny understood immediately, dropping to the slope of the roof and pulling the prisoner with them. Hugh shifted quietly to the next block of chimneys, unused and ornamental now, above the hearths of numbers 15 and 13. He sensed rather than saw movement behind the stack and lurched aside as a razor-edge arced at his neck.

Hugh kept his balance and raised his pistol. His close-quarters attacker ignored it and stuck at Drummond's left foot, ruining its grip and sending him slithering down to the overhanging rain gutter. Hugh had to drop his weapon to grab a handhold. The Glock skittered off the roof and vanished.

Light plastic guttering held by thin modern clips would have broken, sending Drummond plunging to his end, but this was a solid old

Edwardian property with stone buttressing for heavy tar-painted timber gutters. Hugh's boot found a toehold and his fingers caught at the gap where a slate had gone.

Christophe Rosca came in again. The assassin was annoyed that his initial ploy hadn't worked. Everything about Captain Drummond annoyed the killer, from his boss' admiration of the graceless soldier to Irma's inexplicable desire for the Englishman. It was a pleasure to murder him.

"Bulldog Drummond. I have orders to make your demise public and spectacular."

There was a message to send. Besides, Carl Peterson had felt that his adversary would prefer to go out with a bang, fighting to the last, with a brave funeral pyre. Since Drummond had somehow withstood three shoulder-launched grenades, Rosca would give him a personal, bloody death.

Drummond gripped the fragile roof and manoeuvred for a more solid position. "So far you're doing well on the 'spectacular', okay on the 'public', but not so good on the 'demising'," Hugh graded him. "You're the vandal with the grenade launcher, are you?"

"It doesn't matter that you survived that. This is more satisfying. This is what I will describe to Irma."

"Irma, who's she? Is she cute?"

"*Irma Peterson!*" Rosca shouted, lashing out with his knife again, going for the hand by which Drummond clung onto the roof. "You dirtied her!"

Hugh scrabbled back, almost slipped again, and found purchase on a stone water-channel. "You'll have to be a lot more specific, I'm afraid."

"Phyllis Benton! You... She..."

"Filly? So she's Irma, is she? Relation of Carl, by any chance? Please don't say wife."

Rosca managed to score a line down Drummond's arm. "His sister! His lovely sister. I will kill you for her."

"I don't think I dirtied Filly. I'm pretty sure she was pre-dirtied. That's why we had so much fun. But a gentleman never tells."

Along the line of the roof, Algy tried to get a bead on the assassin, but Hugh was in the way. As he lined up his revolver, Madison elbowed Denny to pitch him off the tiles and grabbed at Longworth's weapon.

Denny teetered, unable to regain his balance. Algy let the gang-lord have the Smith & Wesson Centrefire and grabbed his imperilled comrade. As Madison twisted the revolver round to cap them, Algy swung Denny round into Madison. The former orderly didn't rely on his fifteen years of extensive military combat training but reverted to his troubled street youth, pistoning his fist into the American's groin, grabbing him by his broken wrist, and kicking him off the ledge.

Nugent Madison II discovered that all the lawyers in the world couldn't argue with gravity.

"Oops," Denny said insincerely.

Twenty yards along the rapidly-heating slates, Drummond slid again, allowing Rosca to press close with his knife. The assassin fell for it and was surprised when Hugh tore loose one of the roof tiles and smashed it into his forearm. Rosca's hand opened involuntarily, dropping the blade. Drummond pulled him in for a wrestling grapple.

The two off them rolled along the angle of the roof, each trying to gain a foothold that would allow leverage. "This was... much more fun... with Irma," Drummond told the grimacing assassin.

Rosca let out an animal scream and slammed Hugh down. "You don't talk about her!"

"It was you who brought her up. Could you let me have her contact details? I feel I owe her flowers or chocolates or something. I mean, she fooled me and drugged me and sent me off to Iceland but other than it, it was a great date."

"Shut up!" Rosca slid a flick-knife from his epaulette and tried to carve his enemy's face.

Drummond had been waiting for the assassin to divert his attention for even the briefest second; pulling the weapon did it. He took a chance, kicked away from the wooden gutter, and slithered right off the roof, taking Rosca with him.

The only difference was, Drummond had been expecting it. His left hand closed on a capstone promontory, leaving him dangling precariously above a four-storey drop. Rosca flailed and grabbed at the only support available, the ex-soldier who was already hanging on by his fingertips.

Drummond poked a pair of fingers into the assassin's eyes. Rosca screamed, flinched, and instinctively let go.

He vanished into the darkness, crashing onto a concrete patio and the railing around it.

Hugh realised that his sweaty hand was slipping too. He kicked out and managed to get a brief toehold, then caught the gutter with his other hand to stabilise himself. Heart pumping fast, not looking down, he hauled himself back to the pitched slates. Algy and Denny got there just in time to help him stand up.

"We misplaced Madison," Algy apologised.

"I owe Filly a new boyfriend," Drummond replied.

They followed the line of the roof until they found another external fire escape. At the front of the building, fire engines had arrived to tackle the conflagration.

"Recover our weaponry, secure Newton's body," Hugh told Denny. "Peterson doesn't need to know that Madison's not alive and talking. I'll get the Chevy from the garage. Bundle Madison in the boot. Algy, get the car we came in, head off to Tanya's place, and see that she's all right. Tell her sorry from me. Rendezvous at Goring tomorrow at noon, taking the usual precautions."

★★★

Peter Darell was understandably surprised when he returned from his night out to find his house ablaze, the street closed off with fire engines and police cars. He was less surprised to find DCI Mary McIver at the scene.

"I take it I have an insurance claim to make," he began.

"Who was in there?" the policewoman demanded urgently. "Do you know? We need a body count."

"My second floor neighbours are away. Denny and Mrs D are on holiday too. Bulldog is, well, who knows where Bulldog is, but why would he come back here when he's your Person of Interest?"

"Then why would anyone blow up his place?"

"And my place," Dare objected. "I'm a bit cross about that. Frankly, I... Ah."

He paused mid sentence and touched Mary's shoulder, directing her covertly to the slow-moving traffic passing the emergency barriers and police cones on Piccadilly. A sleek blue Chevrolet C4 Grand Sport with a broad white stripe along its bonnet slowly progressed past the road end. The driver offered a brief thumbs up as he followed the queue.

"Bulldog and Denny," McIver spotted. "Allegedly. Although I couldn't be certain. Not certain enough to report it."

"Quite so," Dare agreed. "Now, I want to make a complaint about why the police aren't doing more to stop houses exploding in Mayfair and St James."

★★★

"Then why would anyone blow up his place?"

"Commander Johnstone, I apologise for the intrusion. You know who I am?"

The harried senior officer in charge of the Metropolitan CID looked up from his strong black coffee and mound of paperwork at the gaunt elderly intruder in his private office. "You're Major Hannay, MI6. Etcetera."

"Et-as you say-cetera. May I come in?"

"As I understand it, you have the clearance to go wherever you want."

"Yes. Forgive my attempt at manners. Especially since I am here to be rude to you." The wiry old man entered and, without asking, lit up a pipe in the non-smoking building. "The last vice I'm allowed," he explained.

"What brings you here?" Sir Bryan demanded. "Other than polluting my workspace? This is a busy time."

"So many Hugh Drummond-related disasters, yes? The man is a disaster magnet. I respect that about him. It is he whom I wish to discuss."

"You have information pertinent to my enquiry?" the Commander asked sceptically. Hannay and his ilk were not known for their forthcoming exposition.

"Perhaps. I was Drummond's C.O., you know, back when he was seconded to 21 (Mobility) Troop, G Squadron, of the 22nd Special Air Service Regiment."

"And his record was sealed," Sir Bryan added sourly.

"Do you know how one joins the SAS? Twice a year, two hundred applicants from existing army personnel are brought to Sennybridge and the Brecon Beacons. They undertake personal fitness tests and cross-country exercises against the clock. This culminates with a 40-mile march in full kit scaling the 2,709-foot summit of Pan y Fan and descending again. Any man who cannot run four miles in thirty minutes or swim two miles in ninety minutes is eliminated at that point."

"Fascinating. What has this...?"

"The remainder are taken to Burma, Malaysia, or Brunei to learn navigation, patrol formation/movement and jungle survival, then back to Hereford for education in battle plans and foreign weapons, and for the world's harshest combat survival exercises. At last we dress them in World War Two uniforms, give each patrol a tin can of survival equipment, and hunt them while they go to capture a flag. The reward for success is a 36-hour resistance-to-interrogation course. Typically 30 of our 200 candidates survive to the end of the tests and are inducted into a squad."

"Your point?" Sir Bryan insisted.

"I have never seen anyone pass those tests like Hugh Drummond.

They called him Bulldog at school and we came to understand why. His instructors reported him stubborn to a fault, refusing to quit until he had mastered every skill. He is tenacious beyond sanity. Tough amongst the hardest men I know. A natural leader. A dying breed, and a killing one."

"He is a dangerous man, yes. And the army cut him loose and unleashed him on society."

"22 Troop SAS averages around 500 personnel," Hannay went on. "They are divided into four squadrons, each with four kinds of troops—Boat, Air, Mountain, and Mobility. A mobility unit specialises in rapid deployment infiltration and wide-field warfare. That's what Drummond led, the finest mobility troop I have ever had at my disposal. There is good reason their work is classified. Were it not, every man of them would have a knighthood, Sir Bryan. I see you are getting impatient, so my point is this: I do not want Drummond arrested. Or distracted. He is too useful."

"There was a major incident at his residence tonight. Firefighters are still attending. Military ordinance may have been used in a major domestic terror attack, two days before the State Opening of Parliament."

"Yes. Somebody wanted Bulldog to get out of their business that badly. If the grenades didn't do the trick, do you really want to do the job for them?"

"I want to uphold the law. I'm a policeman, a copper. I… wait, the orders from On High that we give Drummond a pass for that French stuff and the rest… that was you?"

"It came through me. Look, Sir Bryan, I'm not a fool and neither are you. I could threaten you, but you're not a man to cave to that. I could ruin you, destroy your career and see you disgraced, but that would be very poor reward for a life of bravery and service. So I am asking you as a gentleman, as a patriot, and as a chap of conscience, to weigh your country's need against your own personal desire to stick to the rulebook. Sometimes the rules can't apply."

"You want me to give your Bulldog a get-out-of-jail-free card?"

"I want you to recognise that he already has one, even if he doesn't know it. Sir Bryan, we may be days, hours, off a catastrophe unprecedented in human history. This is not hyperbole. There is a strong possibility that this city will not be here next week."

"Then why are we not mobilising? Evacuating? At least warning the public?"

"Because our enemies are not stupid either. Recent events have convinced me that our police, our armed forces, our military intelligence, are thoroughly penetrated. They cannot be trusted; not with this. If I mobilise ground forces, launch aircraft, it will be known and reported. I cannot rely on institutions of state for now, Sir Bryan. Only upon individuals within those institutions."

The Commander stared at his report-strewn desk and wondered how much worse it could get. He didn't want to find out. "What are you asking?"

"I need Bulldog to keep sinking his teeth into a man calling himself Carl Peterson. I need him to do the impossible. You are good enough at your job that you just might stop him. Don't."

"Or else?"

"Or else millions might die."

Sir Bryan glowered. "I do not like Captain Drummond. Or you."

"I don't like kidney dialysis, but it keeps me alive."

★★★

"Rosca confirmed Drummond dead, but Rosca has vanished," Peterson reported to Irma and Koh Zhenkai. "Bulldog may have survived, may still have Madison. And Madison knows about our farm laboratory."

"Hugh is alive?" Irma asked with a satisfied little smile.

"If the man lives, he may be coming here," Koh worried.

"I'd expect so, yes," Peterson admitted. "If so, we need to make suitable preparations."

Irma raised a brow. "Preparations? Why won't he won't just call the authorities on us?"

"If he does, I will have ample warning to evacuate to a fall-back position. Contingencies are in place. We might need to trigger our attack precipitously. But I assess that Drummond will know that. He will pursue an off-the-books, personal solution."

"And we will be ready for him?" Koh Zhenkai demanded.

Irma wondered if anybody could be fully ready for Bulldog Drummond.

★★★

CHAPTER XIV:
IN WHICH HE GOES TO WAR

By noon, Drummond's allies had assembled again at the Thames-side cottage in Goring. Mrs Denny gave her husband a hard hug before she began scolding him about his life. Mary McIver took a seat beside Fi Benton, still unable to understand how she had been dragged into all this as an accomplice.

"How's the flat?" Drummond asked Dare.

"You owe me a couple of townhouses," Hugh's ground landlord insisted.

"Talk to Algy. He extracted Chapter 51's millions before pushing their boss off a roof. That should cover a rebuilding project. I'd quite like the whole of number 17 when it's spruced up, though. Elbow room. We'll fix up 19 for you. How's the lovely Tanya, Algy?"

"Tanya says she wishes we were still married, so she could divorce me all over again," Algy complained. "She says I'm an unhealthy association."

"We all knew that," Bangbang told him. "We always thought that was your best feature."

"Settle down," Hugh told his comrades. "This is a council of war. There are some interesting new developments in our case, and then we need to blow things up."

"I'm okay with that," agreed Dare, former demolitions specialist of the Black Mask Gang, 21 (Mobility) Troop, G Squadron. "I owe Carl Peterson a bunch of grenades."

"I've been talking with my counterpart in Iceland," T.S. told the room. "They're been picking over that base that Bulldog planted a boat in, and questioning the survivors. From the equipment and what little they could get out of the prisoners, it looks like there was a major operation planned for very soon. They were training mercenaries in hazmat gear for smash-and-grab operations and mass extraction of materials."

"Contaminate an urban area and then send in bandits to pick it over," Bangbang considered. "Empty bank vaults, jewellers, loot museums of anything that can be scrubbed, that kind of thing."

"There were also some pretty sophisticated electronic hack devices there, until someone moored on top of them. The sort of thing that could crack a secure terminal that is sole access to top secret security data: submarine codes, missile sequences, that kind of thing."

"Once a city is undefended, it's secure terminals could be wide open,"

Algy reasoned. "I've been combing the Chapter 51 files. I think I know what Madison's part in the plot was to be—still might be."

"I thought Madison was street pizza?" Jez Seymour objected.

"But the people he's paid and set ready aren't. It looks like Chapter 51 had placed people or paid third parties to undertake a round of mass assassinations across the country at a set time after a trigger event."

"There's a colossal anthrax attack, and in the chaos a bunch of people who might otherwise step up are also bumped off," summarised Hugh. "That we pass on to Mary, right?"

"If you don't, I'll arrest you all now," the DCI promised. "That's the sort of information we can act on, a co-ordinated take-down across the nation."

"But not yet," T.S. cautioned. "Everything I've been doing has given me a tingle in my spine. I don't trust all the people involved in the widescale investigation. Don't set anything going until whatever Bulldog is planning is already underway."

"There's another angle," Dare chipped in. "I've been reading the financial markets. There's another name I want to toss into the ring: Koh Zhenkai, international financier out of Taipei. He's quietly shifting a lot of assets around—in ways that only make sense if the UK took a major economic hit. If it does, he will make tens of billions on it."

"Do we have a location for him?" Bangbang wondered.

"He entered the UK two weeks back. 'Business trip'."

"So we have the other corner of the operation," Drummond recognised. "The way to beat him is to stop a disaster. And that's where Mrs D and Fi's deductions come in. Jezzer?"

"Right, aye." The hairy pilot spread a set of aerial photos out on the coffee table, then unfolded a large-scale Ordinance Survey map. "I found it—the place where they held Ms Benton. Also the lab where they processed the anthrax, if I'm reading this imagery right. Bangbang?"

Teddy Jerningham pushed back his dreads and pored over the photos of Coldbrook Farm. "Looks like some kind of research base, for sure. Certainly not a domestic farm. Cosmetics testing centre, or something like that?"

"Anthrax breeding ground," Dare corrected him.

"And here's a nearby airfield," Jez went on. "SoarBrite was recently sold to a new owner. The vendor, a bloke called Rupert, won't take my calls."

Hugh whistled. "That's quite a selection of aircraft."

"And quite a lot of work being done on them," Algy spotted. "Expensive maintenance and refits."

"And a lot of delivery trucks there at the perimeter," Mary added. "I should call this in. We can have Special Forces…"

"We have Special Forces," Drummond declared. "Just not the ones Peterson is waiting to be called. Bangbang?"

The proprietor of Jerningham Enforcement Solutions added a list of typed names to the coffee table. "Here are fifty-two recently discharged, highly-trained soldiers on my books right now, looking for gainful employment. SAS, Special Boat Service, Special Reconnaissance Regiment, Special Forces Support Group, 18 Signal Regiment, or Joint Special Forces Aviation Wing. And three U.S. Marines and an Australian Ranger commando for variety. You know some of them. We've worked with them back in the day. The rest I've used before and they're sound. You remember Mullings?"

"I still have teeth marks on my shin where Mullings bit me in a bar fight in Malay," Dare exclaimed. "You have that mad bastard on payroll?"

"Him and a lot of his friends. I could have them in Norfolk by nightfall if someone has a passenger transport plane available?"

"Something might be arranged," the owner of Falcon Flights agreed. Jez thought again and added, "but you cover the cleaning bill."

"We'll use them," Hugh decided. "See they come with full hostile terrain gear for action in a toxic environment. Army grade—or better. We're going into a place where we *know* there's anthrax."

"You… you're going to attack the farm?" Fi ventured. "Privately?"

"Well, I want Carl Peterson to know that it's nothing personal, but… yes. I'm taking him down! Tonight."

★★★

At 2102 hours, a highway maintenance truck arrived at the junction of the B113 Norwich Turnpike and Church Lane, opposite Bunwell Village Hall, half a mile from Coldbrook Farm. The works foreman wore overalls and a high-visibility orange jacket, along with a balaclava, ear protectors, and safety goggles; and he bore a striking resemblance to former Loamshire Private Denny, J.

The crew laid out traffic cones and tape, and placed a *Road Closed: Flooding* sign that diverted traffic up Church Lane and Bunwell Street then along a scenic tangle of rural lanes before setting travellers back on the B113 two miles further along. A similar warning and blockage established the other end of the detour. If anyone called the toll-free customer service number to complain about the closure they would get to speak to Mrs Denny.

At 2221 hours, a vacuum tanker truck, the kind used to empty out the private sess pools on properties not attached to mains sewage drainage, misjudged a sharp corner right outside The Jolly Farmers pub in Forncett End, tipping over and cracking open, spilling 400-odd gallons of pungent effluence across the road, making the air so foul that the entire village was forced to go inside and close their windows. That driver also resembled the same former soldier.

The practical effect of these actions was that before ten p.m., a section of the Turnpike was closed to road traffic and the stench from the sewage spill deterred the locals from going outdoors. Only a handful of households were cut off by the diversions, but that stretch of highway did contain the turnings to the private lane to Coldbrook Farm and to the SoarBrite hangars and airstrip.

At one minute past ten, DCI Mary McIver was unsurprised to find her commanding officer still fretting at his desk in Scotland Yard. She enhanced his day by passing on the illegally-obtained Chapter 51 material from the hard-drives of the late Nugent Madison II. The documents would never be admissible as court evidence, but they presented a clear and present indication of conspiracy to commit murder on a grand scale. The correspondence implicated over three hundred and fifty people who had been solicited to inflict harm on one hundred and seventy-three subjects across England, Scotland, Wales, and Northern Ireland.

Whatever Sir Bryan Johnstone's reservations about Captain Drummond, he had none about taking down murderers-for-hire, and he held exactly the rank and clout to get on the phone to twenty regional Chief Constables and share his ruined evening. By 2300 hours, Operation Parzival was underway, a joint simultaneous-arrest action by combined police forces across the United Kingdom.

At the same time as the CID Commander was shouting down the line to fellow senior officers of the law, Major General Richard Hannay II DSO KCB was speaking quietly to chosen colleagues about information he had received regarding the possibility of a Black Alert terror attack on the crowds gathered for the State Opening of Parliament the following day. Certain protocols that had been quietly prepared by quiet men in quiet rooms were dusted off and triggered - quietly.

In the face of possible aerial attack, additional surface-to-air Rapier and Starstreak missile launchers were placed overnight at key secure locations around the capital. The Rapiers had first been deployed like that on tower blocks around the site of the 2012 Olympic Games. Additionally, first deployment authorisation was released to place seven next-generation Wildscream X2 infrared-homing drone-supported short-range multi-target warheads, with their advanced Identification of Friend of Foe systems that were deemed vital to intercept low-flying hostile targets over an urban environment.

Any one of these preparations was likely to trigger warnings to Carl Peterson and his terror cell; all of them were certain to—but by then a scratch team of specialists were already in action at the laboratory and airfield sites.

It was the reunion of the Black Mask Gang.

★★★

"We should have brought the tank," Algy reconsidered.

"Peterson knows about the tank tactic," Hugh Drummond reminded him. "He'll have placed anti-tank charges all over the place in readiness. That's why we're going in on foot, without any vehicle that would set off weight or metal content triggers."

"Algernon knows that," T.S. interjected. "He just doesn't like jumping out of aeroplanes. I'm doing it, Algy old boy, and I've only got half the number of legs you have."

"Don't you hold your leg over me, Long John," Algy told him. "Anyone can win a Victoria Cross if they throw their limbs at the enemy. I'm jumping, aren't I? I don't have to like it. We're not all adrenaline junkies like Bulldog Drummond."

"Wouldn't that be a better world, though," Hugh asked his comrades, grinning widely. "Stow the pre-match now, lads. Game on. Equipment check, and go to hostile environment protocols."

"We're approaching the drop site," Jez called from the pilot's seat of his classic 1986 Piper PA-46 Malibu. This was hardly the first rich charter party he had taken up in it for skydiving, but it was the one that mattered. "Wind is ten degrees west of southwest, point three knots at 7,000 feet, weather is clear. Confirm ready to go."

Each jumper checked a partner's gear and then pronounced them okay.

"Paladin One to Paladin Two," Hugh spoke into his encrypted headset, "We're ready to go."

The reply came back from Peter Darell on the ground, in cover a hundred yards from the farm's electric fence perimeter. "P2 to P1, roger. Try not to miss the ground."

"Paladin One to Paladin Four. Confirm status."

"Status is good," Bangbang responded. "We're getting real-time IR imagery from Archangel's plane. There's a heavy guard presence out there but we know just where they are. We're holding, but some of the lads are already wanting the pub."

"Paladin One to Lucifer. How's the smell?"

"Bloody awful," Denny told him from the sewage spillage site. "My nose is the first casualty of this conflict. I thought this hazmat gear was supposed to keep toxics out? I wants me money back. But the perimeter is secured of civvies, I suppose. Call it okay."

"Bangbang's ready for a drink, Denny's complaining, and Dare's being 'witty'," Hugh told Algy and T.S. "It's time to take a walk."

"Yippee," said Algy, unenthusiastically.

Drummond opened the side door.

In July 1941, Lieutenant Colonel Sir Archibald David Stirling DSO OBE proposed a specialist commando force to operate behind enemy lines in the North African Campaign. Men would parachute-drop into hostile territory to commit sabotage, or else to seize a military objective, opening the way for conventional troops to follow up. The first mission was a disaster, with a third of the force captured or killed, but the second destroyed sixty aircraft and was deemed a major success. The doctrine was proven, and four British squadrons, one Free French, one Greek, and a Folboat section were incorporated as 1st Special Air Service.

Jumping from a plane looking for trouble was where the SAS had started. Their regimental crest showed King Arthur's sword Excalibur, depicted as a blazing winged dagger on a crusader shield, over the motto that might as well have been tattooed on Bulldog Drummond's heart: *Who Dares Wins*.

Drummond, Algy, and T.S. leaped into the darkness. Jez banked the Piper and came back round, mission-shifting from delivery to oversight. The PA-46 Malibu wasn't equipped as a combat aircraft but it could detect and paint up any aircraft that tried to lift from SoarBrite for attention from Dare's surface to air deterrents.

The infiltration team free-fell to less than 900 feet before deploying their parachutes. Night vision goggles lit up the landing zone, a cattle field behind the main farm block; had Corrie Dalglish's attic window not been blocked she would have overlooked that very spot. The advantage of alighting in a field used for grazing livestock was that it could not be land-mined.

The Black Mask Gang of 21 Troop, G Squadron had lost none of their old skill. The three night-camouflaged infiltrators landed within twenty feet of each other and gathered in their black parachutes. Sinclair scanned the perimeter while Algy did a tech-check for electronic surveillance and Drummond cased the objective.

"That window," Hugh pointed, indicating the attic room where infrared suggested a person was confined, a room that matched the configuration that Fi Benton had described from her captivity. "As we modelled it, boys."

There were armed guards in the rear courtyard, dressed in dark gear and carrying Taiwanese Hsing Hua Arsenal Type 77 submachine guns. They never knew intruders were near until Drummond and Algy took them down.

Hugh pointed to a former coal shed, with thick brick walls still half-plastered, now reduced to a bin store. "That's your hard point, Paladin Three," he told Sinclair. "Set up shop there."

"Roger, boss. Good hunting." Toby Sinclair peeled away to prepare his position.

Algy shifted to below the target window and prepared a grapple-gun. The compressed-air launcher drilled an extending claw-spike through the wooden window frame and secured a cable. Hugh tested the line. It held, so he swarmed up it. His combat knife pried away the planks covering the glass.

He peered inside the attic room. One heat-shape lay on the bed, undisturbed by his efforts. Drugged? That would be a complication, but they had already prepared for lowering the octogenarian by harness safely down to Sinclair's strongpoint.

Knowing the sill to be screwed down, Drummond pressed an adhesive plastic sheet to the glass and simply kicked out the whole four-pane window, complete with its wooden crosspiece. He lowered it quietly to Algy and slipped through the gap, across to the bed.

The woman in it pushed back her sheet and smiled at him. "Bulldog, is this a booty call?" Irma Peterson asked him. "Very Romeo and Juliet... in a kinky military cosplay sort of way. Should I find my nurse's uniform?"

"Filly! Or... Irma. Where is Miss Dalglish?"

"Well, obviously elsewhere. Aren't I woman enough for you?"

Drummond levelled his pistol. "Where is she?"

"At a safe-house in Norwich, Hugh, miles away from here. She's fine, honestly, if a bit peppery. She's well out of Carl's trap for you."

"What?"

Irma raised her hands in mock surrender. "Are you going to handcuff me to the bed? Yes, Carl guessed you'd be coming. Either Madison survived and blabbed to you, or Dare chased the money for the SoarBrite purchase, or Algy was clever with hacking e-traffic about materials purchases. Which was it?"

"None of the above. Get up. You're coming with me."

"A dinner date? Or stay here; we might have time for a quickie while Carl kills your friends."

A rattle of gunfire came from the distance, from the direction of the airfield.

"I usually get hot at the sound of bullets," Irma confided, "but I suppose that means you're going to do something heroic. That's the din of your chums finding that all the heat-forms you thought were residents of local households were actually Asian mercenaries who had captured those houses earlier today and evacuated the residents to join Miss Dalglish. Now Carl's minions are all coming out to play, surrounding your chums in an iron-clad killing zone."

"How many mercs?"

"About a hundred, according to our ally who provided them. Plus the fifty-eight guards already at the airfield, and the ones we have at the lab here. And you brought your *four* war buddies? They're good, but thirty-to-one good?"

"Maybe," Hugh considered. "Don't move. Don't make any noise. I don't like shooting girls I've slept with, but I will if I have to." He touched his comm-link. "Paladin One general. It's an ambush. Hostiles estimated strength one hundred approaching from adjacent domestic housing to your rear. Engage the Templars. Tally-ho!"

As Peterson's surprise forces broke cover and attacked Dare's and Bangbang's positions, two things happened. The line of explosives that Peter Darell had laid along the likely lines of ambush detonated in a glorious sequential cascade, turning the enemy advance into a chaos of flame and shrapnel. And the fifty-three ex-special forces men that Teddy Jerningham had brought in broke cover from their own ambush points and closed on the airfield from two sides, flanking Peterson's surprise force.

"Archangel alert!" Jez called from the Piper. "I'm not alone up here. They have a bloody Chinook!"

"Do I need to say take evasive action?" Hugh replied. "Do what you have to, Archangel. Lucifer, deploy fireworks."

Half a mile from the combat zone, Denny thumbed the automatic start on a commercial fireworks show, the sort of set that high-end weddings or rich-kid birthday parties commissioned. Suddenly the sky over the village was bright with a cascade of rockets; a licence for the display had even been acquired, and air traffic control was aware. The air was filled with colourful bursts of streaming gunpowder and the screech of starbursts.

And a layman couldn't really tell the difference between gunpowder in airburst firecrackers or machine guns, or distinguish the flare of combat explosives from the strobe of thunderflash pinwheels.

The bright display lit up the farmhouse, painting the attic room with green and red light. "That's a nice touch," Irma admired. "Am I to take you to my leader?"

"Where is Peterson? Is he really your brother?"

"Half-brother. He's not here. Why would he be? The man in charge on site is Doctor Henry Lakington, as creepy a mad scientist as you could hope to hire to more-weaponise a weaponised virus. Brrr! Security is provided via our sponsor Koh Zhenkai, and he'll be joining us soon since I triggered my attack alarm when you started breaking in."

"Paladin Five, fall back to Paladin Three," Hugh ordered Algy. "This is a foobar now. Head for the lab, secure it, identify the guy in charge, and try to question him. But don't take unnecessary chances. They have the numbers and the terrain. Watch out for traps and some serious resistance."

"Hello Paladins Five and Three," Irma called at Drummond's microphone. "Bulldog will be with you presently. He's just frisking me. Well, I hope. He does enjoy it."

Drummond relieved Irma of two knives, her phone, and a small remote alert button. "Down the hall," he ordered her. "You first. Move."

"I'm your human shield? Is that very heroic, Hugh?"

"You're a pretty package, Irma, but you're trying to kill millions. Don't count on your being cute saving you when I have to make a calculation."

"You think I'm cute? Aaw!"

The first guards to clatter up the attic stair met a grenade bouncing down the other way. Drummond pushed Irma past the gory mess and cut down a rear passageway for the back stairs. According to the best schematic that Algy and Seymour had been able to come up with, there was a way from there into the former milking sheds, now set up as a laboratory and testing area.

"Archangel to P1," came the call, "This flamin' Chinook has been refitted for combat. It's weapons-hot. I can't stop it. It's heading for our people on the airfield."

"I'm calling them back now," Bangbang responded. "Paladin Two?"

"Nearly finished," answered Darell. "One more… that's it. Try and lure that chopper in low, P4."

Hugh had no more attention to spare for the air battle or the landing field combat. As he descended the rear stairs to the ground floor kitchens he was nearly taken down by a spray of machine-gun bullets.

"I've got Irma Peterson here, dammit!" he called back to the men in cover in the kitchen.

"They don't care, Bulldog," Irma explained to him. "Koh Zhenkai doesn't mind if I live or die. That's why Carl left him in charge of security. I'm no good as a hostage if Koh is willing to sacrifice me. Carl might cave, but not him."

"Your brother sacrificed you?"

"He risked me, as I risked myself. We're both rather gambling on you being the man we think you are. You're going to rescue me."

"Why would I do that?"

"Because you're you, darling, and I love you for it. And I don't want to die, so I'll tell you now about the bomb."

Another cascade of machine gun fire ricocheted off the opposite wall from where Drummond and Irma sheltered. Hugh decided enough was enough and rolled another grenade at the opposition; there was little chance a kitchen explosion would release any anthrax container.

"What bomb?" he demanded of the mystery blonde beside him as the dust settled.

"Carl set a failsafe in case you found this place. I can't stop it. It's counting down now, so even if you win here you lose. Bulldog, it's an anthrax bomb."

Drummond led the way into the shattered kitchen. "We came prepared for that."

"I'm not," Irma pointed out. "Nor are all the civilians in a three-mile radius. And since the bomb is also packed with suit-shredding shrapnel, nor will be any of the people whose protective gear gets compromised. So ideally, stop the detonation, please, hero."

"Carl set this up?"

"You and he both like grand gestures. If the game is up then he'll slip away and leave a calling card. A disaster to cover his tracks, distract from his escape. Or a disaster to prevent, if you're able."

"What do I have to do?"

"The bomb is in the lab. Koh and Lakington don't know about it, so they'll be trying to stop you taking the place."

Another pair of guards appeared at the broken window. Drummond took them out with single shots through their foreheads. "Paladin One to Paladin Two. When you're done there, get to the Coldbrook Farm lab. There's a bomb to dismantle."

"Bit busy being shot at now, Paladin One, old chap, but I'll add it to my to-do list," Dare promised.

"We're outside the lab now," T.S. called in. "We're encountering heavy resistance. We're pinned."

"That Chinook is closing on us," Bangbang reported. "I think Mullins wants to bite it to death."

"Right," growled Hugh, grabbing Irma by the wrist and dragging her on. "It's you and me to take down the villains and stop the bomb. Come on!"

★★★

CHAPTER XV:
IN WHICH THERE IS A COUNTDOWN

The Boeing CH-47 Chinook was a twin-rotor heavy-duty helicopter still painted in the faded colours of the Royal Netherlands Air Force. It had been brought back into use only days ago, after Peterson's purchase of SoarBrite, and it was re-equipped with its three pintle-mounted M240/ FN MAG machine guns. It swung in low over the airfield hangars, turning to bring its port shoulder window and rear armaments to bear on the intruders caught between perimeter fence and landing strip.

Dare waited for the chopper to commit before warning Bangbang and his units to hit the deck. Then he began to thumb the detonators on the plastic explosive charges he had attached to the row of planes and copters arrayed on to tarmac.

The aircrafts exploded sequentially, their detonations larger and hotter than Darell would usually have set because he wasn't taking risks about biohazard materials. The Chinook veered away from its attack vector, thrashing sideways to avoid the course of the explosions.

That put it near the fuel silo. When Paladin Two judged that the helicopter had edged as near as it was likely to get, he sent that up too.

That explosion was so loud and large that it could not be mistaken for fireworks. Car alarms two miles away began to screech. The nearby conning tower crumpled and fell, shredded apart like a kicked dandelion.

The Chinook was caught in the shock wave, slapped hard so it tilted almost horizontal. It should have died, but its pilot somehow miraculously righted it thirty feet off the ground and twisted it away. Small fires still blazed along its fuselage, but it was operational. It gained altitude and swivelled vengefully towards Jerningham Enforcement Solutions' exposed ground forces.

The PA-46 Malibu blurred in at 350 miles per hour, scarcely topping the treeline. This was the plane model that had set world speed records in the 1980s, and while Jez Seymour wasn't approaching Steve Stout's 439.13 miles per hour between Chicago and Toronto, the world champion pilot hadn't been aiming to skim his fixed undercarriage across the rotors of a combat helicopter.

The Chinook's rear blades sliced through the Piper's landing gear but were reduced to useless scrap. The helicopter lurched again, this time in an uncontrollable spiral, and ditched hard in the rapeseed field next to the airstrip.

Jez's howl of triumph screeched out of his comrades' earpieces. "Archangel has brought the wrath of God," he added, "but I think I've busted my wings. I'll have to ditch."

He coaxed the Piper to a thousand feet and checked there was only pasture below before he quit the ailing craft and chuted down to drop on a field of cabbages.

★★★

"We're getting confirmations of the first arrests, governor," DCI McIver reported to Sir Bryan. "Also, there appear to be explosions in East Anglia. A full military engagement."

"East Anglia is out of my jurisdiction," the Commander replied in satisfied tones.

★★★

"I'm telling you there's a major gas leak up there," James Denny insisted to the uniformed police officers at the traffic barrier. "Didn't you hear them explosions? Now go check with your station as to whether they wants you going in there and exploding an' all, that's good lads."

★★★

"Yes, deployment of counter-terrorist forces and special measures is approved," Major Hannay agreed down a secure phone line to Whitehall. "Downing Street is aware. Deploy at will; but be aware that we already have assets on the ground. We've deputised a cohort from Jerningham Enforcement Solutions as an advance recon force. Link up with their C.O. in the field. How long will you take to scramble?"

★★★

"There's something on the news," Fi told Mrs Denny. "Some sort of gas main problem near Norfolk, they're reporting. It's just breaking."

"Well, that'll make for an interesting news cycle," Mrs D noted. "Another cuppa?"

★★★

"What is happening?" Koh Zhenkai demanded angrily in Mandarin over his headset. "Tell me what is going on!"

Gǔ Cāng was beside him and didn't need communications equipment to answer. "No contact with the men at the airfield. They are lost. Fighting is happening now outside this farm."

The sound of shooting was too near for the financier's comfort. The noise was coming from just beyond the perimeter of the lab itself.

"Where is my security? Did I not pay for protection?"

Koh Zhenkai's exact words to his guards had been, "If you fight well I shall pay well. If you die, your families will be rich. If you fail, your families will be executed."

"*Niútóu quǎn* has brought soldiers too," Gǔ Cāng explained, using the Mandarin Chinese for 'Bulldog'. "His men are well-trained."

"We set an ambush!"

"So did he. The helicopter is down, but so is their plane. They have destroyed the airfield and captured the trucks with the chemicals on board. We still hold the laboratory and there are few of *Niútóu quǎn*'s men here."

"Where is Peterson?"

"Our sentries report that he left some while ago."

Koh Zhenkai was not reassured by the news. "Peterson fled? But his sister is here! He left her?" The financier's hard face hardened more. "I am betrayed. Get me out of here, Gǔ Cāng. Kill Drummond. Kill Irma Peterson. We are leaving."

★★★

Algy Longworth and Toby Sinclair were making slow progress against the defended positions outside the former cattle shed. Half a dozen of Koh Zhenkai's men were in sheltered positions behind a low wall and a line of metal milk churns, where they could use their machine guns with little fear of reprisal. They were too close to the laboratory to be flushed out with hand-grenades.

Algy fell back, fingering the hole in his combat armour where it had stopped a 5.8x42mm/DBP87 rimless bottlenecked 'standard rifle cartridge' entering his stomach. "Those things sting," he objected.

Sinclair nodded agreement. There was another bullet hole in his right leg—the prosthetic one. "If they'd only shot the other leg I could have had another medal."

"We're pinned down here. No way forward, no way back."

"Now I remember why I retired and joined the Diplomatic Corps," Sinclair sighed as he fitted another clip. "Perhaps I should send these fellows a stiffly-worded note of reprimand?"

"It would do as much good as our gunfire. Look, we have to get past those thugs. Any ideas?"

"Smoke grenade. Lob it on the corrugated roof, let it roll down right on top of them. Then flashbangs. We have night scopes. They don't."

"Cheating," Algy admired. "I like it. Here goes." He peeled an L-84 white phosphorous smoke grenade from his combat harness and placed it with such accuracy that even avid cricketer Hugh Drummond could not have found fault with his bowling.

The canister rattled down the slope of the byre roof and landed right behind the shooters. As they reacted to the sudden thick roil about them, Sinclair stepped out to apply the signature SAS stun grenades they colloquially called 'flashbangs' or 'thunderflashes'. Each of the non-lethal devices detonated with a light-burst of around seven million candela, effectively blinding its victims for five seconds or more, and with a noise greater than 170 decibels, sound equivalent to standing next to a space shuttle launch, enough to shatter eardrums.

T.S. and Algy moved as soon as the flashbangs went in. They flicked back on low-visibility enhancement goggles that would have been burned out by the light explosion, and Algy crossed the yard and vaulted the low wall in the five seconds' grace the attack offered him. T.S. dropped to his good knee and held his rifle to his shoulder, sniper-style, picking off the defenders who staggered out of the smoke cloud.

Twenty seconds later, the door was clear. T.S. joined Algy, applied an "opening package" of magnesium strip to the metal barrier's hinges, and mimed a three-count. As soon as the burn-strips flared and melted their way through the metal pins, Algy kicked the barrier in. T.S. was already in position to shoot down the surprised men behind the floor-mounted Chinese Type 80 general-purpose machine gun.

The way was clear into the narrow hallway, with one door each way to left and right and double doors at the end behind the late machine-gunners. Paladins Three and Five reported that they were moving in, but Algy hand-signalled T.S. to keep behind him and move slowly while he checked for tripwires, laser triggers, or pressure pads.

What the team's tech-expert was not anticipating was the partition wall at his side breaking apart as massive hands punched through. They grabbed him by the head and pulled, slamming him hard into the remaining brickwork. Algy's combat helmet protected him from a broken skull but the impact was enough to knock him out. He slumped to the ground as Gǔ Cāng shattered through the lath and plaster to face Sinclair.

T.S. managed to bring up his L129A1 sharpshooter rifle, but before he could fire it, the Barn hurled the section of wall he had brought with him. Sinclair's shots went wild and Gǔ Cāng closed the distance too fast. The huge Asian was unbelievably quick for his bulk.

T.S. ducked one shattering fist only to be grabbed by the giant's other hand and swung round into the wall. More plaster crumbled from the force of the impact. Something painful happened to T.S.'s ribs. His rifle was knocked away and meaty fingers closed around his throat.

"Hey!" shouted Hugh Drummond from the doorway, "pick on someone half your own size!"

Gǔ Cāng looked over his shoulder and grinned. He could snap Toby Sinclair's neck with a twitch. "Just you, then, *Niútóu quǎn*" he told Drummond. "No weapons."

"Let him go, then."

The Barn allowed his captive to slump to the floor. He gestured with his fingertips that Drummond should come on.

"Oh, this will be worth watching," Irma Peterson anticipated. "Any

Algy's combat helmet protected him from a broken skull...

chance you could take your shirt off first, Bulldog?"

Hugh paused long enough to handcuff her to a drainpipe, out of reach of any of the many discarded weapons on Koh's dead security forces.

He approached Gǔ Cāng cautiously. Anyone who could take down Algy and T.S. that easily was a foe worth respecting.

Barn and Bulldog closed.

★★★

Denny had scarcely seen off the police patrol when an elderly man approached him from the inner side of the security cordon on a rickety pedal cycle. "I say!" the cyclist called. "I say! Hello!"

The two 'workmen' with Denny ranged out so that they were watching his back while he handled the old man.

The cyclist braked to a stop. "What's all this road block for, eh? It says flooding but I've just ridden the whole road and there's no water. There's a nasty sewage spillage at the Farmers but that's not blocking this road. The radio says gas explosion, and there was a big bang after the fireworks, but… look, it doesn't make sense and it's deuced inconvenient. Who's your gaffer?"

"I'm sorry, sir," Denny began, "but this is…"

The cyclist lifted a pistol and neatly killed both watchmen flanking Drummond's orderly. "Don't even twitch, Mr Denny," he commanded in quite a different voice. "Mrs Denny would be devastated if anything happened to you."

Denny froze. The old bike and the doddering appearance had fooled him. He saw now it was a disguise. This fellow was no older than he was, fit and lean, with an old scar down one side of his face.

"You have a fast escape vehicle stowed somewhere nearby. I require it. Give it to me without dispute and I will let you live. Understand?"

"I get you. 'Oo are you supposed to be, then?"

"I'm supposed to be Carl Peterson. The villain. It's time for my big exit. The car?"

"You din't 'ave to kill these blokes."

"I wanted you to take me seriously. *The car.*"

★★★

A good big man can always beat a good little man. That was the old saw that Master Olaki has begun with when he had started to train then-Lieutenant Hugh Drummond in Jujutsu and other forms of unarmed combat. Bulldog was already a serious British boxer, as his nose attested, with inter-school trophies to national level, but the pseudonymous martial arts instructor showed his pupils a whole new range of ways that a little man such as himself could knock down opponents of any size.

Hugh relied on those techniques against Gǔ Cāng, using a range of deflections and jab-strikes against the Barn's sumo-like bulk. He never used the same attack twice and shifted through half a dozen techniques so that his opponent would never know what was coming next.

Drummond had taken a lot of beatings against Olaki. Every one of them had taught him something, until at last he was the only man in the training square who could take the master five falls out of ten.

Gǔ Cāng accepted every blow, seemingly oblivious to nerve-cluster punches and pressure points, striking back with engine-like precision and persistence. Only Hugh's combat armour distributed the force of those sledgehammer blows enough to keep him in the fight.

"Stop... playing with him..." H.S. grunted from the corner where he had crawled to nurse his broken ribs.

Drummond wasn't playing. It was deadly earnest, two strong, highly-trained, very determined fighters doing their best to kill each other. It was one of the rare times when Bulldog was the good little man against a bigger, more powerful opponent.

"Come on, Hugh!" Irma cheered him from the doorway, as far as her cuffed arms could stretch. "Do remember there's a bomb counting down."

Drummond didn't need reminding, but nor could he divert even the attention it would take to answer the femme fatale. His combat with the massive Taiwanese bodyguard was that well matched. Drummond could fight. Gǔ Cāng's punches shattered walls.

Hugh risked a grapple. He dived onto the Barn, toppling them both into a sluice room store. Buckets and mops clattered down around them as they rolled. Drummond scarcely broke free before Gǔ Cāng flopped his unmovable bulk down where he would have crushed his enemy.

The opponents rose cautiously and regarded each other.

"I don't suppose you'll come quietly," Hugh surmised.

"I am under orders. You must die, and then Miss Peterson."

"What did I do?" Irma protested innocently. "Oh wait, there's a list."

"You won't have either of us," Drummond promised, shifting so that the sinks were at his back.

"Oh, save me, Bulldog Drummond!" Irma called out, enjoying the fight.

Hugh gritted his teeth, hurled a pile of discarded pans to distract his target, then went in low for Gŭ Cāng. The huge bodyguard didn't fall for it though, sidestepping and returning a crane kick that propelled Drummond into the sluice sinks. One ham-fist powered straight at Hugh's head.

Drummond jerked aside almost too late. The Barn's punch passed his face by a whisker and crashed into the brickwork behind him—just where Hugh had calculated the water pipes ran. The blow burst the main, spraying the surprised giant in a blinding torrent.

Drummond launched himself off the sinks, aiming at the tangle of lighting wires that dangled from the half-ruined ceiling. He dropped down to the now-wet floor, dragging them with him, and touched them to the water.

His combat boots were insulated, but the spraying pipe still washed freely over Gŭ Cāng. The Barn stiffened as his muscles lost voluntary control, but then a fuse blew and the circuit went dead.

Any normal foe should have been downed by that shock. It delayed Gŭ Cāng perhaps three seconds. Drummond used them. He took out the giant's right kneecap, then swept the left foot away. As Gŭ Cāng fell, Drummond wrenched a sink off the wall and slammed it down on the Barn's head.

He kept smashing it down until Gŭ Cāng stopped struggling.

So intense was his survival rage that he didn't notice Koh Zhenkai's last security guards shift into position around him until their guns were aimed.

"Captain Drummond," Koh hissed. "You have cost me dearly. Very dearly. For that you will die slowly. You and Peterson's sister. All who have crossed me will suffer!"

"It's over, whoever you are," Hugh told him, wobbling to stay upright after the Barn's beating. "And there's an anthrax bomb you don't know about, ticking down to exploding right here in that lab of yours. We have to stop it."

"Do you think me stupid?" the financier demanded.

"Yes," Irma Peterson replied. She had slipped her cuffs and retrieved one of the discarded QBZ-03 gas-operated selective-fire assault rifles from a guard's corpse. She placed deadly precise single shots into each of Koh Zhenkai's four remaining guards and turned the weapon on him. "I don't think you should have included me on your threat-list," she told the businessman.

"Miss Peterson… Miss Franklyn…" Koh stammered. "Wait! I am a rich man…"

"No. You were a rich man." Irma shot him through the centre of his temple.

She turned the QBZ-03 on Drummond. "And now you, Bulldog. What am I going to do with you? Bullets or bed? I admit I'm conflicted."

"You can drop the gun and stand still, honey," H.S. suggested, wincing as he pushed a pistol to the back of her neck. "I prefer brunettes."

★★★

Dr Lakington regarded the anthrax bomb with surprise and a strange masochistic anticipation. "Isn't that a thing of beauty, Miss Peterson?"

"Give me my gun back and I'll shoot him too, Bulldog," the blonde offered.

Drummond looked at the surviving test subjects coughing and shaking behind their one-way glass and gave the offer serious consideration.

The device was housed in a conical tube disguised as a chimney vent near the lab incinerator. A shrapnel-filled canister uncomfortably similar in shape and size to R2D2 would be shot to a position about thirty feet above the cattle-shed before it detonated, distributing biosuit-ripping needles over 500 yards and highly infectious Vollum 21136 spores over two or three miles, depending on the wind. A disappointingly mundane liquid crystal display offered a numerical countdown in tenths of a second; it was currently passing below 8,400.

"It won't go all the way down to zero," Irma predicted. "Carl is always amused when people presume that will happen. He likes to set his detonations off at, say, 3,122, while the bomb disposal people are still unpacking their tools. The bigger number is just to comfort people."

Drummond touched his earpiece. "Paladin Two, where are you? I need you here, stat."

"Hello, P1," Dare responded. "We're just disengaging now. The chopper's gone, thanks to Jezzer being completely insane, and we've pinned down the last of the mercs. Paladin Four has just linked up with the cavalry along the main road, so it's coming under control. I gather you have a bit of a bomb problem?"

"And not much time to stop it. Hoof it here, Peter, and don't stop for a drink on the way."

"That mechanism is a very nice piece of design," Lakington continued his encomium. "A truly worthy home for my work! Do you know it took over two years to clean up what Dr Ivins did to the U.S. Postal Service, and that was just a little scattering of material. *My* strain is so much more effective."

"You're proud of this?" Drummond snarled. "Proud of these people you murdered?"

"People? No, these are test subjects. They stopped being people when I started the tests." The chemist blinked and turned back to Irma. "I don't suppose you know where Miss Benton is now, do you? Only I was rather promised I would be able to have her for my experiments, you know."

"Stop talking now," Hugh cautioned him. "If you like having teeth."

"Ignore him," Irma advised. "He'd see being punched on the nose as a chance to study blood-flow rates." She examined the mechanism. "He's right that this is a work of art. Carl likes to use the best. That's the selfsame anti-tamper equipment as they use on the new Wildscream missile arrays. Go near it without a code, vibrate it, send the wrong signal to it, and the whole thing goes off. Brrr!"

"So how do I stop it?"

"I really don't know how you'd shut it down. I wasn't kidding when I asked you to save me, Bulldog. But there must be a way. Carl wouldn't leave me here if he didn't think you might stop it while he escapes."

"Dare is our demolitions man. Algy's our hacker. One is too far off and the other is out cold."

"We don't have time to run."

"How would this thing get stopped officially?" Hugh wondered.

"Well, keypad disarm, I suppose," Irma considered. "With a countdown-skip if the entry-code is wrong, of course. It can't be my birthday, because I don't know when that is."

"So I can get near enough to it to punch some buttons. Okay, what happens if I just rip out the whole panel?"

"Dead man's switch? If the hold signal stops then the whole thing detonates?"

"And what detonates it? There's got to be propellant, to push it up the launch tube. There's got to be accelerant to set off a percussion explosion, but not enough heat to sterilise the contaminant." Drummond looked about the lab, then at Lakington. "What do you have here that's very cold?"

"Apart from you," Irma clarified.

"You mean like... LN$_2$?" the scientist replied. "Liquid nitrogen? Those white tanks over there." He smiled reminiscently. "You can make wonderful ice-cream with that, you know. I was going to make some for Phyllis, when we took a break from our investigations."

"How fast does it freeze stuff?" Hugh demanded. "If I dragged a tank of it to that keypad, beside the bomb, and set it off, would it be able to freeze everything before the detonation?"

"I don't know. It would be an interesting test."

"The Drummond approach," Irma said. "Blow something up."

"Yeah. It's worked for me so far. Step back. If you try to leave the lab, T.S. will shoot you."

"T.S. is a huge spoilsport."

"Find shelter behind that metal table. Take Dr Creepy with you. If you have to kill him, do."

"Don't take me too far," Henry Lakington pleaded. "I want to see this."

Drummond tested the heavy LN_2 container. There was a distribution nozzle but it was too thin for his purposes. He put his shoulder to the canister and heaved it, walking it scrape by scrape across the lab's concrete floor until it was stood beside the code pad.

There was a clatter at the door and Peter Darell dashed in. "Where's the fire?"

"Get down behind this bench," Drummond warned him. The countdown was already dwindled to 1400, a little over two minutes to 'official' detonation time. There was no leeway left.

Dare asked no more questions but joined Hugh, Irma, and Lakington in cover. T.S. was still sat in the hall with the unconscious Algy, covering the only unsealed entrance and exit.

"That thing's under pressure, right?" Drummond checked with the mad scientist.

"Extreme pressure. The liquid-to-gas expansion ratio of nitrogen is 1:694 at 20°C. When the tank at Texas A&M University went up in '06 it shattered the concrete beam below it, went through the roof, and the blew the lab walls half an inch off their foundations." Lakington giggled.

Drummond shot the tank.

★★★

Denny was expertly disarmed and stripped of his communications gear. He led the way to the church hall car park where a well-preserved silver Rover 827 'Fastback'—the last exciting genuinely British-made motor vehicle to ever be produced—was parked between a battered camper van and a Boy Scout minibus.

"Why did you go an' try to blow up London?" Danny asked his captor. "Bloody mass-murderer!"

"Business, Mr Denny," came the reply. "The keys?"

"In the tailpipe. Shall I get 'em?"

"No. I'd prefer if you stood with your hands where I can see them at all times. Don't let your loyalty to Captain Drummond overcome your good sense. You want to get home to Claire in Gorham, don't you?"

Denny's heart leaped. How did Peterson know about the hideaway?

The villain read his face. "Locator chip on DCI McIver's police-issue vehicle," he supplied. "Friends in the force. It took a while to get the data and make some additional enquiries but… I know where you live. Where you live now, after I blew up your townhouse. If you want to continue living—anywhere—keep quite still, please."

"I'm supposed to believe you'll just let me go?"

"I'm a man of my word. The game's no good if you don't keep to some rules. A superior man need not cheat to win. I said don't move, Mister *aaaaagghh!*"

The villain's declaration was interrupted by the twin tines of a police issue X2 taser hitting him in the right buttock and delivering 50,000 volts at 25 watts through his body. He shuddered, dropped his firearm, and toppled insensible to the ground.

"If 'e's so clever, how come 'e didn't know this was our camper van?" asked Mrs Denny from the door of the Autotrail Apache 700SE 6 Berth Motorhome. She was at the other end of the 30 metre cables. "As if we'd stay in Gorham while you was out on exercises, James!"

"I do like 'aving the van nearby in case I wants a sandwich," Denny agreed.

Fi Benton peered over Mrs D's shoulder at her previously-unseen kidnapper. "I thought he would be taller."

"Yeah well," Denny said to them, "maybe he'll grow a bit if I kick 'im enough."

★★★

CHAPTER XVI:
IN WHICH THE PIECES ARE PUT TOGETHER

"What was the butcher's bill?" asked Major Hannay.

"Do I want to speak with you?" Drummond asked down the telephone he had just been handed by an anonymous functionary in a smart grey suit.

"I daresay not. But you need to. The casualties?"

"We lost five friendlies," Hugh confessed, "including the two that Peterson shot at the road block. Another fourteen injuries, including Algy and Hugh, but they'll all make it."

"Jerningham Enforcement will offer substantial packages to next of kin?"

"The best, but it doesn't ever make up for the losses."

"True. The farm and airstrip are now locked down?"

"Your boys are crawling all over them. Bomb squad is thawing out and defusing that anthrax launcher gizmo I froze up. The anthrax canisters in the transport trucks are secured for incineration. The remaining mercs are under arrest. The surviving test victims have been rushed to hospital under strict quarantine."

"The Petersons?"

"Gone to the Norfolk Police's Secure Interview Suite in Norwich. Irma told us where Miss Dalglish and the locals were being held and they've been retrieved. Peterson's not spoken a word since he woke up."

"What can he say? Denny's *wife* took him down."

"You don't know Denny's wife. You said I needed you. Prosecutions?"

"Nothing to prosecute. You're only getting back to England this afternoon, after your extended stay in Reykjavík. Welcome home. Meanwhile, it turns out that your comrades were commissioned for an intelligence operation codenamed Appleblossom Harvest and were acting entirely under government licence."

"Nice to know. Thanks, I suppose."

"Thank you, Captain Drummond."

"Since you're communicating, what about the mop-up? Mary McIver had a list…"

"Operation Pilgrim? That will certainly help meet police serious-crimes arrest quotas for the current quarter. My sources tell me that Sir Bryan Johnstone very nearly smiled."

"The finance trail?"

"That will take longer. I'd have preferred Koh Zhenkai alive. We'll know more when we crack Peterson."

"Peterson is still dangerous."

"We will take him seriously. Hugh, you have done well. Her Majesty thanks you. Take the rest of the day off. Take some contraband to your friends in hospital. Take the real Ms. Benton for dinner. Go see about getting your house rebuilt. Leave something for the rest of us to do, will you?"

"I don't work for you any more, Hannay."

"Really, Bulldog? Are you quite certain?"

★★★

"You do not have to say anything; but it may harm your defence if you do not mention when questioned something which you later rely on in court. Anything you do say may be given in evidence. Do you understand your rights?"

Irma Peterson sat at a grey interview table, handcuffed to a restraining loop. "Hello, DCI McIver. Nice to see you again."

"This interview is being taped, commencing at 0916 hours…" She gave date and time for the official video record and told the prisoner about her right to have a representative present.

"There's a solicitor on the way," Irma promised. "I'd better keep quiet until then."

"You already made a statement. You revealed the location where your brother was holding hostages."

"Well, yes. Poor Miss Dalglish needed releasing. She has hens to feed. I hope you're not going to charge her with anything about what she did all those years ago."

"That's above my pay grade. And there's a queue of people waiting to ask you about what you planned with your anthrax terror attack. I'm just tidying up my case, the nightclub incident and what followed. You made false statements, alleging assault and other things, and stole the identity of Phyllis Benton."

"I was a much more interesting Phyllis than she ever was. She needs to think about that."

"And I wanted to stare you in the eye and see what kind of person would deceive me while she prepared to kill eight million people."

"Take a good look."

"You might as well co-operate, Irma. It's over. We have you, we have Carl, we have Lakington. We can put together a case that'll keep you in prison for the rest of your life—a *proper* life sentence. How hard that life is, that depends upon how much you help us now."

Irma smiled. "And with that threat, we come to the end of the conversation. It was nice to see you again, Mary. I'm sorry we didn't get more chance to know each other—you seem interesting. Now I'm going to exercise my right to remain silent until my brief gets here."

★★★

"Ouch," complained Algy as he crawled back to consciousness.

"See, Lauren?" Dare told the young, attractive attending nurse at Norfolk and Norwich University Hospital. "Some people would swear or groan when they wake up from a head injury, or maybe ask what happened, or where they are. Mr Longworth actually says 'ouch' - the word - as if he was in a comic-book."

Lauren moved over and shone a torch at Algy's pupils. "How are you feeling, Algernon?"

The wounded man managed a sideways glare at the comrade who had informed the hospital that Algy preferred to be addressed at all times by his full name. "Ouchy," he grumbled.

Dare grabbed his jacket and prepared to head back to Drummond and Denny. "I'm glad you're back with us, Algy. And with no worse brain damage than before you got slammed into a wall. Besides, you helped me win a bet with Lauren here, about your waking remark." He gave the nurse a winning smile. "Dinner, wasn't it? What time does your shift end?"

"Oh, I'm *so* glad you were concerned about me, Peter," Algy spat.

"Dare likes dating nurses," T.S. chipped in. Algy hadn't realised that his comrade was laid in the next bed. "Medical women can usually identify his latest STDs for him."

"Should you be speaking, what with your broken ribs?" Dare asked him maliciously. "Why haven't they wired your jaw shut?"

★★★

"I can't believe it's all over," Fi Benton admitted to James and Claire Denny.

Denny had moved his motorhome to the visitor carpark outside the Norwich police headquarters, where it was parked beside Drummond's Chevrolet C4 Grand Sport, newly delivered by Hugh' occasional chauffeur Jenkins. Fi emerged from the camper van into the warm Norfolk sunlight, under a wide blue sky.

"There'll be a lot more tedious questions yet," Denny warned her. "The Sweeney like their statements."

"Nobody calls them the Sweeney any more," Mrs D warned her husband. "That's just sloppy writing, that is, lacking research. Derivative."

"Well I call them that, so it's true to life."

"Ignore 'im, Fi. It's generally best. They can't keep interviewing you forever, and then you can put all of this behind you."

Phyllis Benton sighed. "I don't know where to even start putting my life back together. Four months held in a room, and none of my friends or family cared enough to even notice that somebody else was living my life! 'Filly' was even better at my job than I think I would have been."

"But then again, you didn't plan to murder every soul in London, lovie," Mrs Denny pointed out. "So there's that."

★★★

Bangbang packed the last of his staff onto a coach back to London.

"Remind Mullings that they now put ring-pull tabs on the tops of beer-cans," he instructed the driver. "It is not necessary to open them with one's teeth," He rapped his hand on the side of the bus and watched it pull away from the security perimeter.

Jez Seymour limped over, favouring the leg where he'd landed heavily from his emergency bail-out. "It was a good scrap, it was," he told Bangbang. "Sorry about your lads, though."

"Worst part of the job, informing the families. I know now why Bulldog always hated it." They paused a moment, remembering absent friends.

"If I was going to go, though," Jez considered, "I'd want to go out doing something like this. Didn't we just save about a million people?"

"Eight million, if you're counting. And now they want us to fill in eight million forms about it."

"There's no justice. Do you think Bulldog's doing forms?"

Bangbang tried to picture it—and failed. "I doubt it somehow," he eventually answered. "Do you hear any explosions yet?"

★★★

The captive in prison greys was handcuffed to an interview desk. "Carl Peterson, huh?" Drummond began. "I wanted to see what you looked like, before you disappear off after Lakington to a black-ops detainment site forever."

The prisoner met his stare without malice or fear. In fact he seemed to be entirely uninterested.

"Nothing to say, now? Suddenly it's 'Right to remain silent' and all that? You had plenty to mouth off with when you were planning to slaughter millions."

No response. The killer wasn't playing.

He wasn't playing.

DCI McIver saw Hugh tense "Easy," she warned. "I got you in to see him on promise of your best behaviour. Don't do anything that gives his defence any material for a misconduct case."

Drummond frowned. "One question," he said to the policewomen. "One stupid nagging itch at the back of my mind. I've never seen Carl Peterson before. We've spoken, but I've not seen his face. And this guy's not talking so I can't compare voices."

"He identified himself to Denny as Peterson."

"So? He could have claimed to be Jason Statham; doesn't make him an action star." He leaned in to the prisoner. "How about it, chum? *Are* you Peterson? Or just a well-trained decoy?"

The prisoner with the face-scar made no response.

Hugh's gnawing doubt grew. "All respect to Mrs D, but you went down really easily for a fellow with your rep. *Too* easily. Who are you really?"

McIver stirred unhappily. "You're suggesting that Peterson could still be at large? This perp's physical description matches what little we have on Carl Peterson but... well, it would do if he was Peterson's substitute."

"Another plan, is it?" Drummond challenged the prisoner. "Like the anthrax cache and the crop-duster bluff and the bomb at Coldbrook Farm that..."

He stopped because McIver had gripped his shoulder hard. She had thought of something. "Distractions. His sister...!"

"Irma!" Drummond rose quickly. "Get me to her. Keep eyes on him at all times."

★★★

"Irma sends you her love," the blonde lookalike who had replaced Peterson's sister in her security cell told Drummond. There was no sign of the lawyer who was supposed to be having a private interview with her, or of the legal assistant who had accompanied him.

"Where is she?" McIver demanded.

"She just had to step out for a bit. Grey's not her colour."

★★★

"Both of them on the run, getting away scot free!" Hugh raged at Denny and Dare. "Lives lost, millions threatened, and he just walks away laughing, leaving a murderous decoy for us to chew on!"

"I thought we 'ad 'im," Denny confessed. "We still got that bastard as killed our men, though, whether 'e's Peterson or not."

"But not the bastard who sent him."

The three of them sat around the drop-down table in the Dennys' battered camper. Mrs Denny handed out mugs of sweet tea. It was clear that things were not as over as she would have liked.

"There will be a manhunt, a huge operation," Fi suggested. "I mean, for something like this..."

"That Carl Peterson 'as shown 'e's pretty good at getting past that sort of thing," Denny predicted gloomily.

"But Irma Peterson, she can't be more than fifteen minutes away from here yet," argued Mrs D. "If they set road blocks..."

"This is quiet, rural Norfolk, love, not some big target-hardened city," Denny cautioned her. "They'll set stuff up, yes, but... 'ow quickly?"

"And all the extra resources and fast response teams are over at Coldbrook Farm right now," Dare added. "Damn."

Hugh gripped his mug as of it was Peterson's throat and he could throttle him. "Dare, is there anything you can rake from that mass of financial data we took, or the stuff about that Koh Zhenkai character, to give us a lead where to chase? Anything at all?"

"There's probably a hundred leads if I only had time to trawl thought it," Dare admitted. "It's clear that Zhenkai bought up a lot of stuff for

Peterson to help their plot along. Not just SoarBrite and Coldbrook Farm. A construction unit to dig the soil. A haulage firm to shift it. Aviation engineers to fix up the planes. Dozens of companies, with big controlling shares in hundreds more. It's hard to know which were for the plan and which were investments for when London got hit."

A nasty connection occurred to Drummond. "The bomb he left at the lab. State-of-the-art tech, Irma said. You agree?"

The demolitions and explosives expert considered the device he had been too late to disarm the conventional way. "It was a pretty piece of lethal engineering, I'll say that for it."

"And it had some top-line anti-tamper stuff. Irma named it."

"You mean the same proximity and attack protection systems as the new Wildscream launchers?"

"Yeah. That."

"What about it?"

"Those Wildscreams are brand new, aren't they? 'Bleeding edge', as the yuppies say. Their systems are about as classified as it gets. So how did they end up on a terror weapon at Coldbrook?" Hugh's pulse quickened at a deeply unpleasant idea. "Where's Algy? Get him on the phone for me. And somebody get him a laptop."

***

Sir Bryan Johnstone was not a swearing man, but he went silent as he heard Mary McIver's update.

"They're not letting me in on what's happening here, governor," his DCI on the spot told him. "Closed ranks and local protocols. You know the score. It's not helping that the blokes from MI5 or whoever Major Hannay dropped on the investigation are trampling all over lines of responsibility. It's chaos."

"That seems to be Carl Peterson's signature," grouched Sir Bryan. "How did the woman get exchanged right there in secure holding?"

"From the security footage, she had a visit from her solicitor and his assistant. Looking now, I see the secretary was the same size and body shape as Irma. When the cameras were off for a private interview the women must have switched. The officers on the cells didn't spot the wigs. Simple as that."

"And after that?"

"Took a cab from out front. They're tracing it."

"The substitute woman?"

"Not speaking, guv, same as the substitute Peterson. Well paid or well frightened, or both. Pros, I'd say, given how they're holding up."

"Any leads on the brief? Do we know who he is—was supposed to be?"

"Some old chap with a grizzled white beard, from the cam-footage. Tweedy suit, old-fashioned document case... Wait! Hold on."

"McIver?"

"I need to get them to run that lobby video of him again. He had that briefcase when he came in. I don't remember if he had it when he left."

"It was checked through security?"

"Not sure if it came in with him, but we know that Peterson is nothing if not..."

The bomb went off.

★★★

A few minutes earlier, still parked outside the County Police HQ, Drummond, Dare, and Denny were hooked up by conference call with Algy and T.S. in the local recovery ward where Bangbang and Jez were visiting them.

"Some of us are trying to recover here," Algy complained. "And convince Nurse Lauren not to make a terrible life choice."

"You keep away from my nurse," Dare objected. "And particularly, don't marry and divorce her before I get back."

Drummond suppressed a growl. "I have an itch between my shoulder blades," their former commanding officer told them. "I don't like it."

His serious tone warned them that things were turning grim again. "What is it, old man?" T.S. asked.

Hugh tersely outlined development about a likely-fake Peterson and the substitution of Irma for a lookalike supposed legal secretary.

"She's free?" Bangbang worried. "And we never had Peterson? Now I'm nervy too."

"What can we do that the police can't, though?" T.S. asked. "They have the numbers and organisation for a huge manhunt. We have Algy and Denny, and Algy isn't allowed out for bed for another twenty-four hours."

Drummond tried to prise what was bothering him out of the back of his head. "Peterson's plan. He steals the anthrax deposit, improves it, makes it vaccine-resistant. He buys a bunch of spraying planes that might deliver it all over London. But we catch wind of the plot to abstract the poison and we stop the aircraft before they ever leave the tarmac. Nice work, Dare and Bangbang, by the way. The anthrax gets recovered, disposed of, and we all breathe a sigh of relief."

"I thought we did," Jez muttered.

"But?" Dare waited for the other shoe to drop.

"But from the moment we first suspected an aerial attack on Westminster, at the State Opening, the chances of that plan working properly went way down. Why?"

"Once the threat was known, we have countermeasures," Bangbang reasoned. "As soon as the warning went out, the number of building-mounted surface-to-air missiles protecting Parliament was about doubled."

Hugh slammed his palm on the van wall. "That's right! The only thing that failed Peterson plan actually did was to get a lot more missiles fitted round Central London."

"The only beneficiaries are Wildscream shareholders," Dare joked.

"But chaps…" Algy cut in nervously, "Koh Zhenkai was a Wildscream shareholder. A major one. He had access to…"

"To cutting edge new Wildscream tech like we saw in the farm bomb," recognised Hugh. "Irma even pointed it out to me!"

"So Peterson has Wildscream tech?" T.S. observed. "Disturbing, but…?"

"So he owns the company that designed all those missiles we just put on rooftops across London!" Drummond thundered. "Why bother with planes that can get shot down, when you can use the missile launchers put right there to stop them? What could those brand new suddenly-deployed Wildscream X2 rockets be packed with?"

"There's no records to show just how much anthrax Lakington was able to culture before we shut Coldbrook down," Bangbang realised. "If we didn't get it all, just the stuff still on site…"

"That Peterson fellow does like 'is decoys," contributed Mrs Denny.

"He never intended to go with the plan he sold Filchenkov, Madison, and Koh!" Drummond gasped. "Everything, even the lab you discovered, was all a fake-out. It's the missiles! And they are there *right now!*"

There was a TV on in the corner of T.S.'s ward, right in his line of sight. "And the royal carriage has just left Buckingham Palace."

"We have to warn Hannay!" Dare insisted. "We need to…"

Then the frontage of the police station beside the camper van exploded in a bright ball of fire.

★★★

CHAPTER XVII:
IN WHICH THE PETERSONS TAKE A DRIVE IN THE COUNTRY

"The State Opening of Parliament more or less took its present form in the 16th century. First the Yeomen of the Guard arrive at the Palace of Westminster to search the cellars for explosives, a tradition stemming from the 1605 Gunpowder Plot. The Lord Great Chamberlain pays for the Yeomen's services with a small glass of port wine."

Carl Peterson listened to the radio and drove a Porsche 718 Boxter S at just under the legal limit along the pleasant dual carriageway, towards the small east coast seaport and beach resort of Lowestoft.

The BBC commentator continued his education of the masses. *"The Peers of the Realm, robed and coroneted, gather in the House of Lords, along with summoned guests, the Queen-in-Council (appointed ministers and Privy Councillors), the Queen-on-the-Bench (senior judges representing the judicial system), the Chief of the Defence Staff (representing joint chiefs of the armed services), Gold Stick-in-Waiting (the honorary Colonel of the Household Cavalry), and the* Corps Diplomatique *of accredited foreign diplomats."*

The road signs said it was 19 more miles to Lowestoft, 26 to the larger seaport of Great Yarmouth. Peterson made for the older, smaller destination. A fast motorboat awaited him at the marina to convey him to a larger and more luxurious getaway ship ten miles offshore. Once that vessel vanished into the North Sea, one of the world's busiest shipping corridors, he would be almost impossible to trace.

"The members of the elected House of Commons gather in their own chamber in everyday formal dress," BBC Radio 4 lectured. *"The Vice-Chamberlain of the Queen's Household, one of the government's 'Whips', is sent to Buckingham Palace and is kept under guard as a hostage for the monarch's safe return; a practice first instituted by King Charles I for non-ceremonial reasons."*

"So it's alright when a king takes hostages," Carl said to his sister. "That's a real double standard."

Irma sat beside him, enjoying the wind whipping her yellow hair behind her. "When has life ever been fair?" she asked him. "All you can do is enjoy what's offered while it lasts."

"*Under supervision by the Crown Jeweller, the Imperial State Crown is taken from Victoria Tower and is passed by the sovereign's Bargemaster to the Comptroller of the Lord Chamberlain's office, to be placed in the Australian Imperial State Coach along with the Great Sword of State, the Cap of Maintenance, and maces for the Sergeants-at-Arms of the royal procession. These are taken for display in the Palace of Westminster's Royal Gallery, where...*"

Irma turned down the radio.

"This is rather nice," she told her brother. "This countryside, I mean. I'm glad we're not anthraxing this area. Is anthraxing a word?"

"It soon will be," Carl promised her.

He shifted into sixth gear and cruised away from the bomb he had planted in the police station foyer. It should be detonating right about *now*.

★★★

The electronic timer in the briefcase concealed under a sofa in the police station waiting area reached 1020 hours. It triggered a small commercial detonator wrapped inside four 2x1½x11" M112 demolition blocks of C-4 plastic explosive. The C-4 was custom-made to exclude any DNMB 'tagger', the legally-mandated additive that gave the material its distinctive odour and allowed its detection by explosive vapour detectors.

The detonation rippled outwards, propelling non-metallic polymer pellets packed around the device at 8,090 m/s, like seven thousand lethal seed-sized bullets. The fragments peppered the whole reception area like buckshot, cutting down everybody there. The supporting column directly behind the sofa failed.

A fireball bloomed with the shockwave, washing across the police station's public area and bursting out through fragmented windows to vent across the car park. The whole frontage of the modern glass and steel building blossomed with flame.

DCI McIver, heading back to reception to review the security video again, was caught by the shockwave, then hit by the double doors leading into the foyer as they were blasted from their hinges. She was hurled back hard, but the same heavy doors that fractured her arm and collarbone shielded her from the plume of searing fire that welled along the lift lobby where she fell.

The blast rocked the Autotrail Apache 700SE 6-Berth Motorhome a hundred feet from the building, spattering dents along the side of the

The detonation rippled outwards...

vehicle, starring the windows, actually lifting one side from the ground before the van rocked back heavily onto four wheels.

"Bomb!" Denny shouted by reflex, diving to cover his wife.

"In the police station!" Drummond called. He was already halfway through the door, with Dare behind him.

The front of the building was a mess. The whole of the smoked-glass façade was gone, exposing upper offices and shocked police personnel. Flames emerged from the former reception area, through they would blaze themselves out for lack of material soon. Choking black smoke welled from the wreckage.

Hugh shouted instructions. "Dare, Danny, search and rescue. Mrs D., comms. Warn Bangbang and the others, contact the hospital direct—I think 999 emergency calls route through here. Have Bangbang and Jezzer alert security over there, too, in case there's another package."

"What about you?" Dare asked as he rushed into the devastation behind Drummond.

"Like we just said, Peterson loves a decoy. Where are his body-doubles during all this, eh? I'm on that."

Hugh groped across the smoky, wrecked entrance hall. There were some survivors behind the reinforced reception desk, crying for assistance. Part of the suspended ceiling was down, covering what were clearly corpses.

He trusted to Dare and Denny to co-ordinate some kind of rescue and triage. He saw Fi Benton preparing the van's first aid kit for the first survivors. Sure that his comrades were on the job, he pushed on through the blast zone, working towards the back of the building.

He found McIver in the lift lobby behind the entrance hall. She was caught under one of the doors, clutching her painful left shoulder.

"Hold still," Drummond called. "I've got you, Mary!"

The reinforced door was half-wedged into the wall from the force that had ripped it from its hinges. Drummond heaved with his full strength and managed to pull it clear of the injured policewomen.

"Thanks," she gasped. "What happened?"

"I'd say IED, but I'm not sure about the 'improvised' part. Are you okay for me to leave you? I need to check…"

"On fake Peterson and fake Irma? First floor detention rooms. Use my key card. Go!"

Drummond took the pass, gave McIver a nod that substituted for so many words, and scrambled up the stairs.

★★★

"The sovereign travels from Buckingham Palace, nowadays in the Diamond Jubilee State Coach, passing through crowded streets lined with tourists, guarded by a dress military escort. As she arrives at Westminster, the Royal Standard replaces the Union Flag atop the Houses of Parliament. She dresses in the Parliament Robes of State and Imperial State Crown in the Robing Chamber, on the wall of which hangs in warning the death warrant of that same Charles I, who was beheaded by Parliament in 1649."

The TV in the corner of the two-bed hospital recovery room was still tuned to the State Opening of Parliament, but the occupants of the ward were focussing their attention elsewhere. "What's the status now, Mrs Denny?" Bangbang asked urgently.

"The station's being evacuated. We've got a triage point going in the car park. James, Mr Darell, and Captain Drummond have gone in."

"Should I get over to you?" Bangbang asked Mrs D.

"You couldn't do anything that's not being done," Claire Denny judged. "The Captain was clear that the hospital needed to be on alert, though."

"That's done. I've called back the coach with my lads on. It should be here in half an hour. Jez is with the security guards now."

"And we are stuck in hospital beds," T.S. objected on behalf of himself and Algy.

"Well, you might 'ave to share soon, sirs," Mrs D warned them. "We'll be sending a lot more over to join you."

★★★

Two officers in the stricken police station did not rush to evacuate or to assist their injured colleagues. DI Fleming and DC Corcoran proceeded to the secure interrogation suite, where the fake Peterson who had murdered two men in cold blood and the former legal secretary that had impersonated Irma were held in custody. They relieved the alarmed PC on station there to go and help with the emergency and released the prisoners from their confinement.

"Tell Mr Peterson we did out jobs," Fleming said.

Faux-Peterson nodded. "Which way out?"

"Back fire route. Look for a green Ford Mondeo near the exit gate. That's yours."

Another nod. The escaped prisoners moved quickly and efficiently to the fire escape and sought their vehicle.

"Now we cover our tracks, Ben," Fleming told Corcoran. "Then it's just deciding what to do with all our payday."

Someone used a priority key-card to enter the custody suite.

"You aren't authorised to be here," Fleming told the civilian. "This is a restricted area that…"

Drummond punched him, a smart uppercut that actually lifted the officer from his feet and sent him sprawling across a desk. Before the bent copper's surprised companion could reach for his baton, Drummond caught Corcoran by the neck and slammed him down into a photocopier.

"Where are the prisoners?" Hugh demanded. "Where?"

Fleming rallied, reaching to his belt for a taser. Drummond kicked his legs from under him and stamped down on his hand.

"Where?" he asked again, adding a boot between the legs to keep his opponent down and catching an attempt from Corcoran to grab him from behind. Hugh dislocated Corcoran's arm and introduced him to Fleming's taser.

"Where?" he asked again, pinning Fleming in a half-Nelson that threatened serious multiple fractures.

"Gone…" the DI gasped out through clenched teeth.

"*Where?*"

"Green Mondeo. Let me go!"

"Let him go," DCI McIver said, limping up as quickly as she had been able to follow. "You go get the killer, Bulldog." She pushed her phone at him. "Stay in touch." She glared at the downed officers. "As for you two puddles of scum, I am placing you under arrest. You do not have to say anything…"

★★★

Major Hannay was surprised to receive a call back from Lieutenant Theodore Jerningham on behalf of Captain Hugh Drummond. He was dismayed to hear his former subordinate's theory about the Wildscream systems. "Hold in place," the old soldier commanded curtly. "I will call you shortly. Keep this line clear."

"Well?" T.S. asked.

"I'm on hold," Bangbang snarled.

Algy and Sinclair could see the coverage on the BBC's 24-hour news channel.

"*Waving at the crowds, the sovereign is accompanied by the Royal Household Cavalry as she progresses along Birdcage Walk, past Regent's*

Park and Audley House, towards the Palace of Westminster, the Houses of Parliament. It's a fine clear day and I can see a lot of people clapping and cheering as her carriage passes by..."

"She's halfway to Parliament," Algy warned. "She'll be there in five, ten minutes."

"And we're in bloody Norfolk!" Bangbang objected. "We can be there in about, what, three hours on the M11?"

"*When Her Majesty arrives, she will take her throne in the House of Lords, and will motion the Lord Great Chamberlain to dispatch Gentleman Black Usher of the Rod to summon the House of Commons. However, the door to that chamber is slammed shut to keep Black Rod out, reminder of the House's independence since Charles I's unsuccessful invasion of it in 1642. Black Rod strikes the door with his mace three times—the indentations of many such blows may be seen on the wood—and the Commons agree to admit him to give his summons. These days, a defiant topical jibe is usually returned from Labour MP Dennis Skinner.*"

"Come on, Hannay!" Bangbang shouted at his phone. "What the hell do you think you are doing?"

★★★

Major Sir Richard Hannay regarded the pale-faced security officer who hastened into his office at the SIS's Vauxhall Cross Building overlooking the Thames. "Not good news?"

"Sir, the Wildscream X2 arrays' anti-tamper systems are all activated, fully operational, but they are not responding to stand-down transmissions."

"Briefly," Hannay commanded curtly.

"We can't turn them off. We can't approach them. If they believe they are being tampered with, threatened, hacked, they will self-destruct—or, if they have been thoroughly compromised, they may possibly launch."

"Who authorised... no, question for later. How can they be disarmed?"

"We're looking at that, sir. They can't be physically approached closer than four metres. They have advanced countermeasures against missile and firearms attack."

"In short, they are as difficult to capture or kill as we could possibly make them, and they seem to do their job well," Hannay observed. "A shame they were supplied by and do the work of a major terrorist, eh?"

"We can inform the Metropolitan Police, activate Condition Sigma Four, have them evacuate Parliament," the aide proposed.

"Don't," Hannay insisted. "You start that, on live television, and Peterson will launch his missiles straight away. And, since he clearly has back-channels into our defence arrangements, he will know if we attempt any kind of planned covert measure. We need… an unplanned one."

"Sir?"

"Go to Condition Sigma Two and Black Setting Five. Do all the things you need to do for that, but quietly, not in general circulation. And leave me alone. I have some calls to make."

★★★

Drummond scrambled for the fire stairs and took them three at a time. The rear car park was for police vehicles only, and there were still three or four black and white "panda" cars and a dozen staff vehicles lined up there. There were few people, though, as all the rescue and recovery efforts were centred on the front of the stricken building.

Hugh scanned the area: no green Mondeo.

He sprinted round the outside of the station, to the side where Dare was pulling another injured officer from the wreckage. Fire engine sirens were audible now; the situation here was coming under control.

A green vehicle vanished through the gates onto the Norfolk ring road beyond.

Drummond's Chevy C4 Grand Sport had been sheltered from the blast in the lee of Denny's camper. He leaped into it and reverse-swerved the car out of its slot with a screech of rubber. The 5.7 litre engine growled like the wrath of God. The Chevrolet twisted onto the main road and hit 60 miles per hour in 4.4 seconds.

Denny saw Hugh go. "The Captain's onto something," he told his wife, even before his phone registered an incoming call from DCI McIver's number. He thumbed *accept* and pressed the phone to his ear to hear over the din of the rescue and the emergency sirens. "It's 'im!"

"Denny? Can you do something technical and patch me through to Algy? And Bangbang, if he's available?"

"Yessir. Just give me a second to get back to the van. I takes it that you are in some kind of 'ot pursuit?"

"The man who killed our comrades, and the impostor-impostor-Filly. I'm chasing a lime green Ford Mondeo along the Norwich bypass after the man who killed our comrades, and the impostor-impostor-Filly. Ah, he's spotted me and speeded up!"

Drummond gunned the engine, closing the distance to the far-less powerful Mondeo but reserving one last burst of speed.

As he came up behind the escaping prisoners, the Peterson-lookalike in the passenger seat leaned out and aimed a pistol that must have been waiting for him with the getaway vehicle. That was what Hugh had been waiting for. He squeezed another few drops of acceleration from the Lotus Engineering-designed double overhead cam LT4 engine, unexpectedly bringing the Chevy right alongside the speeding Mondeo. Hugh caught the gunman's wrist and relieved him of his weapon, then swerved across onto the pavement, dragging the escapee's captured arm with him.

The substitute Peterson screamed as his limb was wrenched from its socket. Drummond used the Glock 17 he'd taken from his enemy to fire a round into the Irma-impersonator behind the Mondeo's driver's wheel.

Knowing what was to come next, Hugh stamped on the Grand Sport's brakes, letting the out-of-control escape vehicle swerve across the road ahead of him. The Mondeo hit the central barrier at speed and flipped over, scraping to a slow halt on its roof on the other side of the road.

Hugh screeched to a stop and checked the lookalikes. Neither of them was going anywhere.

"Talk to me, chaps," Drummond called down the phone to Denny and whoever his adjutant had connected him to. "Algy? Bangbang?"

"It's Hannay," came back the crisp, clipped voice of their former commanding officer.

"We're here too," Dare added over the line. "Algy, Bangbang, T.S. and Jez at the hospital, me with the Dennys and DSI McIver here at the bomb site."

"Your surmise may be accurate, Captain Drummond" the Major said succinctly. "The Wildscream units are all locked in proximity defence mode, which means they will launch if anyone goes near them. They are receiving a constant non-recurring radio code stream—an electronic dead man's switch."

"If the signal is blocked or shut off then they go to attack," Algy understood at once.

"Quite so. The signal is being transmitted on standard mobile phone frequencies. We cannot copy it. We cannot get near enough to freeze the units as Bulldog did with the bomb he found. We cannot destroy the arrays without their payloads being detonated and probably distributed."

"And you can't stop the ceremonies without tipping Peterson that the game is up," Drummond recognised.

"But the Queen's at the Palace of Westminster right now!" T.S. objected.

"Won't Peterson trigger his devices now?"

"We might actually have a bit of time left," Drummond estimated. "Remember, Carl likes his big moments. If his ego holds up, he won't trigger things until the most dramatic climax. That's *after* the Queen's Speech to the joint houses, when she's about the progress back to Buck House in state, when the crowds are biggest, just as rush hour get going."

"So we have time to get about half way there before Peterson blows his wad," Dare objected.

"Your presence in London would be quite irrelevant," Hannay told them. "Peterson is hardly going to be at ground zero when he switches off the delay-signal, is he?"

"And he can control the Wildscreams from anywhere with phone coverage," Bangbang added.

"He's near here, I'm sure of it. He just came for his sister," Drummond insisted. "Let me find him."

"The only way to shut those anti-tamper systems down safely would be to get the control box off him," Algy recognised. "Major, sir, can you trace the phone signal back to source?"

"Menwith Hill is on it now," Hannay replied, referring to the RAF's satellite ground station, communications intercept, and missile warning site, the world's largest electronic monitoring installation.

The scream of approaching police sirens warned that the Mondeo wreck had been called in. Drummond climbed back into his Chevy. "Find me Peterson's location," he called down the line.

"He must not know that he is being followed," Hannay insisted. "All he need do is shut off his phone signal and everything is lost."

"How the hell did Peterson get his anthrax into missiles deployed by our own security forces anyhow?" Bangbang demanded.

"You said that he had our establishment penetrated," McIver pointed out. "We only got this far by using 'non-traditional' resources.

"And he still played us, so he did," Jez objected.

"I reckon there will be some hard questions asked later," T.S. surmised, "If anyone survives to answer them."

"We have a fix," broke in Hannay. "He's using a relay spoof system and all kinds of technical tricks but... A146. He's beyond the Norfolk Ring Road, heading for the coast."

Drummond demonstrated the Grand Sport's acceleration again, leaping forward to begin the chase. The hunt was on.

★★★

"How's the Opening progressing?" Peterson asked his sister

"There's something called a Black Rod banging on a door?"

"It's a person. An office. It's historical. A rich tradition dating from the sixteenth century right up to, well, literally until today. This is the last time."

"The Commons process to enter the chamber of the Lords in two ranks led by the Prime Minister and Leader of the Opposition, though they must stop at the bar and not enter the floor," the BBC advised. *"By tradition, the procession is straggling, jocular, and informal, to show that the MPs are not intimidated by the summons."*

Irma sighed. "I'm sorry we have to get rid of all of it. I mean, I liked the ravens in the Tower of London, and the cream teas at Harrods. The Royal Ballet. Trafalgar Square. Carnaby Street. I'm glad we got Hugh out of there."

"Still obsessed with your Bulldog, are you? You should know better."

"He saved my life, Carl, when you left me with your nasty bomb."

"You could have entered the deactivation code at any time. You just wanted to see what your hero would do."

"And what he did was save my life. As far as he was concerned, the risks he took were real."

"Which is why I haven't killed him. I rather like him too, Irma. I've enjoyed matching wits with him, even if he is hopelessly ill-equipped for it."

"The Lord Chancellor approaches the throne, bends to his knee, and hands the monarch a goatskin vellum parchment on which is a speech written by the Prime Minister and Cabinet that outlines their intentions for the next parliamentary session. Her Majesty reads the document in a neutral tone conveying neither approval nor opposition and the joint Houses make no comment at the time; they separately debate the contents over several often-contentious days afterwards."

"You are such an intellectual snob, Carl. What will your next cover identity be? A professor? A tech-genius wunderkind? Another baron? It's sure to be something posey."

"Nothing European, I think. Not till this situation plays out. The political map of the Continent will be changing radically after today. South America?"

"I do like a tan. By the way, the Queen is making her speech. 'My Lords and Members of the House of Commons...' How long now?"

"Depends on the speech. It'll end with her saying 'My Lords and

Members of the House of Commons, I pray that the blessing of Almighty God may rest upon your counsels.' Then there's a bit more processing out, a nice photo opportunity, and that's when things go rapidly downhill."

"Non-traditional!"

"I'm afraid so. But we set out to bring this nation low, didn't we? This is how and when."

They slowed for a roundabout but then the road went straight, cutting across the flat Anglian fenland with nothing but the occasional slow caravan and container lorry to navigate.

"What do you think Bulldog will do in the savage new world?" Irma speculated. "I think he'll fit rather well. A bit of shadow will suit him."

"I doubt he'll ever come to our side," Peterson warned his sister. "Bulldogs are notoriously loyal to their owners, and this nation is his master. He's been trained too well, with his public school morals and his military codes. It might have been kinder to kill him after all, before he sees it all end."

"Well, he survived Alonya and Viera, and Nugent, and Gŭ Cāng. He killed Luigi and Christophe. He's a hard man to get rid of, Carl."

"Then we won't try. We'll just kill our millions and sail off for Rio. Our work here is done."

Peterson slowed down to 30 as he entered the outer environs of seaside Lowestoft.

The Queen's Speech continued.

★★★

CHAPTER XVIII:
IN WHICH HE MEETS CARL PETERSON

Drummond covered the twenty-five miles from Norfolk to the coast in 12.6 minutes, averaging 119 miles per hour on roads with a legal limit of sixty or seventy. The Chevrolet Grand Sport's LT4 V8 engine produced 330 horsepower and 340 lb-ft of torque, and Drummond let the beast have its head. Passive speed camera traps snapped the Admiral Blue racer—Norfolk is notorious for its obsessive traffic enforcement—but did nothing to deter the last and greatest of the C4 Corvettes.

"Keep following the main road through town," Arty told him over McIver's phone from his hospital bed. He had arranged for the tracker feed to be passed through to his laptop so he could guide Hugh from there. "Try and get visual on him. Peterson's not using geolocation or navigation features on his mobile. We can only ping him by cell towers. His phone's a Dark Matter KATIM, which means it's uncrackable. I'm amazed and slightly terrified that the Menwith Hill boys were able to trace it this well; that's not a known capacity of theirs. But it means that we can tell where Peterson is to about three hundred yards."

"So where is he now?"

"About three hundred yards ahead of you, due east. Carry on across two roundabouts, toward the water front."

"A port?"

"Not so much these days, more a seaside resort, but there's a marina behind a sea-wall. Lots of motor-boat slips."

"If he heads out to sea, how far will his phone connect to a signal tower and keep sending that code?"

"Twenty to forty miles, depending on terrain and weather. Don't worry about accidental signal drop. Worry about deliberate shutdown if he spots you."

Drummond saw an expensive sports car ahead, standing out from the local traffic like a rare orchid amidst a common hedgerow. The driver didn't seem that remarkable from this distance, but his passenger seat companion had billowing blonde hair.

"I see him. And Irma. Red Porsche convertible heading to the seafront. I'm keeping back for now until I can get a clear shot."

"You need him alive," Hannay cut in over the line "If the phone is protected—and those Dark Matter models are very protected—there will be a cypher to access it. And another code to shut down the signal. We don't have those codes. You have to get them from him."

"Because otherwise this would be too easy," Dare complained.

"Any chance of getting Bulldog some backup, sir?" Bangbang asked the Major.

"As much as ever," Hannay answered curtly. None, then.

"Hold on!" Hugh called urgently. "I've lost them. I can't see where they've gone!"

He screeched his Chevy to an emergency stop on Pier Terrace, blocking the traffic over one of the two lanes of what was actually a swing bridge over Lowestoft Harbour.

"There's a slip road down to the marina and railway station," Mrs Denny called in from her station at the camper van. She had online area maps booted up too. "You missed it, Captain. It's before the bridge, fifty yards back."

Hugh spotted the Peterson's bright red convertible on the docking slip below, beside the marina wharf. Unable to reverse because of the summer holiday traffic, he just abandoned his vehicle and the protesting drivers behind it. He vaulted off the elevated road, over the safety railings, and dropped-and-rolled the ten feet to the lower level behind the British Rail terminus.

There was a security gate blocking off the private boat slips but Drummond burst the padlock with the butt of his Glock 17 pistol. He had no leeway to be subtle; Peterson might shut off that signal at any moment, or escape to sea where he would never be found.

"What's going on, Bulldog?" Algy pleaded over the speaker of Mary's phone, but Drummond had neither time nor breath to answer him. Hugh sprinted to the parked Boxter S and cast about for the Petersons.

The sun flashed on a glimpse of golden hair that vanished down a flight of stone stairs at the pier side. These old steps led right down into the water, where a boat could be moored on rings let in to the sea-wall. A sleek steel-blue Fairline Targa 62GT speedboat waited there, a thoroughbred amongst the usual leisure crafts and hobby boats crowding the harbour.

Drummond dodged round a trio of jet skiers in baggy Bermuda shorts and raced to the lip of the raised sea-wall. Irma Peterson was untying the aft line on the 64-foot luxury motor launch. A broad-shouldered man with a shock of black hair, beard, and moustache was warming up the engines. As he turned, Drummond saw the old carved scar on the man's face, identical to that of the prisoner that Denny had captured last night who now lay bleeding on a Norfolk highway

"The real Carl Peterson, I guess?" Hugh asked, aiming the Glock at the deadliest man in Britain.

"Captain Drummond?" Peterson recognised. He raised one bushy eyebrow. "I am rarely genuinely surprised, but I am now. Congratulations on finding me."

"Stop talking." The expensive security phone might have voice-command recognition. "Don't move. Irma, I don't want to shoot you. So keep still."

"If you don't want to shoot me, then don't, darling," the mystery blonde suggested. "But please tell us how on earth you found us. Carl was being ever so clever."

"I said quiet. Peterson, take that gun from your pocket, slowly, with two fingers. Drop it over the side into the water. Now you, Irma. Lose the weapons."

"I'm straight out of police custody, my hero. I didn't have time to go shopping yet, not even for guns and knives. How many clothes do I have to peel off before you'll believe me?"

"This isn't the time for games, Irma. Not with your brother's anthrax rockets primed to launch from his phone."

"You worked that out too?" Peterson was impressed. "I warned Filchenkov, Madison, and Koh not to underestimate you. I should have listened to my own advice. So what now? You shoot me and save Britain?"

"You take out the phone as slowly and carefully as you did the gun. You don't touch the screen. You don't speak. Final warning."

Peterson nodded in understanding. Holding one hand clear, he carefully edged the black KATIM out of his pants pocket.

"Mummy! Mummy! That man has a *gun!*"

Drummond was standing in a working marina on a busy, hot summer's day, pointing a firearm at two boaters. He was bound to be spotted. The child clutching an ice-cream and pointing at him was only the first.

The momentary distraction was enough. Irma Peterson jumped in front of her brother, shielding him with her body. Drummond could only get him if he shot her in the back.

That second's hesitation to fire was all that Peterson needed. He tossed the phone in a short arc towards Hugh, deliberately pitching it short so that it splashed into the water by the steps. "Oops," he mocked.

Drummond had to make a split-second choice: take down both Petersons or go after the phone. If the device had landed on the barnacled-steps below the water line then it might still be functional. If it sank into the murky depths of the harbour it was lost forever. If he diverted his attention from the deadly Petersons then they might escape.

The jet-ski brothers were moving over to heroically challenge the mad gunman. Other holidaymakers were running away or towards Drummond. Hugh jumped off the steps and splashed down to search for the drowned Dark Matter KATIM.

Peterson gunned the Targa's twin Volvo Penta d13-900 evc-d engines and sped from the mooring, leaving a wash swell that pushed Drummond up against the sea-wall. In that moment Hugh saw the illuminated rectangle of the phone's screen twist and vanish down into the dark silty harbour-water. He took a lungful of air and dived after it.

The speedboat slalomed at illegal speeds round the outlet to the river mouth, then slewed hard starboard into open sea.

Hugh struggled against his own buoyancy, kicking downward in pursuit of the electronic glimmer of the sinking phone. If the sea breached the instrument's casing, if the transmission had ceased, eight million people might be dead men walking.

As Drummond's breath ran short and his lungs screamed, his fingers brushed against hard smooth metal—the finished surface of a protective phone sheath. He almost lost it, but fumbled it into his hand and stroked for the surface before he blacked out.

He broke water six yards from the sea wall steps. The jet-skiers were waiting to seize him until the police could arrive.

Hugh let them drag him from the water, then he took the three of them down as gently as he could, tipping them into the harbour; all except the last—from him Hugh took the keys to his ride.

The Sea-doo GTX LTD 230 was a little over eleven feet long, a top-line three-seater sports jet ski with Bluetooth sound system, USB port, removable dry bag, depth finder, water temperature gauge, and high-performance variable trim system. Drummond didn't care about any of that. What he needed was the 230hp Rotax 500 HO ACE engine that offered acceleration comparable to that of a Porsche 911.

He ignored the cries of objection from behind him, revved the throttle, and jetted the craft out of the marina after Peterson.

★★★

"Where is he?" Major Hannay demanded.

"He's not responding, sir," Bangbang reported; answering Hannay's questions was a deeply ingrained habit. "DCI McIver's phone has gone dead."

"Is the hold signal still being sent?"

"Yes," Algy confirmed. "That phone is now moving again, somewhere east of the easternmost cell tower in Lowestoft."

"The marina," Dare assessed. "Or open sea."

Algy checked his screen to confirm what he was seeing there. "Sir, lads… Peterson's phone is receding from the cell tower—at about fifty miles per hour!"

★★★

Drummond could tell when he pursued the speedboat beyond the harbour mouth. It was the difference between riding a seaside donkey and a raging bull. In open water the breakers came in hard on a ten-foot swell that would only get worse further from shore. Hugh's jet ski half-sailed, half-flew over the watery canyons, crashing down to almost submerge before leaping again like a struggling salmon.

Far ahead, a mere blur in the sea-spray, the Targa 62GT gunned its engines and left a spreading V-trail as it made away from land.

With a few moments to spare before the next rough channel, Hugh pulled the two phones from his jacket and checked them. Peterson's secure model seemed unharmed by its dive. The screen remained a dull luminous green rectangle except for an input keypad. DCI McIver's mobile had not survived its encounter with salt water. There was no way to contact Algy, Dare, or anyone else.

"On the plus side, while I have the phone, Peterson can't switch off the delay-kill signal," Drummond told himself, because who else could he consult? "In the minus column, I can't stop the missiles from firing eventually without Peterson inputting some code. And he's haring off towards the horizon."

A particularly nasty wave caught the Sea-doo sideways-on, nearly pushing Hugh from the saddle. For a moment Drummond was turned around, unsure of the direction he had been chasing, but then he spotted the speedboat again, haring off through the rising seas.

"On the plus side, this contraption is faster than Peterson's getaway toy. On the minus side, his boat has a nice cabin and a decent beam, and it can cope with heavy waves so much better."

Drummond also considered that he had lost his Glock during his phone-diving. If he caught up with the Petersons, even if they remained unarmed, it would be two to one.

"On the plus side, if I do catch him, I *will* kick his arse," Bulldog Drummond growled.

He plunged the water-ski on, trying to match the turbulent North Sea waves' natural rhythms as he slowly gained on the speeding Targa. He felt pleased until he spotted the petrol gauge dipping down into the red zone. The speedboat had a fuel tank more than forty times larger than his.

He had no option but to plough on through the fifteen foot swell, enduring the savage pounding of the breakers, closing from five hundred yards to fifty, near enough that he could again see Irma's hair blowing in the wind, see her waving to him.

At the distant smudge where sea met sky, a larger vessel came into view.

It was an expensive motor yacht, no mere speedboat but ten times the size of the craft in which the Petersons were fleeing. Carl was making directly for it. Presumably he had henchmen aboard, and all of them armed.

Drummond pulled the jet ski alongside the Targa. The Sea-doo was running on fumes now, and he was running on adrenalin, grinning like a lunatic, madder than Mad Mullings the leg-biter. "Carl Peterson," he called across, "I'm making a citizens arrest!"

Peterson swerved the motorboat hard towards him, trying to run him over. Drummond veered sharp to starboard, scarcely avoiding bone-shattering collision. The GTX LTD 230 spluttered, choked, then started again, its fuel almost exhausted. Hugh revved it to top speed again, running on fumes, knowing his time was almost up.

Peterson swung again to hit Drummond's tiny craft, but this time Hugh did not even try to avoid. He yanked what he needed from the Sea-Doo's dashboard, stood on the front seat, and jumped. As the side of the motorboat rendered the dying jet ski to scrap, he landed on the open rear deck of the Fairline Targa and rolled to his feet.

Peterson cut the motor, slowing the craft down to a virtual stop. "Well, that was spectacular," he applauded. "What a lot of effort just to give me my phone back."

Drummond looked up into the muzzle of a .44 Remington Magnum; of course Carl Peterson had another gun aboard.

"Her Majesty has just finished boring the nation. She's coming out of Westminster now," the villain told Hugh. He checked his watch. "Yes, we are exactly on schedule for launching a new world order. And once again you have helped play an important part in my plans."

"And once again I'm going to stop them," Hugh said. He held up a small black box he'd brought aboard with him. "You're not the only one who can play the hostage game."

"What do you mean?" Irma puzzled. "Hugh, what is that?"

"Your brother's not the only one with access to C-4. Here's enough explosive to take out this boat and all of us. On a dead man's switch, in honour of Carl here. Shoot me and you go bang too. Let the missiles off and I'll kill us all. *You don't get to walk away after murdering a city.*"

"You would kill Irma?" Peterson asked.

"Not by choice. How about you?"

"I feel so loved and wanted," the blonde declared.

Drummond and Peterson faced off against each other.

"What's it to be Carl? Do you shoot me and go boom? Or finish your plan and go boom? Or do you unlock your phone, turn off the Wildscream systems so they can be defused and disarmed, and live to plot another day?"

Carl Peterson studied Hugh Drummond. "I cannot tell if you are bluffing," he confessed. "I rank the chance at fifty-fifty. Those are not sufficiently good odds to warrant a fatal gamble." He reversed the Magnum and held it out for Hugh to take. "I yield."

"Just like that?"

"Just like that. As you say, there will be another day. The phone, please."

"You'll only disarm the devices, not trigger them?"

"My word on it. This plan is over. It has failed. Others will not."

"He means it, Bulldog," Irma advised. "You've won this round. Well done!"

"This is the disarm code," Peterson said. "02-04-79, the date of the accidental release of anthrax from a biological weapons complex in Sverdlovsk, Russia, with sixty-eight deaths. There, it's done. You can telephone your allies to confirm it."

Hugh realised he was being distracted. The larger ship had turned towards the speedboat and was closing the distance between them.

"Nice try, Peterson," he told the villain.

Drummond turned the Targa around and ran towards the nearest Coast Guard station.

★★★

"And that's how I broke your phone," Hugh finished his long explanation to Detective Chief Inspector McIver. "Algy's finding you a nice new one."

Mary shifted in her shoulder cast and tried not to wince. "That's one hell of a story, Bulldog," she admitted. "One that I suspect is going to get so classified that you won't even be allowed to dream about it without breaking the Official Secrets Act."

"What 'appens to Peterson now, then?" Denny wanted to know. "Tower of London's still good for beheadings."

"He's been detained under some obscure section of international anti-terrorism treaties. Serious men in black suits and unnecessary sunglasses whipped him and Irma away to wherever they took Lakington. I hope it's Guantánamo Bay's less-pleasant bastard cousin."

"And that's our end of it done," Drummond concluded. "All the interesting parts are over. Now it's just assigning the blame and arguing about new policies and such. Definitely not our department."

"Not yours, no," Dare agreed. "Poor old T.S. might get roped in, though, once his ribs are back where they should be. And apparently there's about three tons of catch-up paperwork for Bangbang, to show he was working for the government all along."

"And we have a lot of arrests to process," McIver added. "Shame I'm on sick leave while that's going on."

"That's the spirit, Mary," Drummond approved. "We'll get you on-team yet!"

"There's just one bit of your big last stand I still don't get, though, Bulldog," Dare objected. "That self-destruct bomb that made Peterson stand down. Where did you pick thing that up?"

"This old thing?" Hugh tossed the small black box at his old comrade. "It turns out that it was useful having a Bluetooth stereo system in the jet-ski after all."

★★★

Three days later, at an unlisted detention centre outside the United Kingdom, the erstwhile Carl Peterson was led into a sparse, dark interrogation room. But then his bonds were loosed and he was served Columbian coffee in a fine china cup.

"Thank you," he told his visitor. "So, did I pass the audition?"

"We are very impressed, young man. To get so far with such limited resources... yes, impressed is the word. You may consider yourself commended."

"Am I invited to the big table?"

"You are. We are all expecting great things of you, Mr Peterson."

"I do have some very exciting plans," the villain promised. "I can hardly wait to start."

★★★

Hugh set aside Mrs Denny's excellent kidneys and bacon with an uncharacteristic frown. "Something wrong, sir?" Denny checked.

"I'll be glad when we get Half Moon Street up and running again, James," he confessed. "I'm looking forward to having the entire house this time, with Peter safely next door. But now that the excitement with Filly and her follies is all over bar the recriminations, I find myself a bit bored again."

"Oh, Lord!" Denny groaned.

"Place a call to *The Times* for me, please," Drummond said. "I wish to place an advertisement."

★★★

AFTERWORD:
ON THE RETURN OF BULLDOG DRUMMOND
I.A. WATSON OUTLINES THE CASE

Bulldog Drummond? Why him? Why *now*?

After all, Hugh Drummond is a rather old-fashioned hero, a puncher and a hitter where modern protagonists are more sophisticated and subtle, a patriot in an age where we doubt our nations and governments, a ladies man at a time where gender politics has sensitised us to patriarchal privilege. In his original 1920s incarnation, Hugh was an archetypal "rich dilettante does good for fun and *nobilesse oblige*" character, rooted in the values and expectations of class, sex, and culture of his age. To some more contemporary critics, he is "a bundle of chauvinisms, hating Jews, Germans, and most other foreigners"[1]—a problematic figure for some modern readers.

However, at his core, Drummond offers qualities not easily available for writers of new contemporary characters. No new detective can offer the sort of deductive leaps that Sherlock Holmes can without inviting reader disbelief; Holmes, established in a different time, with the weight of many years of established literary expectation on him, may do so without breaking suspension of disbelief—and must. Likewise, Bulldog can evince values and opinions and perform prodigies that might cause more modern creations to appear cartoonish or unrealistic.

One might create a pastiche character in homage to Drummond and his ilk, to take advantage of that literary licence—but why use an inferior substitute when the real thing is available for reinvention?

Bulldog Drummond gets around. He has enjoyed a public profile of the sort that many modern fictional characters would envy. Bulldog's creator H.C. McNeile, writing as Sapper, briefly debuted him as a policeman in a short story for *The Strand Magazine*, but the author was unsatisfied with the result and went back to the writing desk. The reworked Bulldog was framed into his regular form for his first novel, *Bulldog Drummond* in 1920.

This version of Bulldog found his audience, in ten books and four short stories. In the 1920s, McNeile was the highest-paid short story writer in

1 Michael Denning in *Cover Stories: Narrative and Ideology in the British Spy Thriller* (1987).

the world, earning £10,000 per year, the equivalent of $867,000 today.

Like Sherlock Holmes before him, Drummond became a dilettante living a gentleman's life in London, turning his hand to investigating mysteries and righting wrongs. Like Richard Hannay, he was a military man of patriotic bent, upholding civilisation against those who plotted society's downfall. Like the Scarlet Pimpernel he was assisted by his loyal band of old friends, and later by his wife Phyllis.

And like his templates and literary inspirations, Captain Drummond made the transition onto the stage and into movies. *Bulldog Drummond* was adapted by McNeile and Gerald du Maurier for Wyndham's Theatre, starring du Maurier in a run of 428 performances. Three other stage productions followed.

Bulldog made his cinematic debut in 1922 and featured in twenty-four films between then and 1969. Alfred Hitchcock himself intended to make a Bulldog Drummond film but could not agree a rights deal; that movie became the Drummondless *The Man Who Knew Too Much*.

The American radio station Mutual Broadcasting System put out Bulldog adventures from 1941 to 1949 and again in 1954. *Douglas Fairbanks, Jr. Presents* put Drummond on TV in "The Ludlow Affair" in 1956.

After Sapper's death in 1937, seven more books were released by McNeile's friend Gerard Fairlie and two by Henry Raymond.

Perhaps his most unnoticed contribution to world cultural history was that in the 1930s the tenacity and Britishness associated with the nickname 'Bulldog' was applied to another hard-drinking, implacable, problematic, dauntless British patriot, Sir Winston Churchill; although physical appearance perhaps also played a part. Even today, the UK insurance firm Churchill uses an animated bulldog as its advertising mascot.

Bulldog Drummond has somewhat disappeared from the public eye now, but his legacy lives on in the series that took elements of his stories and found new use for them. Drummond's echoes linger in Simon Templar's Saintly doings, in Biggles' patriotic exploits, and in James Bond's womanising for Queen and country. Indeed, Ian Fleming admitted that Bond was "Sapper from the waist up and Mickey Spillane below."

Drummond entered the public domain in 2012, seventy-five years after his creator's death. Was Bulldog now out of fashion, yesterday's hero, with little to offer a cynical and jaded modern audience? Could he only be used ironically, satirically, to show how much cleverer and more sophisticated we have become since his glory days? Or was there some core truth to the character that could speak to us from our literary roots and offer new readers something of the thrill and rush that made Bulldog a staple of adventure fiction in books and films ninety years ago?

In reintroducing Drummond to a modern audience, the main hurdle is what might be called "The John Carter Effect". In 2012 Disney movies released a big-budget adaptation of Edgar Rice Burroughs's iconic Mars-explorer, only to see the film fail at the box office. *John Carter* was criticised by less informed critics as derivative of many science fiction movies from *Star Wars* to *Avatar*. The truth is that Burroughs's *Barsoom* stories, published since 1912, have been strip-mined for inspiration so often than they now too easily appear to be cliché-filled and more-of-the-same, when they actually established the tropes that many more recent tales have reused.

In the same way, the adventures and adventure-types of Bulldog Drummond have become the regular fare of Saturday matinee cliffhangers, of pulp action fiction, and of big budget summer blockbusters. Bulldog was there early on, but many others have come after him and made him less distinguishable from a crowd of square-jawed, two-fisted, hard-to-kill heroes. The rich secret adventurer has become Bruce Wayne. The flawed, big-hearted, unsubtle, unstoppable tough guy has become John McClaine.

So what to do?

Arguably the most successful relaunch of a beloved public domain character in recent years has been the BBC's *Sherlock* TV series. The reimagining of the familiar characters in a contemporary situation was at first shocking; until one remembers that Conan Doyle was writing *his* Holmes in the present day when he set pen to paper in 1882. Somehow the juxtaposition of the essence of the original Canon with a heady chunk of modern-world to interact with offered a chance to bring those stories home to a new audience with new force.

Or so the eleven million UK viewers and hundreds of millions who watched in 224 other TV territories seemed to feel.

A modern Drummond then, with an old-style (and perhaps a bit old fashioned) hero in a modern complicated world. Friends who are a bit more diverse and distinctive than the Darell, Sinclair, Jerningham, and Longworth of Sapper's volumes, in line with modern readers' expectations of more shaded, developed characters. A broad global scale allowing for Bulldog's values to crash into realpolitik and the spirit of the times. But let's not leave out the fun, either!

Airship 27 publications never forgets its pulp roots, so our new Bulldog

Drummond aims for fast-paced high adventure, with a dash of *Sherlock*, a pinch of *Fast & Furious*, a spoonful of *Mission Impossible* and a sprinkling of Tom Clancy. We want the heart, we want the clashes, we want Hugh Drummond at his most Bulldoggish in a world that is no more ready for him today than it was in 1920. We want him irrepressible and implacable and unstoppable.

That's why.

IW
Considering advertising in *The Times*
August 2018

★★★

THE AUTHOR:

I.A. Watson has forayed into offering new tales of well-known characters before, starting with his four Robin Hood novels, offering contributions to thirteen (and counting) anthologies of *Sherlock Holmes, Consulting Detective*, one story collection about *The Amazing Harry Houdini*, and a novel about both, *Holmes and Houdini*, along with versions of other neglected pulp and legendary heroes. His next major release will be the fantasy epic *The Dark Lord*. A full list of his sixty-plus published works appears at http://www.chillwater.org.uk/writing/iawatsonhome.htm

COVER ARTIST:

Ted Hammond is a Canadian artist who has been creating amazing art for over twenty years. His work has appeared in magazines, ads, books and graphic novels just to name a few. Go to (www.tedhammond.com) to contact him and check out more of his work!

INTERIOR ILLUSTRATOR:

Howard Simpson - I was born in Newark, NJ. My mom says I started drawing when I was two years old. I found come old, discarded comic books in the basement. Upon reading these four-color treasures I decided on my life's course. I would become a storyteller. And with all of my artwork I'm endeavoring to tell a story. Sometimes it's a personal story and others it is the character's story.

Today I am using more digital tools such as a Wacom tablet and stylus. Usually using software such as ArtRage, Adobe Illustrator and Photoshop. I'm always including more in the mix, such as Sketchbook, Clip Studio Paint, Procreate, Medibang Paint Pro, Mischief and Krita. I am creating my own future now with my creator owned web comics which can be viewed on Tapas at https://tapas.io/abbastudios

You may find me online at http://abbadabba.com/ and https://www.instagram.com/abbastudios/.